MICHAEL BAISDEN

THE MAINTENANCE MAN

It's midnight, do you know where your woman is?

SCRIBNER PAPERBACK FICTION
PUBLISHED BY SIMON & SCHUSTER
NEW YORK LONDON TORONTO SYDNEY SINGAPORE

SCRIBNER PAPERBACK FICTION
Simon & Schuster, Inc.
Rockefeller Center
1230 Avenue of the Americas
New York, NY 10020

Published by arrangement with the author.

Designed by Stacy Luecker
Manufactured in the United States of America

Library of Congress Cataloging-in-Publication Data is available.

ISBN 978-0-7394-1361-6

DEDICATION

To my energetic and passionate aunt Dorothy Wilson

who passed away on October 31, 1997

I'll never forget you, Sweet D.

ACKNOWLEDGMENTS

As always I have to begin by giving thanks to God for guiding my life and my career. Without a strong sense of spirituality, none of this would have been possible. To my mother, Alicia Parham, for bringing me into this world and for always supporting me. I hope you're around for many years to come so I can continue to spoil you. And to my feisty grandmother, Florence Adams, the matriarch of the family. You've taught me what it truly means to love unconditionally. Thanks for always being there for me. I love you, Grandma!

I must also give thanks to the countless radio station personalities who made it possible for me to reach so many of my fans. First of all, to my folks at Majic 102 in Houston. Funky Larry Jones, Val Wilson, and producer Carla Boatner. Thanks for having me on the morning show on a regular basis and for making me feel so welcomed in the studio. Also, thanks to the Breakfast Brothers on Power 98 in Charlotte, North Carolina: B.J. Murphy, Tone X, Tyrone, and producer Lori Mack. Also, in Charlotte on V101.9, D.C., Derrick Corbett, holding down the P.M. drive. And to Janine Davis, for always offering to take me out to breakfast when I'm in town.

To my girl from way back, Bev Smith. Thanks for the great late-night interviews on *The Bev Smith Show*. Over the years, you've been there for me and I appreciate it from the bottom of my heart. I wish you all the best. You deserve it. Of course, I have to send a special shout-out to my folks at KYSS FM in Washington, DC. To crazy Russ Parr, my girl Olivia Fox, and their producer Ted Carter. It's been an experience sitting in with a such a talented group of lunatics. Much success in syndication. And of course, I have to thank my boy, Jeff Fox, on WBLS in New York. We always get the phone lines lit up on the P.M. drive.

Thanks to everyone at Q93 and WYLD in New Orleans for being down to earth over the years. C.J. Morgan and Monica Pierre, L.B.J. LeBron, and Karen Hence in promotions for being so helpful in sponsoring my relationship seminars. To my folks at KISS 104.7 in Atlanta, especially Mellisa Summers for always promoting my book signings on her show. And also to smooth Jeffrey Charles for holding down the P.M. with the ladies. And how could I forget, Si Man, Baby! I sincerely appreciate all the shout-outs and support over the years. You've always been a good friend.

And of course, my family at V103 also in Hotlanta, Frank Ski, Griff (you do the math), comedian Wanda Smith, and producer Tara Thomas, who always keeps it spicy when I'm in the studio. Also, to my special ladies Joyce Littel (on the late-night talk) and Porsche Foxx. Thanks for supporting me on numerous occasions and making Atlanta feel like home.

I have to send a special thanks to Tavis Smiley and his producer Jaci Clark at *BET Tonight*. Thanks for having me on the show and for allowing me to sit in as host while Tavis was on the road. It was an honor and an experience I'll never forget. Last but not least, I want to thank everybody at the *Tom Joyner Morning Show*: Sybil Wilkes, J. Anthony Brown, Myra J., and especially producer

Yolonda Starkes, for doing such a wonderful job of promoting African-American literature in our community. Thank all of you for helping to prove once and for all that black folks do read!

—*Michael Baisden*

THE MAINTENANCE
MAN

PROLOGUE

Confession

(1988)

CHICAGO
SEPTEMBER 1988

Just as the casket was being lowered into the ground, the clouds darkened and the rain began to fall. It seemed so appropriate. Malcolm's mother grasped his hand tightly and began to cry.

"I can't believe he's gone, I just can't believe it!"

"It's gonna be all right, Mama."

After the minister said a few last words, Malcolm exchanged emotional hugs with friends and family then escorted his mother over to where his best friend, Simon, was standing.

"Are you okay, Malcolm?" he asked.

"I'll be fine. I just need a minute alone. Can you take Mama to the limo and wait for me?"

"No problem."

Malcolm handed over his umbrella and told his mother to go with Simon to the car. She smiled and gave him a gentle kiss on the cheek. "I understand, baby. Take all the time you need."

The rain began to come down even harder as Malcolm kneeled at the edge of the grave. He turned his head toward the stormy sky and reached out his hands as if to confirm the rain was real. He wanted to break down and cry, but he fought it. This was as close as he was ever going to be to his father and he wanted to spend those last moments talking the way they used to. Malcolm had unresolved issues and needed to release. Deep down in his heart he knew his father could hear him.

"Dad, I've always admired you for being strong and providing for our family. I never wanted for anything, not money, not attention, and definitely not love. But despite how great you were as a father, I hoped and prayed I would never be like you. As far back as I can remember, you cheated on Mama, not with one or two women, but with five and sometimes six. I hated you because I saw the pain in her eyes that you never did. I kept my resentment toward you buried deep inside, which is why I always neglected to call you on Father's Day.

"Ever since I was seven years old, I've been listening to you lie, cheat, and break women down. There was a vent in the basement that led directly to my bedroom. I remember a conversation you had with a woman named Rachel. I was thirteen then. You were arguing because she suspected you of sleeping with her sister. You were cold busted, but instead of confessing, you took the offensive. Ten minutes later you had everything turned around and she was apologizing to you."

Malcolm paused to regain his composure. His voice choked and the tears began to well up in his eyes. He quickly leaned his head back and allowed the rain to wash them away. He took a deep breath and continued.

"I'm making this confession because my prayers went unanswered. Not only have I become you, I've become worse than you. I'm a gigolo. Now, don't start with your preaching. I'm not some cheap prostitute hanging out on street corners.

My job is escorting rich women out to business functions and social events. I've already earned twenty thousand dollars. Not bad for a twenty-five-year-old rookie. I lied to you and Mama because I didn't want you to know that I dropped out of music school. I thought about calling home for help with tuition but my pride wouldn't allow it.

"So, I decided to make it the best way I knew how, and that meant playing women. Everything I needed to know I learned from watching you: how to walk, talk, dress, and how to use sex to control women. By the time I was fifteen, I was charging my classmates fifty dollars each to escort them to prom."

Malcolm paused again, this time only for a second, then he burst out laughing.

"It's great to be able to joke around with you like this. Too bad we didn't have a chance to do it more often while you were alive. But isn't that the way life always seems to work out. People don't appreciate how precious something is until it's been taken away."

The tears began to well up in his eyes again; this time he allowed them to flow.

"Before I go, I want you to know that I love you and I forgive you. And I hope you will forgive me, too. I know that I can pull my life together and make something of myself. I want you and Mama to be proud of me."

Malcolm stood up and brushed the mud off his pants. Then he pulled a neatly folded piece of paper out of his suit pocket. On it was a song he had written especially for his father entitled "When Players Pray." He kissed it and threw it on top of the casket.

"I was hoping to play this song for you when I came home for Christmas," he said. "I've been practicing it every day on that Steinway piano you gave me on my eighteenth birthday. I've gotten pretty good, too. Who knows, maybe I'll get a chance to play it for you at Carnegie Hall. Rest in peace, you old player."

As Malcolm walked toward the car, he was haunted by the lie he had told his family. His father wasn't shot by a burglar, like it read in his obituary. He was killed while cheating with the married woman who lived next door. The woman's husband came home early from work and shot them both—his wife once in the chest and Malcolm's father twice in the head. The wife survived. When she was asked why they didn't go to a motel, she said Malcolm's father was too cheap to pay for a room.

PART I

Players

LOS ANGELES (2000)

Chapter 1

It was 9:10 P.M. when my flight arrived in Los Angeles right on schedule. I grabbed my garment bag from the overhead compartment and rushed to meet my limo. My appointment with Helen was at 1:00 A.M. and Tina was waiting downtown at the Marriott. I was determined to kill two birds with one stone.

When I arrived at baggage claim, there was a tall distinguished-looking black man holding up a cardboard sign with my name neatly printed on it.

"Excuse me," I said, while extending my hand. "I'm Malcolm Tremell."

"Hello, Mr. Tremell. Allow me to take your bag."

"Thank you, Mr. . . . ?"

"My name is Allen," he said, "but everybody calls me Big Al."

"Well, let's go. I'm in a hurry!"

When I stepped outside the automatic doors, the brutal Los Angeles heat welcomed me home. June was always humid in southern California, even at night. Big Al wiped his forehead with a towel as he laid my garment bag inside the trunk of the freshly waxed black limousine. Then he politely opened my door.

Once inside the car, he buckled his seat belt and put the car in drive.

"Help yourself to a cold drink," he said while pulling out into traffic. "The bar is stocked with everything from cranberry juice to Moët."

"Don't mind if I do."

I poured myself a shot of Christian Brothers brandy and leaned back against the soft leather interior. As we merged onto Highway 105, I tuned the radio station in to 102.3. The deejay's sexy voice serenaded me as we maneuvered through the dense L.A. traffic.

"You're listening to KJLH," she announced. "Coming up next, your request for Anita Baker and Barry White. But first, an old-school classic by Kool and the Gang, 'Summer Madness.' " She paused as the intro began to play. "This song goes out to all you children of the night."

It was as if she were playing that song especially for me. I was definitely a child of the night, a moon child, a Cancer. It had been three days since I last saw daylight. My workdays began after 8:00 P.M. and ended before sunrise. On the days when I had no appointments, I kept my blinds shut and curtains drawn—I lived like a vampire.

The drive downtown to the Marriott took thirty-five minutes. It was 9:55 P.M. and the clock was ticking. I gave Big Al instructions to pick me up at eleven-thirty then rushed into the hotel. Tina checked into Room 1001, like always. I hopped aboard the elevator hoping she was ready.

As I approached the room, I could smell the familiar aroma of jasmine incense burning. I knocked on the door and put my hand over the peephole.

"Who is it?" she asked apprehensively.

"It's the plumber, ma'am," I said, trying to disguise my voice. "We received a call that the sink was backed up."

"There's nothing wrong with my sink. Are you sure you have the right room?"

"I'm looking right at the job order, ma'am. It says Room 1001. Guest needs drain unstopped."

When I burst out laughing, she was on to me. Tina opened the door buck naked and popped me upside the head.

"Malcolm, you scared the hell out of me!"

"I'm sorry, baby. Let me make it up to you."

I backed her into the candlelit room and dropped my garment bag. Then I lifted her by the cheeks and carried her over to the bed.

"I love a man who knows how to take control," she said.

"And I love a woman who knows how to let a man be *The Man*." I gently laid her down on the bed and began taking off my clothes.

"Hurry up, Malcolm," she said while pulling at the buttons on my silk shirt. "I'm horny as hell."

"Slow down, baby. These clothes aren't cheap," I said while backing away. "Let me do this."

"Why are you worried about your damn shirt?" She sounded upset. "I can afford a thousand shirts."

What she really meant was her husband could afford a thousand shirts. Tina was going through an ugly divorce with a star point guard in the NBA. Every dime she had came out of his bank account.

I didn't want to ruin the mood so I poured two glasses of the Moët champagne she had chilling out on the terrace. Then I proposed a toast.

"Here's to six months of good conversation, good company, and great sex."

"I'll drink to that!" she said.

While I sipped on my drink, I casually looked over at the clock on the nightstand, it read ten-fifteen. I excused myself to the bathroom and immediately went into action. I hung my clothes neatly over the shower rod, brushed my teeth, shaved, and took a quick shower. Within ten minutes I was ready.

"It's about time," Tina said with an attitude.

"I promise you, it will be worth the wait."

I pulled a Trojan condom and a metal flask of baby oil out of my garment bag and heated the flask by the fire from the candle. "Turn over on your stomach, baby," I told her.

I poured the warm oil on her back and massaged it into her shoulders. Once she relaxed, I slowly ran my tongue from her lower back to the base of her neck.

"*Ssss,* do that again, baby," she begged.

"Say please," I insisted.

"Please, please, please, with sugar on top."

I used my tongue like a wet probe, boldly going where no man had gone before. Twenty minutes into the foreplay, Tina couldn't take it anymore. "Stop teasing, baby," she said, sighing. "Give it to me." I pushed her legs back toward the headboard as far as they would go then I dove in. The candlelight cast an erotic shadow onto the hotel room wall. It was like looking into a smoked mirror. I tried to concentrate but I kept staring at the silhouette of her body. With every flick of my tongue, she winced and quivered.

In a slow circular motion I ascended from her pierced belly button to her supple nipples. She inhaled, then turned her head to the side and let out a soft moan. "Oh, Malcolm, you feel so good. Don't stop. Please don't stop."

I moved my hand slowly down her long, smooth leg until I felt the warmth from within. I paused briefly to massage her, then I put on my condom and slid inside. Her head sprang up in one quick motion.

"Wha—what are you doing?" she stuttered.

"I'm doing my job," I replied confidently.

She flopped back down onto the pillow and began to shake violently. Seconds later she let out a loud scream. "Oh, shit, that's the spot, baby, right there!" Her legs tensed as she grasped the sheets into her small fists. "I'm cumming. I'm cumming!" Tina bit down on her lip and frantically tossed her head from side to side. If there was an

Academy Award for best orgasm she would have won, hands down. When it was over, she rolled onto her side, clutched the pillow between her legs, and dozed off. Talk about perfect timing. The clock read 10:55 P.M. Her time was up.

I grabbed my garment bag and stepped into the bathroom. While the bathwater ran, I pulled out my black book to confirm my next appointment. I recalled writing 1:20 A.M. but my notation read: Helen—Melvin's Jazz Club—12:00 A.M. "So much for a long, hot bath!" I said in disgust.

I pulled the shower lever and quickly jumped in. While I washed in the hot drizzle, I tried to relax. The four-hour flight in from Chicago had me worn out. I thought about canceling my appointment, but Helen was a priority customer. According to the article I read in *Fortune* magazine, she was worth ten million dollars. I wasn't going to disappoint my golden goose, not for a basket case like Tina. She had more drama in her life than a soap opera: death in the family, relatives in jail, the dog being run over by a car, and an impending divorce. I couldn't help feeling sorry for her. So, I penciled her in as a courtesy fuck.

By 11:15 P.M. I was rejuvenated and ready to go. When I stepped out of the bathroom, I expected Tina to still be asleep but she was standing outside on the terrace buck naked, smoking a cigarette. The moonlight accentuated her tanned skin and long silky hair that extended to the middle of her back. I paused to admire her one last time. As I was about to announce I was leaving, she muttered something.

"Did you say something, Tina?" I asked while walking toward her.

"You heard what I said, men are no damn good! All they do is tell lies, get you pregnant, and then move on to the next young piece."

"I don't know what kind of drug you're on, but I don't have time for another one of your tantrums, not tonight. Now, if you don't mind, I'd like to collect my money and leave."

She turned suddenly, her eyes filled with tears. "Fuck you, Malcolm!" she shouted. "I knew you didn't give a damn about me. All I am to you is another trick."

She tossed her cigarette over the balcony then stormed past me looking for her purse.

"Here, is this what you want?" Tina pulled five crisp hundred-dollar bills out of her wallet and threw them in my face. "Take them!"

I looked at her like she was out of her mind. Then I calmly took my black book out of my suit pocket and began writing.

"What are you doing?" she asked, sounding concerned.

"I'm scratching your name out of my book."

"But I want to see you next month." Tina quickly composed herself, clearing her throat and wiping the phony tears from her eyes.

"Next month? I'm scratching your crazy ass out for good," I said. "I'm sick and tired of these dramatic episodes. This is the third time in six months I've had to deal with this shit. Enough is enough!" I put my book inside my pocket and headed for the door.

"Where do you think you're going?" She tried to block my way with her naked one-hundred-and-twenty-five-pound frame. "I paid you for your time, plus a hundred-dollar tip."

"You think you can throw money at me like I'm some kind of cheap prostitute? I couldn't buy a decent pair of shoes with that chump change."

"I'm sorry, Malcolm. Don't go. Please don't go." Tina gathered the bills off the floor and handed them to me. "You know this divorce has me under a lot of pressure."

"I can't believe you're still dealing with this nonsense," I said. "Let it go and get on with your life."

"I gave that bastard the best ten years of my life. I'm not about to let him walk away scot-free."

"Scot-free?" I asked sarcastically. "He offered to settle

out of court for five million dollars, the house, the Mercedes, and twenty-five thousand dollars a month in child support. What more do you want?"

"I want to break that son of a bitch, that's what. He just signed a twenty-five-million-dollar contract with Nike. I'm not going anywhere until I get paid!"

I lifted her by the waist and tossed her onto the bed. "You're nothing but a gold-digging tramp."

"You'll be back, Malcolm," she said seductively while caressing her breasts. "I'll give you a call when I get my first million. We'll spread it on top of the bed and fuck on it."

"You're pathetic," I said. Then I picked up my garment bag and rushed out the door.

While I waited on the elevator, I searched through my bag for aspirin. The stress of playing the role of lover and psychiatrist was getting the best of me. My reflection in the corridor mirror spoke volumes. My eyes were red and my hair was graying in places I didn't recall. For the first time in twelve years I contemplated retiring from the business. As I stepped onto the elevator I popped two Tylenol and nervously laughed at the thought.

Chapter 2

We arrived at Melvin's Jazz Club at 11:50 P.M. The line wrapped around the corner and the valet parking was full. I told Big Al to blow the horn and flash the headlights three times. The valet stepped aside and the bright orange partitions parted like the Red Sea.

"You must be a regular," Big Al said.

"Let's just say it's a popular place for people in my line of work," I replied with a sly grin.

Every city has its professional hangouts. In Los Angeles, musicians and gigolos congregated at Melvin's. It was just a coincidence that Helen wanted to meet there. I'm sure she was unaware of its infamous reputation.

"Good evening, Mr. Tremell," the valet said as he opened my door. His name was Rosco. "I can see you remembered the signal."

"Sometimes it comes in handy, Rosco," I said as I slipped him a ten. "Thanks for the hookup."

"You're welcome, sir."

Big Al was standing on the driver's side of the limo with his mouth wide open. The women standing in line were attractive and dressed provocatively, most of them wearing miniskirts that barely covered their asses.

"Excuse me, Big Al!" I shouted to break his concentration. "Would you like to join me for a drink?"

"Am I off the clock?" he asked.

"As far as I'm concerned."

"In that case, it would be my pleasure!"

He rushed a comb through his graying hair and popped a Tic Tac in his mouth. After he handed over his keys to the valet, he escorted me through the rowdy crowd. Big Al stood six-five and weighed at least two hundred and sixty pounds. His wide body made for a perfect wedge. I never saw people move out of the way so fast.

When we entered the club, Melvin, the man himself, was waiting to greet us. He was sporting a white pinstriped suit, a matching brim, and like always, he was chewing down on his trademark Cuban cigar.

"Hey, Cool Breeze!" he shouted in his deep, raspy voice. Then he threw his arm around me. "When did you get back?"

Melvin was like a surrogate father to me. Ever since I came to L.A. back in 1991, he had taken me under his wing, teaching me about the music business and about life. At seventy years old, he was the closest thing I had to a father. The nickname Cool Breeze was his idea. He said I stroked the piano keys so smoothly that I sent chills down his spine.

"I flew in a couple of hours ago," I told him. "I had business on the East Coast, then I stopped off in Chicago to check on Mama."

"How's she doing?" he asked, sounding genuinely concerned.

"She's fine. I'll be sure to tell her you said hello."

"So, what's up with the big fellah." Melvin looked at Big Al from head to toe. "Don't tell me you've hired a bodyguard to keep the women off you."

"This is my driver, Big Al. Big Al, this is the famous Melvin Butler."

"It's an honor to meet you, Mr. Butler," Big Al said nervously.

"Thank you, young man," Melvin replied while shaking his hand. "But, please call me Melvin. Any friend of Malcolm's is a friend of mine."

"Are you in the mood to jam on the piano tonight?" Melvin asked. "I've got it tuned just the way you like it."

"You play the piano, Mr. Tremell?" Big Al asked.

"He does more than just play the piano. He makes love to it," Melvin boasted. "Malcolm is the most talented jazz pianist in L.A. And I should know, I've heard the best."

"Okay, that's enough ego stroking for one night. My head is starting to swell," I said, smiling with pride. "But I'll have to take a rain check, old man. I'm here on business tonight."

Melvin knew what I meant and didn't press the issue. He chewed down on his cigar and gave me an inconspicuous nod.

"Let me get you a table in the VIP section." Melvin signaled the host. "I'll be over to check on you later. Meanwhile, enjoy yourselves. Drinks are on the house."

As we walked through the dimly lit room, I felt right at home. The rhythm of the music, the aged brick walls, and the chatter of the crowd created a cool ambience. There's no place on earth like a jazz club, especially one with a history like Melvin's. You could practically feel the ghosts of the immortals like B. B. King, Ella Fitzgerald, and Billie Holiday.

The VIP section was situated across from the stage and consisted of six tables and two booths. Some people perceived this as a place of status. For me it was a comfortable seat away from the disgusting cigar smoke and annoying conversations. Melvin's was a haven for wanna-be players who wore makeup and expensive jewelry to compensate for their lack of class and self-esteem. I always got a kick out of watching them talk on their cheap cell phones as if they had important business.

"They should call this place Perpetrators R Us," I said, laughing.

"You can say that again. This place is a circus," Big Al said, as he glanced across the room, "and we're sitting in the center ring."

Beautiful women from all sides of the room smiled flirtatiously trying to get my attention. I caught the eye of a blonde who dipped her finger in a wineglass, pulled it out, and sucked on it. Another woman, who was with a date, gestured for me to meet her at the bar. She thought it was cute, but to me it was disrespectful.

"Do you always attract this much attention?" Big Al asked while watching the performance.

"In my line of work, attracting attention is considered free advertising. You'd be surprised how far an expensive suit and the scent of cologne can get you."

"I hope this isn't too personal a question, but what is it that you do exactly?"

As a rule, I never discussed my business, the only exceptions were Melvin and my best friend, Simon. Even my mother didn't know what I did for a living. She thought my full-time job was selling real estate. But I felt comfortable with Big Al. Call it intuition.

"I own an escort service," I said.

"Escort service? Is that a fancy way of saying you get paid to have sex with women?"

His ignorance was not surprising. Most people don't know the difference between a gigolo and a prostitute.

"Any bum off the street can stick his dick inside of a woman," I said defensively. "Being a professional gigolo is about having class and intellect."

"Are you telling me these horny women are spending big bucks for deep conversation over a cup of tea?"

"Sometimes that's all it amounts to."

He paused, looked straight in my eyes, then burst out laughing. "Get the hell outta here! Women today are no different than men. They want to get their freak on."

"This business is not about sex," I told him. "Most of my clients are married women who need an escort to a social function."

"Why would they hire you if they're married?"

"Because their rich husbands are too damn lazy or too busy fucking their secretaries, that's why!"

"So, basically, you're an expensive arm piece?"

"I see myself more as a therapist. And nothing gives me more pleasure then sending my patients home to their sorry-ass husbands feeling beautiful and desirable."

"Sounds to me like you're a high-priced maintenance man."

"Exactly!"

Our conversation was interrupted by the waitress excusing herself to set three glasses down on the table, two glasses of water and a glass of cognac. She placed the cognac in front of me.

"Thanks for the water, but I didn't order a drink," I said.

"The Courvoisier is from an admirer." She pointed in the direction of the bar.

I looked over and there was a beautiful black woman wearing a red sequined dress. She smiled at me and lifted her glass in a friendly toast. I did the same to show my appreciation. I was hoping she wouldn't perceive my gesture as an invitation to get better acquainted. Unfortunately she did. A few seconds later, she gestured to the woman next to her to watch her purse then started toward me.

"Well, Mr. Maintenance Man, I hope you've got your toolbox handy," Big Al said as he stood up from the booth. "Looks like you have more pipe to lay tonight."

"Very funny, Chris Rock. Now, if you don't mind."

"No problem, boss," he said jokingly as he stepped aside to allow the woman in red to sit.

Her timing could not have been worse. It was 12:30 A.M. and I had a feeling Helen would arrive at any moment. Even if she didn't show, I was in no mood for casual conversation. My mind was focused on one thing: getting paid.

"Hello, I'm Stephanie," she said while extending her hand. "What's your name, handsome?"

"Malcolm."

"So, where are you from, Malcolm?"

"Chicago."

"Chicago? I love Chicago!" she said enthusiastically. "In fact, I'm going next week to visit my girlfriend. Her name is Kim Jones. Do you know her?"

I looked at her like she was stupid. How any rational human being could expect you to know one person out of five million is beyond me, especially with a common name like Kim Jones.

"I don't believe I know her," I said while conspicuously looking down at my watch.

"Are you expecting company?" she asked.

"As a matter of fact, I am." I was intentionally being short, hoping she would get the hint. But she was persistent.

"Girlfriend, wife, or just a friend."

"That's personal, don't you think?"

"I thought this was a personal conversation," she said while sliding her phone number over to me on a napkin.

I was becoming irritated by her awkwardness. I was already tired from my flight, Helen was a half hour late, and worst of all I was hungry.

"Look, Stephanie, let's not waste each other's time with all the small talk," I said in a soft but stern voice. "I don't date or fuck for free. My fee is two hundred dollars an hour, plus expenses. Now, if you can afford that then leave me your business card and I'll call you to set up an appointment. If not, please stop annoying me with your boring-ass conversation."

Her cheerful smile quickly changed to a look of disappointment. She covered her face with her hand to compose herself. When she removed it, she was noticeably upset. One look into her big brown eyes and I knew I had made a terrible mistake.

"I don't have a damned business card," she said with contempt. "I'm a cashier at Wal-Mart."

"I'm sorry," I said compassionately. "I didn't mean to come off so harshly."

"You don't have to apologize to me, Mr. Ladies' Man. I'm nobody special," she said as she stood up from the table. "I don't have any money. I don't drive an expensive car. Hell, I can't even afford this dress I'm wearing. I have to take it back to Saks tomorrow for a refund." Her hands were on her hips. "But I'll tell you what I do have, Malcolm, I have a good heart. That probably doesn't mean much to a coldhearted son of a bitch like you." She picked up my glass of cognac and threw it in my face. "By the way, you're welcome for the drink." Then she calmly walked away.

I felt like a complete heel. My face was soaked with Courvoisier and my jacket and shirt were stained. Some of the people in the club saw what had happened and were gossiping and snickering. Big Al rushed over with a stack of paper towels and handed them to me. I could tell by his expression that he had been laughing, too.

"What happened?" he asked.

"I got what I had coming," I said as I stood up to wipe myself off.

"I think I'm going to change your name from Maintenance Man to Rain Man."

We both burst out laughing as we walked out of the VIP section headed for the door. On the way out I said my good-byes to Melvin. He gave me a fatherly hug and told me to stay out of trouble. He didn't say anything about the incident to my face but I heard him laughing his ass off when he closed his office door. It definitely wasn't my night.

When we walked outside, people were still lining up to get inside. The valets were running around like maniacs trying to park all the cars. Big Al decided to get the limo himself. While I waited, I thought about going back inside to apologize to Stephanie. My ego was bruised and my conscience was kicking my ass. Before I could decide, a white stretch limousine drove up and Helen stepped onto the scene wearing a black Armani mini dress with matching pumps and a Branda bag.

For a woman in her late forties, she had one hell of a figure, 36-26-38. No woman should be so rich and sexy, I was thinking. While the men in line gawked, I stepped up to greet her.

"Hi, Malcolm, sorry I'm late," she said nonchalantly. "But you know what they say, business before pleasure."

I looked down at my watch, it read 1:15 A.M., then I pulled out my appointment book.

"Well, I have a saying of my own," I replied as I scratched out her name. "Phone first!"

"Excuse me?"

"You heard what I said. The next time you expect to be late, have the common courtesy to call in advance."

"I know you can't be serious, Malcolm," she said while stroking my face with her hand. "What if I pay you another five hundred. Will you forgive me?"

"I wouldn't give a damn if you paid me five thousand dollars, I don't tolerate inconsiderateness," I told her. "Now, if you will excuse me."

When I turned to look for Big Al, Stephanie and her girlfriend walked right past me. I grabbed Stephanie by the arm to get her attention.

"Stephanie, can I talk to you?"

"I don't think I can afford your time," she said sarcastically and pulled away.

I left Helen standing there looking foolish and I went after Stephanie. She crossed the street and began walking toward the parking garage. I crossed in the middle of the intersection to cut her off and damn near killed myself trying to dodge traffic.

"Stephanie, please wait!" I shouted from behind. "Just give me a minute!" She stopped. I saw her reach inside her purse to give her girlfriend the car keys. Then she stood still and waited for me to catch up.

"What do you want, Malcolm?" she asked with an attitude.

"I just wanted to tell you how sorry I am for being such an asshole. What I said to you was totally uncalled for."

"Apology accepted, now good night," she said abruptly. Then she began to walk away.

"Hold up," I said as I blocked her way. "Don't act like that."

"How do you expect me to act? You hurt my feelings," she said emotionally. "I thought you were a gentleman but you're no different than the rest of these creeps in L.A."

"You're wrong about me, Stephanie! But I can't change your mind, not in one night," I said. "I just need to know that you sincerely accept my apology so I can sleep with a clear conscience."

"I already told you, I accept."

"Can we at least shake hands or hug or something?"

"If I give you a hug, will you leave me alone?"

"I promise, cross my heart and hope to die." I made an X over my chest.

"Okay," she agreed, "but don't try anything fresh."

When she put her arms around my neck I squeezed tight and carefully slipped something into her purse. She was involved for a moment then pulled back. "That's enough," she said while straightening out her dress. "Now leave me alone like you promised." I stepped aside and allowed her to go on her way.

Once she was safely in her car I headed back to the club. Big Al must have seen me coming because he made a U-turn right in front of the club and headed toward me.

"Need a taxi, sir?" he asked as he pulled up to the curb. I took off my jacket and jumped in. Once inside I lay back and took a deep breath.

"So, where do we go from here?" Big Al asked.

"Home," I told him. "I want to go home."

Just as we were about to drive off, there was a knock at my window. It was Stephanie. I cracked my window just enough to hear her.

"Malcolm, I can't accept this."

"What are you talking about?" I asked, playing dumb.

"I'm talking about the three hundred dollars you put in my purse."

"Stephanie, you better put that money in your purse and get your ass back in the car!" her girlfriend screamed from the car behind us.

"Why don't you take her advice?" I said to her.

"Malcolm, let this window down so I can give you this back."

"The window is broken."

"Well, open the door."

"The door is broken, too."

"If you don't take this back, I'm going to leave it here on the street."

"That's your prerogative," I told her. "I would rather you use it to purchase that dress," I said in a serious tone. "You look like a queen in that dress, baby. And I want you to have it. Consider it a gift."

I signaled Big Al to pull off and we sped off down the street. As we merged back onto the expressway, I was feeling good about myself. I lay back and turned on the radio hoping to hear something relaxing. Right on cue, a song by the Ohio Players called "It's All Over" came on.

"Hey, Al, remember this old cut?"

"Of course, I remember. Back in those days I used to throw rent parties in my basement."

"My father used to throw those parties, too. He always played this song right before he kicked everybody out," I said, laughing. "Those were the good old days."

"Where is your father now?"

"He died back in eighty-eight."

"I'm sorry to hear that," he said with compassion. "What did he die of? Cancer, heart attack, stroke?"

"No, he died of an overdose of women," I said sadly. "I just hope I get out of this business before I O.D., too."

Chapter 3

At eight o'clock the next morning I awoke to the clatter of pots and pans. I rolled out of bed and put on my drawers to see what all the commotion was about. When I opened the bedroom door, my maid, Ms. Ruby, was scrambling eggs and frying bacon.

"Good morning," she said, smiling from ear to ear.

"Ms. Ruby, what are you doing here?" I asked while rubbing the sleep out of my eyes. "I thought I gave you the day off?"

"Yes, sir, but today is a special day, so I decided to come over to make you breakfast." She winked.

"The only thing special about today is that I can't get any sleep," I said as I walked into the living room and closed the black satin curtains. "Why are you torturing me? You know I can't stand sunlight."

"Are you sure you don't have a coffin in your bedroom?" she said, laughing.

"As a matter of fact, I do. And if you don't let me go back to sleep I'm going to bite you on the neck."

"Vampires aren't supposed to age," she said as she winked again.

"Ms. Ruby, is there something wrong with your eye?"

"Malcolm, you are a pitiful soul. You can't even take a hint?" She pulled out a white envelope and shoved it in my face. "Here, take it!"

"What is this, a letter bomb?" I asked, laughing.

"I wish it were, you party pooper. It's a birthday card."

"Today is my birthday?" I asked. "I thought it was tomorrow."

I went over to check the calendar on the refrigerator to confirm the date. Sure enough, it was Thursday, June 29. Suddenly I had a burst of energy. I ran over to Ms. Ruby, grabbed her around the waist, and began dancing around the apartment.

"Let me go, boy!" she shouted.

"I'll never let you go, you domestic goddess. I can't live without you or your collard greens."

"Malcolm, you are so crazy. Let me go before I drop this fork."

"Well, drop it and show me what you got, old lady."

She stopped dancing and put her hands on her hips. "Who you callin' old?"

"Did I say old?" I said, checking myself. "I meant experienced."

"That's what I thought you meant. Besides, if anybody is old around here, it's you." She walked back to the stove to turn over the bacon. "One day that young pistol of yours is going to run out of bullets."

"I can always reload with Viagra."

She snatched the damp towel off the refrigerator door and chased me back into the bedroom. For sixty-five she was quick on her feet. Just as I thought I had gotten away, she popped me right on my ass. I let out a scream like a little sissy. "Ouch!"

"You deserved that, you little heathen!" she shouted.

"Maybe next time you'll have more respect for your elders."

I went to get a towel out of the linen closet to return the favor but before I could, the phone rang.

"Tremell residence," I answered.

"Happy birthday, son!"

"Hi, Mama. How did you know I would be up this early?"

"Because I was the one who told Ms. Ruby to wake you up and feed you," she said. "Ever since you stopped eating red meat and pork you've gotten skinny."

"Who you callin' skinny?" I asked as I examined myself in the dresser mirror.

At six-three, two hundred twenty pounds, I was solid as a rock. My chest was a muscular fifty-two inches and my abs were tight, six-pack and all. I thought I was in great shape for my age.

"I swear, ever since Oprah did that show on the beef industry, people have lost their minds," she criticized. "A slab of ribs and some chitlins never hurt anybody."

"Mama, I'm eating just fine. Ms. Ruby is taking good care of me."

"What you need is a wife," she said. "Somebody who's there for you twenty-four hours a day."

"There you go again, trying to marry me off. You're starting to make me feel like an old maid."

At that moment, my other line rang. "Saved by the bell," I whispered. I told Mama I loved her and that I would call her back. Then I clicked over.

"Tremell residence," I answered.

"Tremell residence? I see those white folks in Marina del Rey have you talkin' proper."

That wisecrack could only come from one person, Simon. "Wuz up, fool?"

"You're whuz up," he said. Then he began singing the birthday song. *"Happy birthday to you. Happy birthday to*

you. Happy birthday to Malcolm. Happy birthday to you.
He went on. *"How old are you? How old—"*

"Okay, that's enough," I said, cutting in. "You can't sing worth shit. Thank goodness you went into the nightclub business."

"So, how old are you?" he asked. "Forty-five, or fifty?"

"If I'm fifty, you're fifty-one. Don't forget you're a year older than me."

"In that case, how does it feel to be twenty-one?" We both laughed.

Simon and I had known each other since high school. We met at a talent contest my freshman year. I played the piano and he mixed records. Neither of us won, but we stayed in touch afterward. Later that year Simon got into a fight with a senior on the football team over a girl he was dating. I jumped in to help and we both got our asses kicked. We've been best friends ever since.

"You know damn well I'm thirty-seven," I told him. "But old age must be catching up with me. Can you believe I forgot my birthday was today?"

"That doesn't surprise me one bit? Those women are wearing you out."

"You're right about that. I've had four dates in three different cities this week. I'm beat."

"Why don't you take a break and fly down here to Atlanta this weekend. You can check out the new club and sit in with the band in the Jazz Room."

"The last time I sat in with the band at your club, it damn near burned down, along with the piano my dad gave me for my eighteenth birthday, remember?"

"How was I supposed to know my bartender was smoking crack in the storage room? And by the way, I *did* reimburse you after I got the insurance money."

"No amount of money could replace that piano," I said sadly. "But I'll try to get down there anyway. Just let me check my schedule and I'll get back with you."

"Don't give me that crap about your schedule." He sounded annoyed "I'm not one of your clients you pencil in your little black book. I'm your friend."

"Okay, I'll come," I said, trying to calm him down. "Besides, I've got to check out your new place. What did you decide to call it?"

"Club Obsession, and it's taking off like a rocket. Especially since we added male strippers on Thursday nights. Cynthia came up with the idea."

"Cynthia!" I shouted. "When did you start seeing her again?"

The phone suddenly went silent. "I was saving that surprise for when you got here," he said. "We've been back together for about a month."

"Simon, don't you think it's a strange coincidence that she came back a week before the club opened?"

"What are you trying to say?"

"What I'm trying to say is Club Obsession has made you an instant celebrity in Atlanta. Cynthia just wants to shine in the spotlight," I explained to him. "I guess being a news reporter wasn't enough."

"Don't start preaching to me, Malcolm. I know what I'm doing."

"Open your eyes, Simon. That woman is nothing but a no-good—"

"Stop!" he interrupted. "I love Cynthia and she loves me. And no matter what you say, I'm planning to marry her. Why can't you accept that and be happy for me?"

I wanted to blow up, but I bit my tongue. He was a grown man and had to make his own decisions.

"Okay, partner, I got your back," I told him. "I only want what's best for you."

"Thanks for understanding," he said. "I'm going to let you go. I'll see you Saturday night at the club. Until then, enjoy your birthday."

"I'll try," I told him. Then I hung up.

I stared back at my dazed expression in the mirror and shook my head. "Damn you, Simon," I said to myself. "When will you ever learn?"

Chapter 4

Simon arrived at Club Obsession at 5:00 P.M., two hours before the doors were scheduled to open. He parked his red Dodge Viper in the back lot and took his nine-millimeter pistol out of the glove compartment. Growing up on the Southside of Chicago taught him never to get too comfortable with his surroundings. Although the club was in the affluent Buckhead section of Atlanta, he knew he could get jacked at any time.

After deactivating the club's alarm system, he unlocked the two dead-bolt locks and went inside. Simon was setting a trap. For the last three weekends the cash at the door had come up short. He had a hunch the club manager, Darren, was skimming off the top but he needed proof. So he drilled a hole inside a light fixture behind the cashier's window and mounted a tiny camera, like the ones they used in Vegas to watch the blackjack tables and slot machines. He ran a thin black wire along the ceiling and into his office where he connected it to a monitor. "Now, let's see what kind of fish we catch," he said to himself.

After putting away his tools, he mixed himself a gin and tonic and put on his favorite song, "Mind Blowing Decisions" by Heatwave. He grabbed a broom handle and pretended like he was steppin' at the Fifty Yard Line in Chicago. Those were the good old days, he was thinking as he danced around the freshly waxed floor. Just as he was getting into a nice groove, there was a loud knock at the front door. *Bam, bam, bam!* He turned off the music and walked slowly toward the door with his pistol drawn. "Who is it?" he shouted as he peeped out of the window.

"Mr. Harris, my name is Ariel Daniels. Can I talk to you for a moment?"

"How did you know I was here?"

"I was having dinner across the street and I saw you drive up," she told him. "I was waiting for the club to open so I could talk to you about a job."

Simon put away his pistol and let her in. He was impressed with her poise and beauty. Ariel stood erect at five-nine and spoke with perfect diction. Her cinnamon-brown skin was flawless, and her hair was cut short and natural. She tried without success to cover her firm breasts under the light-blue jacket she wore. Simon tried not to stare as he escorted her into his office.

"Have a seat," he told her. "So, what can I do for you?"

"Mr. Harris, I've been an admirer of yours ever since you opened your first club in Marietta back in ninety-three. I always wanted to work for someone with your vision."

"I appreciate your admiration for my hard work, but what are you qualified to do?"

"I'm currently working as a marketing manager at Coca-Cola. But I've been in the nightclub industry ever since I was in college. I worked as a waitress, bartender, and as a manager," she said. "Here's my résumé."

She pulled a folder out of a black leather briefcase, and handed it to him. While he looked it over, she glanced around the room at the pictures on the walls.

"You mind if I look around?" Ariel asked.

"Be my guest."

She walked over to the poster of Cynthia and stared at it like she was trying to make a connection. "Isn't she a reporter on Channel Five?"

"Yes, she's my fiancée."

"Congratulations! I'm glad to finally meet a man who isn't afraid of commitment."

"I take it that you're single?"

"I'm probably the most single woman in Atlanta." She laughed nervously. "I haven't been on a date in months."

"That's hard to believe. I mean, you're very beautiful. And judging by your résumé, you've got brains, too."

"A home in Stone Mountain, a Mercedes, and a master's degree don't make you an ideal mate. Most men are intimidated by strong, independent women."

"So I've heard."

"Look, Mr. Harris. I want to work for you," she said passionately. "I know I can make Club Obsession an even bigger success. Just give me a chance."

"I would love to hire you, Ariel, but there aren't any positions open for anyone with your qualifications," Simon explained. "But if that changes, you'll be the first person I call."

"Thank you for taking time out to see me, Mr. Harris," she said as she reached out to shake his hand.

"Please call me Simon," he insisted. " 'Mr.' makes me feel old."

Simon escorted her out to her car, and cordially opened her door.

"Before I go, I want to tell you how much I appreciate your professionalism," she said as she let the top down on her convertible. "You don't know how difficult it is for an attractive woman to be taken seriously."

"Well, that's the difference between me and most men, I don't allow my smaller head to make business decisions," he said. "Besides, I love Cynthia too much to do anything to jeopardize our relationship. It's just not worth it."

"Now, there's something you don't see every day," Ariel said as she put her car in drive.

"What's that?"

"A gentleman."

Chapter 5

At 9:00 P.M. hundreds of women stood in line outside Club Obsession to see the strip show. It was Ladies' Night and the first one hundred women would get in free. When the doors opened, they rushed inside to get the best seats near the stage. But the strippers hadn't shown up or even called. The manager, Darren, was sweating bullets. This was the second time in four weeks he had failed to secure the entertainment.

"We've only got an hour before show time," Simon said. "Where the hell are they?"

"I've been trying to contact them all day," Darren explained. "Maybe they're on the way."

Simon knew they weren't coming. Darren had put him in another tight spot. He wanted to fire him right then, but he needed him, at least until he found a replacement.

"I'm going to make some calls to see if I can find someone on short notice," Simon said as he walked toward his office."

"What do you want me to do?" Darren asked.

"You can keep these women from tearing down my place."

Simon frantically scrolled through his Rolodex and called every talent agent and strip-club owner in Atlanta. Thirty minutes passed before he finally contacted a group out of Decatur. They called themselves Hot Chocolate. The manager, Theodore Simmons, was very arrogant and shrewd. He insisted on a fee of two thousand dollars, almost twice the amount of the original group. Simon was in no position to argue, so he agreed.

When he came out of his office to tell Darren the news, the number of women had doubled. Some of them were drinking heavily and getting loud.

"This could get ugly," he said to Darren. "Call the police and tell them we need extra police officers."

"I already did," he said.

"And?"

"They didn't have any available."

"I'll be damned," Simon said with his hand on his hip. "I sure hope those guys show up in time."

"If they don't, then what?" Darren asked.

"If they don't, you're going out there to explain why the show was canceled."

"Why me?"

"Because you're the dumb son of a bitch who got me into this mess in the first place."

• • •

By 9:55, the crowd was getting restless. Some of the women began to demand their money back. Simon stood on the second floor where he could get a view of the front entrance. Every time a car pulled up, he cringed. "Where are they?" he asked while looking down at his watch every two minutes.

At 10:05 he gave up hope and went downstairs to tell

Darren to make the announcement. But Darren was nowhere to be found. He checked Darren's office, the kitchen, and the rest room, but there was no sign of him. "Never ask a boy to do a man's job," Simon said as he walked toward the stage. The overzealous crowd suddenly got quiet. Simon grabbed the microphone out of the stand and cleared his throat to deliver the bad news.

"I want to apologize for the show not starting on time," he said. "It's just been brought to my attention that . . ."

Before he could finish his sentence, the deejay signaled that the group had arrived and was ready to go on. Simon played it off brilliantly and made the announcement seem like a part of the act.

"As I was saying, it's just been brought to my attention that the show is about to begin! Ladies, please put your hands together for the men of Hot Chocolate!"

The lights dimmed and the deejay played the song "Pony" by Ginuwine. The crowd erupted. Red, green, and orange lights flashed in rhythm with the music. When the smoke cleared, four muscular men stood onstage wearing cutoff T-shirts and thongs. Women were screaming at the top of their lungs, "Take it off!"

It was a scene right out of an X-rated comedy. Well-dressed women in business suits were knocking over chairs and one another trying to get to the stage to put money in the strippers' crotches. The deejay turned up the music and began remixing the lyrics, *I'm just a bachelor, looking for a partner.*

The strippers worked their way through the impassioned crowd, bumping and grinding while women stuffed their thongs with dollar bills and phone numbers. Midway through the song, the men tore off their shirts and jumped on top of tables, flexing their muscles and pushing their pelvises in women's faces. Some of them got carried away and pulled their penises out from under their thongs. It was a wild scene.

When the song ended, the strippers ran back onto the stage and took a bow. The women applauded apprehensively hoping the show wasn't over. Three of the dancers went backstage to get chairs while the other grabbed the microphone.

"I have a special treat for you tonight, ladies!" he announced. "Do you want it?"

"Yeah!" they yelled.

"Are you sure you can handle it?"

"Yeah!" they yelled again.

"I can handle it, baby!" shouted an intoxicated woman on the front row.

"Before I give it to you, I want the women who are celebrating birthdays to come up here to the stage."

Several women rushed the stage claiming their birthdays were in June. It took a few minutes to sort out the pretenders. Once they were sorted out, three women sat onstage looking nervous as hell.

"What's your name, sweetheart," he asked the woman sitting nearest to him.

"Crystal," she said shyly.

"That's a pretty name," he told her. "Let me ask you a question, Crystal. Do you keep stuffed animals on your bed?"

"Yes," she giggled.

"Do you have a teddy bear?"

"No, I don't."

"Well, I'm going to give you a teddy bear for your birthday," he said in a sensual tone.

The lights dimmed again, and white smoke blasted from the floor as the song "Return of the Mack" by Mark Morrison echoed through the huge speakers. The beat was hypnotic.

"Ladies, it's my pleasure to bring you the man of the hour. Put your hands together for Teddy Bear!"

When the lights came on, a bald man stood in the center of the stage sporting a long white fur coat, a matching brim, and a black cane. He slowly peeled off his coat revealing his naked and oiled black body. The women onstage fell backward in their seats and the crowd went wild.

"Come to Mama," one woman yelled as she reached out with a twenty-dollar bill.

"Damn girl, look at the body on that man!" another woman screamed.

At six-five, two hundred forty pounds, Teddy Bear was an awesome sight. He had a washboard stomach and muscular thighs. Most of the attention was focused on his midsection. Simon damn near choked on his drink when he saw how long *it* was. "Make damn sure he doesn't get an invitation to the company pool party." He slapped five with one of the bartenders.

Women in high heels and business suits rushed the stage to get a closer look and to touch. Security guards stood in front of the stage to keep them from killing one another. Five minutes later the situation was totally out of control. Simon had to end the show and clear out the club. "That's it!" he yelled. "Party's over!"

The bouncers moved in and directed the frustrated crowd toward the exit. Simon told the bartenders and waitresses to cash out and go home.

"Where in the hell is Darren?" he asked one of the bouncers.

"He was at the cashier's window a minute ago," he answered. "You want me to get him?"

"Get everybody out of here first. Then find him and tell him to meet me in my office."

"Yes, sir."

Simon rushed back to his office to check on the camera he had set up behind the cashier. He pushed the reverse button on the monitor and rewound the tape until Darren came into the picture.

"Well, well, well, what have we here?" he said as he watched Darren take a stack of twenties out of the register.

It was obvious the cashier was in on it, too. She kept looking around very suspiciously, like she was watching his back. When Darren was finished, he gave her a kiss on the cheek and walked out of the booth wearing a sly grin. "Smile you dirty bastard, you're on *Candid Camera*," Simon said as he paused the tape.

Just as he was about to go looking for Darren, there was a knock at the door.

"Who is it?

"It's Darren. You lookin' for me?"

"Hold on a minute."

Simon covered the front of the monitor with a briefcase he found on the floor and he used his suit jacket to camouflage the top. When he opened the door, Darren was wearing the same silly grin he had on camera.

"Have a seat."

"I'm sorry I wasn't there to make that announcement," he explained. "There was a situation at the front door I had to deal with."

"Don't worry about that," Simon said as he blocked the door. "I've got another job for you."

"What's that?" he asked nervously.

"I want you to go to your office and clean out all of your shit."

"Huh? What are you talking about?"

"Don't play me like a chump, you crooked son of a bitch! If I have to repeat myself, I'll throw your ass out." Simon had his fists balled. "Now what's it going to be?"

Simon was only five-eight but he was stocky. He was just looking for a reason to wipe the floor with Darren's narrow ass. He didn't weigh more than a hundred forty soaking wet.

"Okay, I'll go. But first I want my check for this month."

"I'll give you something to take with you." Simon grabbed him by the collar and punched him in the nose, followed by a stiff uppercut to the jaw. Darren fell to the floor like a bag of cement.

While he was lying there bleeding, Simon reached inside Darren's pocket and took back the money from the cash register. Then he picked him up off the floor and threw him out of the door. "Now get out of my sight!" Simon yelled. "And don't forget to tell that thieving bitch she's fired, too."

Theodore was sitting at the bar sipping on a glass of milk watching the drama unfold. He knew it was none of his business but he couldn't help making light of the situation.

"I hope that wasn't the accountant," Theodore said.

"Don't worry. I've got your money." Simon walked over and handed him an envelope. "You must be Theodore."

"You must be Mr. Harris."

"In the flesh," he said as they shook hands. "So, where are your friends?"

"Those are my employees, not my friends," he said smugly. "I try not to mix business and friendship."

"Well, I have a business proposition for you. How about performing here on a regular basis?"

"Give me a call and we'll talk about it," Theodore said as he walked toward the door. "Right now I've got to make it to another gig. A man's work is never done in Hotlanta," he said, laughing.

Simon locked the doors behind him and took a deep breath. "What a night," he said, sighing. He walked over to the bar and mixed another gin and tonic. Then he put his Heatwave CD inside the stereo, advanced it to track six, and turned up the volume.

"Mind blowin' decisions causes head-on collisions," he sang along.

The smooth beat of the music was relaxing and therapeutic. He grabbed the broom handle from behind the bar and began dancing with his make-believe partner. He dipped, turned, and shuffled, just like it was the real thing. Then suddenly, *bam, bam, bam!* There was a loud knock at the door. Simon turned off the music and reached behind the bar for his gun.

"Who is it?" he asked as he walked slowly toward the door.

"It's me, Ariel."

"Ariel? What in the world are you doing here?" He unlocked the door and let her in.

"I'm sorry to bother you, Mr. Harris, but I left my briefcase," she explained. "I would have waited until tomorrow but my driver's license is in there."

Simon went to his office to see if he could find it. And there it was sitting on his desk. It was the briefcase he had used to hide the monitor from Darren.

"Here you go," he said. "It came in handy."

"I'm really sorry for interrupting your little party," Ariel said, trying not to laugh.

"You saw me steppin'?" he asked, looking uncomfortable. "I'm so embarrassed."

"Don't be," she told him. "You're pretty smooth for an old guy."

"Who you callin' old?" Simon stepped back and looked her up and down. "How old are you?"

"Now, you should know better than to ask a woman her age," she said with her hand on her hip.

"I'm going to find out eventually."

"And how is that?"

"When you fill out your application for the manager's position."

"You mean, I got the job?"

"Not so fast," he said. "First you've got to do something for me."

"I hope you're not talking about giving up the booty," she said jokingly.

"Of course not, silly. You have to learn to step."

"You're on!" Ariel set her briefcase down and took off her jacket. "Are you sure your fiancée won't mind?"

"All we're doing is dancing," Simon said as he turned up the music. "And besides, she left today for the Essence Music Festival in New Orleans."

"In that case, lead on!"

Chapter 6

The sun shone brightly as the yellow cab maneuvered through the congested Los Angeles traffic. Even with my sunglasses on I was getting a headache. "How in God's name do people function this early in the morning?" I said to myself as I looked down at my watch. It was eight-fifteen. My American Airlines flight to Atlanta was scheduled to depart at 9:20 A.M. I was hoping to sit down to a nice breakfast before takeoff. But at the rate we were going I wouldn't have time for an Egg McMuffin.

I took a deep breath, put on my Walkman, and tried to relax. I surfed the channels until I heard a familiar voice, Tom Joyner. I remembered him from his days in Chicago on WGCI. Back then he was called "The Fly Jock" because he commuted to Dallas on weekends. He had blown up since then, syndicated in ninety markets last I heard. "Too bad I can't afford to advertise on that station," I jokingly said to myself. "I would have clients lined up from here to kingdom come."

Just as I was getting into the show, my pager went off. *This better be an emergency,* I was thinking as I dialed the number to my voice mail.

"Hello, Malcolm, this is Helen. I want to apologize for showing up late at Melvin's. You were right, there was no excuse for not calling. I promise you it won't happen again," she said seriously. "I'm calling to ask a favor. I need an escort tonight for a benefit at the Fox Theatre in Atlanta. I'm willing to pay a thousand in cash, plus expenses. If you can fit me into your schedule, call my secretary and she'll give you all the details. You know the number." She paused. "And again, I'm sorry for what happened. I hope you'll give me the opportunity to make it up to you," she said seductively. Then she hung up.

My first impulse was to tell her to go to hell, but business was business. Besides, Simon wasn't expecting me at the club until Saturday. I had a whole day to kill. Luckily, I always packed a tux for just such an emergency.

"Hey, my man!" I shouted to the taxi driver.

"Yes, sir?" he replied in a foreign accent.

"I'll give you an extra twenty bucks if you can get me to the terminal before nine. My vacation just turned into a business trip."

Chapter 7

The marquee of the Fox Theatre read: FUND-RAISER TONIGHT—UNITED NEGRO COLLEGE FUND. Hundreds of rowdy fans lined Peachtree Street to get a peek at their favorite celebrities. One by one, freshly waxed limousines arrived carrying famous athletes, actors, and politicians. Flashbulbs exploded and TV camera lights blared as reporters scrambled to get sound bites for the eleven o'clock news. Not being the shy type, I was anxious for my fifteen minutes of fame.

When the valet opened my door, I stepped out onto the scene in my black Armani tux, and posed for the cameras like a seasoned veteran.

"I loved you in your last movie!" a woman shouted, obviously mistaking me for Denzel.

"Can I please have your autograph!" another woman shouted while reaching over the ropes with her notepad.

I stopped for a moment to sign it, then I gave her a hug and proceeded toward the entrance while waving and blowing kisses. "What a ham," I jokingly said to myself.

The lobby was colorfully decorated with red, black, and green ribbons. African-American art was on display along with photographs of prominent blacks such as Dr. King, Malcolm X, Sojourner Truth, and W.E.B. Dubois. And a huge banner was draped over the concession area bearing the slogan A MIND IS A TERRIBLE THING TO WASTE.

"Excuse me, young man," I said to the usher while showing him my ticket. "Can you tell me where this seat is located?"

"Right down the center aisle, Row A. That's the first row from the stage." He gave me a program. "You might want to hurry, the show is about to begin."

I decided to take a leak before going to my seat. There's nothing more awkward then getting up in the middle of a program, especially when you're sitting near the front.

The atmosphere in the bathroom was very stuffy. Men were standing around in little cliques smoking cigars and bragging about their latest business deals. I never saw so many overinflated egos in one place. While I waited in line to take a leak, I tried to tune them out. But as I moved farther into the rest room, it became impossible to ignore their shallow conversations. The two men standing next to the bathroom attendant were particularly obnoxious. One was a short, chubby white man wearing a bad toupee, the other a tall, light-skinned black man.

"How are those stocks doing, Bob?" the black man asked loud enough for everybody to hear. He spoke very proper.

"They're doing pretty well, Eric," he told him. "Thanks for putting me up on it."

"It was the least I could do after you invited us to stay at your condo in Hilton Head," he replied while combing his hair in the mirror. "My fiancée really enjoyed the sauna and tennis courts."

While I was peeing I happened to look over at the guy next to me. We both had that expression on our faces that said, "What an asshole." After I relieved myself, I walked over to the sink to wash my hands. Eric was still admiring himself in the mirror, and blocking the sink.

"Excuse me," I said politely.

"Be my guest," he answered as he stepped back slightly, giving me just enough room to squeeze in.

"You're going to have to move back farther then that, my man." I said with contempt. "I'm too big to fit into this tight space."

He took another small step back and looked over at Bob with a smirk on his face, as if to say, "Who in the hell does he think he is?" They sarcastically slapped five and Eric went back to admiring himself in the mirror. I stood as erect as I could to show off my broad shoulders and wide chest. Although we were about the same height and weight, he was noticeably out of shape. One punch to that weak stomach and he would have folded like a cheap lawn chair.

After spraying himself with cologne, Eric tipped the bathroom attendant and walked toward the door with Bob trailing closely behind, all the while staring at me in the mirror. Once he was gone, I rinsed my face with cold water to compose myself.

"That fool was five seconds away from an old-fashioned Chicago ass-whipping," I said to the bathroom attendant.

"Don't pay no attention to that high-yellow negro," he said as he handed me a paper towel. "He'll get what's coming to him, sooner or later."

"I just hope I'm there when it happens." I put five dollars in his basket and headed for the door. "Have a good night."

"You do the same," he said. "And by the way, I had your back if you would've jumped on that prick. I may be old but I could've taken the chubby white guy with no problem."

"Maybe next time, old man," I said, laughing.

The host of the event was presenting an award for community service as I made my way down the main aisle. The audience stood up and applauded, which gave me the perfect cover to make a mad dash to my seat. Luckily Helen was looking out for me and waved me down as I came jogging down the aisle.

"I'm glad you could make it." She gave me a firm hug and a peck on the cheek. "I thought I was going to need a bodyguard to keep these dirty old men off me."

When I stepped back to get a better look at her outfit, I understood her point. Helen was wearing a black Versace halter dress. The soft silk fabric hugged her small waist perfectly, accentuating her large breasts. Her hair, streaked with brown highlights, was pinned up neatly, just the way I like it.

"I don't know if I can make it through the rest of the show," I said as we took our seats. "How long before it's over?"

"At least two hours."

"Two hours? We'll be lucky to make it through intermission," I whispered in her ear.

"You know I love it when you talk dirty to me, Malcolm," she said while inconspicuously rubbing my penis.

"There's a full moon out tonight," I said. "I hope you took your vitamins."

The lights dimmed in the theater as the next act was introduced. I checked my program to see who was performing. It read: BLACK DANCE COMPANY—SOLO BY MS. ANTOINETTE GRAYSON. While I waited for the show to begin, I reflected on when my mother dragged me to see Alvin Ailey's dance company. I was eighteen then. I was embarrassed because I thought dancing was for sissies. But after that first experience, she never had to drag me back again.

When the long curtain rose, five black women in raggedy clothes stood still in separate spotlights. The backdrop was an urban alley scene, complete with old trash cans and streetlamps, set in the late 1950s. It was a captivating sight. The theater was so quiet you could hear a pin drop. Even I was holding my breath in anticipation.

Suddenly, a funky drumbeat broke the silence and the women began to move to the rhythm. As the tempo quickened, so did their gestures. A piano and a saxophone joined in creating a smooth jazzy groove. Their movements were strong and fluid. I believe the style was modern jazz. The dance was a tale of five women looking for a way out of the ghetto. As the story went on, four con men came dancing into the alley with promises of fine jewelry and fancy cars. Four of the women went away with the men, leaving only one woman behind. She fell down onto her knees in sorrow and the lights dimmed on the set. The audience began to applaud, but the show wasn't over.

A few seconds later, the spotlight came on center stage and she stood with poise, wearing a white leotard and white satin ballet shoes. Her brown skin, light brown eyes, and long, slender frame made her appear even more elegant. "That must be Antoinette Grayson," I whispered to Helen. But she didn't respond. I guess she didn't appreciate my enthusiasm. As Antoinette began to pirouette, the song "Cherish the Day," by Sade played softly in the distance. The passionate beat and poetic lyrics perfectly accentuated the mood.

You're ruling the way that I move
and I breathe your air
You only can rescue me
this is my prayer.

I could practically feel her pain as Antoinette reached toward the ceiling as if praying to God for comfort. From one side of the stage to the other she leaped then landed squarely on her toes. Her facial expression was serious and intense. The more I watched her, the more I became engrossed by her beauty and grace. She was so flexible and strong, yet as feminine as a woman could be.

For the finale, she made a series of turns, which positioned her on the right side of the stage, directly in front of me. As she took her bow, our eyes met. She paused for a split second, then smiled. I smiled back. The audience gave her a standing ovation as the other dancers joined her onstage. I stood and applauded, too, while Helen sat there with an attitude.

I was determined to meet this fascinating woman. I wasn't interested in sex or getting her number. I just wanted to tell her how much I enjoyed the show and that I admired her talent. Somehow, I had to figure out a way to get away from Helen long enough to make her acquaintance.

• • •

When the show was over, hundreds of people gathered in the lobby to congratulate the performers and get autographs. Helen had her arm wrapped around mine like a python, making sure I didn't get out of her sight.

"Let's go to the hotel and get in bed," she said. "I'm horny as hell."

"What's the hurry?" I answered. "Let's get a glass of wine and mingle."

"Okay, but just for a little while. It's been a long day and I'm getting tired." She gave me one of those phony yawns.

We walked over to the concession area to order drinks. While we waited for the bartender, Helen recognized one of her girlfriends on the other side of the bar. She frantically waved to get her attention. For a woman who was supposedly tired, she seemed awfully eager to show me off.

"Helen, darling, how are you?" the woman said as they exchanged hugs.

"I'm absolutely wonderful, Gloria."

"I can see that," she said while looking me up and down like a piece of meat. "Aren't you going to introduce us?"

"Gloria Randall, this is my friend Malcolm Tremell."

"It's a pleasure to finally meet you, Mr. Tremell. Helen has told me some great things about you." She extended her hand.

"The pleasure is all mine," I said as I kissed it.

Gloria was a sassy woman who bore an incredible resemblance to Lena Horne, bright smile and all. She had to be at least fifty-five but she was looking damn good for her age.

"He's even more handsome than you described, and muscular, too." She was still holding my hand.

"Okay, that's enough," Helen said as she stepped between us. "He's already taken."

"Calm down, sweetheart, I was just admiring the merchandise. Besides, I brought my own toy to play with. You want to meet him?"

"Sure, why not?"

I knew Helen wouldn't pass up an opportunity to get her flirt on, especially after Gloria had stepped to me so aggressively.

"Are you coming, Malcolm?" Helen asked.

"I'll be right over after the bartender brings our drinks."

"Okay, baby, don't be long."

The second they walked away, I quickly disappeared in the crowd and headed over to the autograph area. The lines were long and rowdy fans were pushing and shoving trying to take pictures. Being six-three, it was easy to see over everyone's heads. Most of the singers and four of the dancers were sitting down at the draped tables signing autographs, but Antoinette was nowhere to be found. All my energy and enthusiasm went right out of the window. It was like studying all night for a test and the teacher not showing up. I guess it wasn't meant to be, I was thinking.

As I turned to walk away, I noticed a woman walking back inside the empty theater. It was hard to make her out. She was wearing a sheer hood, which partially covered her face. But when she briefly turned, I saw those beautiful brown eyes and I knew it was her.

I fought my way through the crowd, determined not to miss her. "Excuse me," I yelled. "Pardon me." Before I went inside after her, I stopped at the flower vendor's booth to purchase a dozen red roses.

"I've only got eleven," the vendor told me.

"You gotta be kidding me!" I said.

"I'm sorry, sir, this is the last bunch I have left. Take it or leave it."

"I'll take it!"

I threw him a twenty-dollar bill and grabbed the poorly wrapped flowers out of his hand. When I opened the door to the theater, Antoinette was standing on the stage with her back to me.

"I hope I'm not late for the front row," I said.

"Oh, my goodness!" she said as she turned around, looking frightened.

"Sorry if I startled you," I said as I walked toward the front of the stage and handed her the flowers. "I just wanted to give you these."

"You're the gentlemen from the front row."

"That would be me."

"Thank you," she said, looking apprehensive. "But what are these for?"

"For your performance tonight. You were great!"

"I appreciate the compliment, Mr. . . . ?"

"My name is Malcolm, Malcolm Tremell."

"Pleased to meet you, Malcolm." She bent down to shake my hand. "My name is Antoinette Grayson, but everybody calls me Toni."

"Well, Toni, I just wanted to let you know how much I admired your dancing," I said. "I wish you continued success. Have a good evening."

"Wait a minute," she said. "That's it?"

"I'm not going to bug you to death trying to get your

phone number. That's not my style. Besides, a beautiful woman like yourself probably already has a man. Am I right?"

"As a matter of fact, I'm engaged. But . . ."

"You see what I mean?" I interrupted.

"Would you let me finish?" she said, cutting in. "I don't see anything wrong with being friends. I just moved here from New York and I don't know a single, solitary soul."

"The Big Apple, huh? I used to go to school there back in ninety-one."

"Which school was that?"

"Juilliard. I studied jazz piano."

"Yeah, right," she said. "You look more like a model than a musician."

"I'll take that as a compliment," I told her. "But if you don't believe me, why don't you come hear me play tomorrow night?"

"I don't know," she said.

"Don't be such a party pooper. The least you could do is stop by for one song."

"Okay, okay, I'll think about it. But I'm not making any promises." She reached inside her purse and pulled out a pen and piece of paper. "So, where is this place?"

"It's in Buckhead on Peachtree Street, two blocks down from Puff Daddy's restaurant, Justin's. It's called Club Obsession. Just tell the guy at the door you're on the VIP list."

"You've got it going on like that, huh?"

"Stop trippin'. I'm not trying to impress you. My best friend is the owner."

"So are you from Atlanta?"

"No, Chicago, but I live in L.A."

"You sure do get around," she said. "Are you in the military or something?"

"That's a long story." I told her. "I'll explain it to you *when* I see you tomorrow."

"Listen to you, sounding all confident."

"All I want to do is have an intelligent conversation with

you over a glass of wine," I said sincerely. "I promise you I'll be the perfect gentleman."

I politely shook her hand and turned to walk away. Right as I was about to go out of the door, she yelled. "Hey, Malcolm, I'll come on one condition!"

"And what's that?" I yelled back.

"That you have the other red rose to make up this dozen."

"You've got yourself a deal!"

I left out of the theater feeling like I had just hit the lottery. "Yes!" I said to myself. I was already anxious about seeing her the next day. My heart was racing like a schoolboy with a crush on his third-grade teacher. For the first time in years, sex and money were not factors. Toni's presence would be all the stimulation I needed.

When I finally caught up with Helen, she was outside standing next to the limo. She looked furious. I didn't even bother to lie about where I was. She already knew. Before I could open my mouth to apologize, she slapped the shit out of me. *Smack!*

"Here's half your money for doing a half-ass job." She handed me a brown envelope. "Don't expect to hear from me again."

"I'm sorry, Helen."

"I'm sorry, too, Malcolm," she said as she stepped inside the limo. "I hope she was worth it."

"She was," I told her. Then I gave her the envelope back.

PART II

The Situation

Chapter 8

The headboard of the bed slammed against the wall knocking down Cheryl's wedding pictures. "Whose pussy is it?" Teddy Bear asked.

"It's yours!" Cheryl screamed.

"Say it louder!"

"I said it's yours, Daddy! It's all yours!"

"You're damn right it's mine, now turn your ass over and spread your legs!" Teddy flipped her onto her stomach in a doggy-style position and stroked her as hard as he could.

"Take it easy, baby. You're hurting me!"

"It's supposed to hurt!" he told her. "I'm gonna make sure your old man can't get any of this for at least a week."

Cheryl screamed so loud she woke up her six-month-old daughter who was sleeping in the room next door. "Teddy, stop! I have to go check on the baby."

"She's not going anywhere," he said. "Let me get my nut first."

Cheryl used her hand as a brace to keep her head from banging against the headboard. Her long braids swung violently back and forth as Teddy thrust his two-hundred-forty-pound frame against her. She begged him to stop, but that only turned him on more.

"Stop whining! You know you love it, don't you?"

"Yes, baby, but you're punching a hole in my uterus."

"Don't move. I'm cumming! I'm cumming!"

Cheryl buried her face in the pillow and screamed as Teddy jerked and shivered. When he was finished, she quickly put on her robe and rushed to check on the baby.

Teddy laid back comfortably on the king-size bed sipping on a glass of orange juice. Suddenly, his pager went off. "Who in the hell could be calling me at twelve o'clock on a Saturday afternoon?" he said to himself. He grabbed his pager off the nightstand to check to see who it was.

The number on the display read: 2911. It was his girlfriend, Karen's code for an emergency. "What in the world does she want?" he asked while dialing the number on his cell phone.

Karen was a forty-five-year-old attorney he met while stripping at a Christmas party. Although she was an Ivy League graduate making six figures, Karen loved roughnecks, preferably young ones. Teddy went home with her that same night and rocked her world. Two weeks later, she insisted that he move in.

"Karen, this is Teddy. What's the emergency?"

"I just found a pair of yellow Victoria's Secret panties in my drawer," she said angrily.

"Congratulations," he said sarcastically. "What's that got to do with me?"

"They're not mine, that's what!"

"And how would you know that? Do you get your panties monogrammed?"

"Don't play me like a fool, Teddy! I know what my body smells like!" she shouted. "What I want to know is how did this heifer's drawers get in my house?"

"How should I know? Maybe they belong to one of your girlfriends."

"You better get your black ass over here right now before I start throwing your shit out the window. I mean it!" she said, then hung up.

Teddy was cold busted. He knew those panties belonged to one of his women. He just couldn't remember which one. This was the third time in six months that Karen found evidence of his cheating. The phone numbers in his pocket and lipstick on his collar were easy to justify. But he would have to use all of his player skills to get out of this situation.

Teddy reacted with his usual arrogance. He took a long hot shower, put lotion on his body, and calmly slipped into his clothes. When Cheryl came back into the room, he was slipping on his shoes.

"Where are you goin'?" she asked.

"I've got some business to take care of."

"Can't it wait until later? I was ready for another round," she said while unsnapping his pants.

"Sorry, baby, duty calls."

"You are such a tease, Teddy," she said. "Every time you leave here I feel like I'm going through sex withdrawal."

"Just call me *Suuuuu*-per Dick," he said as he put his hands on his hips. "Able to leap sexually frustrated women in a single bound."

"That's not funny, Teddy," she said, pouting like a child. "I need a fix."

"Maybe you wouldn't be so horny if your old man weren't traveling around the country five days a week. He must be crazy leaving a fine young thang like you home alone."

"You leave David out of this. He's a good man," she said, getting defensive. "And good men are hard to find."

"Yeah, but a hard man is good to find, wouldn't you agree?" He collected his things and headed for the door. "By the way, can you loan me fifty bucks? I left my wallet at home."

"I swear, Teddy, you're the most conceited and manipulative son of a bitch I've ever met," she said while handing him the money from her purse. "You think you're God's gift to women."

"Does that mean I'll be seeing you next week at eleven o'clock?"

"Make it ten!" she said as she kissed him good-bye.

•••

Teddy pulled into the circular driveway and parked his Navigator behind Karen's Mercedes. He pulled out a recycled Tiffany's jewelry box from the glove compartment and put it inside his pants pocket. He sat there for a minute to make sure he had his lies straight, then he took a deep breath and got out of the car. "Oh, well, here we go again," he said to himself.

When he walked into the house, Karen was waiting in the living room sipping a glass of white zinfandel. The yellow panties were spread out on the cocktail table like prosecuting evidence in a court case.

"Okay, I'm here. What's up?"

"I want to know what your problem is!" Karen shouted with her hands on her hips.

"You're the one with the problem," Teddy said nonchalantly. "Why don't you relax and have another drink?"

Teddy turned away and went to get a beer out of the refrigerator. Just as he was about to take a sip, Karen came charging into the kitchen and slapped it out of his hand.

"I pay the mortgage, the light bill, the phone bill, and buy the groceries!" she said with her finger in his face. "I'll be damned if you're going to disrespect me in my own house."

"There's no need to get violent," he said, trying to put his arms around her. "I would never do anything to jeopardize our relationship. You're my baby."

"Don't try to charm me, Teddy. It's not going to work this time. I want to know how these panties got into my house."

"Maybe they just floated in through the window and buried themselves in the bottom of your drawer."

"That shit ain't funny," she said, pushing him away.

"Okay, baby, let me explain what happened so we can put this behind us." He was trying to sound serious. "Remember the show I had at Club Obsession Thursday night?"

"Yeah, and?"

"Well, while I was performing, one of the waitresses came backstage and slipped a pair of panties inside my pocket as a joke."

"How does that explain how they got into my house?"

"It was hot that night so I threw my jacket in the backseat. It wasn't until I was looking for the car keys this morning that I realized they were in my pocket."

"I'm still waiting for you to explain how they found their way into the bottom of my drawer."

"You were coming upstairs at that exact moment, and I panicked. So, I put them somewhere I figured you wouldn't look."

"Why didn't you put them in one of your drawers?"

"Like I said, I put them somewhere you wouldn't look," he said sarcastically. "We both know you go through my shit every chance you get?"

Karen wanted to laugh because she knew he was right. She took a long sip of wine then tapped her finger on the glass as if contemplating her next question. Teddy's explanation was weak but it was believable. She knew his job attracted fast women.

"Maybe you are telling the truth," she said calmly. "But

if you knew they were in there, explain to me why you didn't take them out before you left this morning."

"I had my mind on something more important."

"Something more important, like what?"

"Like going by the jewelry store to pick up this."

He pulled the Tiffany's box out of his pocket and handed it to her. She paused, "Is this what I think it is?"

"Open it up and see," he said.

She lifted the top of the small velvet box slowly. Inside was a diamond engagement ring. "Oh, baby, it's beautiful."

"I wanted to get you something bigger, but business has been slow lately."

"That's okay, sweetheart. It's the thought that counts." The tears began to roll down her face. "Please forgive me for not trusting you."

"Don't worry about it, baby, everybody makes mistakes."

She gave him a wet kiss and ran upstairs screaming like a child on Christmas Day. "I'm going to call my mom and my sister, Lisa, and tell them the good news! And when I come back, we're going to the most expensive restaurant in town to celebrate, my treat!"

Teddy got another beer out of the refrigerator and kicked back on Karen's plush leather sofa. While he sipped on his drink, he pulled the pawnshop receipt out of his pocket. When he looked at the two-hundred-dollar charge for the ring, he shook his head and laughed.

"That ought to keep a roof over my head for at least another year."

Chapter 9

I checked out of the Westin Hotel at 1:00 P.M. I thought about going up to Helen's room to say good-bye, but I figured I was the last person on earth she wanted to see. Instead, I wrote her a short letter apologizing for last night and left it at the front desk. When the valet came down with my luggage, I boarded the shuttle to go pick up my Budget rental car. On the way over to the terminal I called Simon on my cell phone to let him know I was in.

"Hello," he answered, sounding groggy.

"Wake up! Rise and shine!" I screamed.

"Man, stop screaming in my ear. I'm not deaf."

"Well get your lazy butt up! The eagle has landed!"

"The eagle better learn to land more quietly before I hang up on his ass."

"How can you be asleep at one o'clock in the afternoon? You're almost as bad as me."

"The club was a madhouse last night. We ran out of beer halfway through the night. And I had to break in two bartenders and a new manager," he said. "By the way, Ariel is looking forward to meeting you."

"What the hell is an Ariel?" I asked jokingly. "Sounds like the name of a laundry detergent."

The four passengers who were riding on the shuttle bus laughed at my joke. Even the driver thought it was funny. I could see her laughing through the rearview mirror.

"She's the new manager of the club, you comedian. I fired Darren Thursday night after I caught him stealing."

"I hope you whipped his ass, too."

"You know I did," he said, laughing.

"Glad to see you haven't forgotten where you came from," I said while throwing up my hands. "Chi-town in the house!" we yelled in unison, "Southsiii-eede!"

The white man sitting across from me turned red as a fire hydrant, probably thinking I was throwing up gang signs. I wanted to tell him it was a black thing, but I thought to myself, fuck'um. That's what he gets for being so damn ignorant.

"Man, I can't tell you how much I miss hanging out with you," Simon said. "How long has it been, anyway?"

"Too long," I said seriously. "We've got a lot of catching up to do."

"Why don't I meet you downtown at the Shark Bar for brunch?"

"I've got a better idea. Let's go to Youngblood's R&B Cafe in the Rio Mall. I've got a taste for barbecue ribs."

"I thought you stopped eating red meat and pork."

"I didn't say I was a Muslim," I told him. "A little swine every now and then won't kill me."

"You're probably right," Simon laughed. "Let me get dressed and I'll meet you there in thirty minutes. Last one there has to foot the bill."

"That's a bet!"

• • •

The parking lot at the Rio Mall was jam-packed. It was no wonder with two beauty salons, three restaurants, a health club, and Chris Tucker's Comedy Club sharing the same mall. I drove around in circles for fifteen minutes before I finally found a spot. I grabbed my cell phone and pager and stepped out of the car. Right away I could feel the ferocious Georgia sunshine burning the back of my neck. "Damn, it's hotter than Africa!" I said to myself as I walked toward the mall entrance. The deejay on the radio said the temperature was eighty-nine degrees, but it felt more like one hundred.

When I came up the escalator, I could see Simon sitting at the bar of the restaurant. He was wearing a pair of white shorts and a Chicago Bulls jersey with number 23 proudly displayed on the back. I waved to get his attention but he was too busy checking out this fine young sistah who was walking by. Her shorts were cut so high they barely covered her ass. I walked up behind him quietly hoping to surprise him.

"You want some of that young stuff, don't you?" I said in his ear.

"Malcolm, you scared the shit out of me!" He turned around holding his chest. "I was just admiring her, uh, her outfit?"

"It's good to see you again," I said as we shook hands and embraced.

"It's good to see you, too, partner," Simon said. "I see you're still pumpin' iron."

I had on a polyester body shirt that showed off my firm thirty-inch waist and defined chest. "My body is my business," I told him. "You can't have a potbelly and flabby ass and expect women to pay two hundred an hour."

"Is that how much you charge for a date?" he asked. "I remember when you were struggling to make two hundred dollars a week."

"Thank God those days are over," I said. "I was afraid I would have to get a real job."

Simon had already called ahead to reserve a table. He picked up the glass of iced tea he was drinking and we walked toward the back room. Youngblood's was very relaxed and had a cultural appeal. The walls were covered with photos of famous black musicians such as Stevie Wonder, Peabo Bryson, and B. B. King. Old-school music played softly in the background blending in perfectly with the lively chatter of the customers. It reminded me of the soul food joints back home.

After being seated, the waitress came over and handed each of us menus. I ordered the Otis Redding baby-back ribs, a salad with ranch dressing, a baked potato, and two sweet teas with extra lemon. Simon had the Bobby Womack wings and fries.

"Damn, you must really be hungry," Simon said.

"I'm starvin' like Marvin," I said, holding my stomach. "I haven't eaten since yesterday afternoon, and that was lousy airplane food."

"Wait a minute, I thought you flew in today."

"Actually I got in last night," I confessed. "I was going to surprise you but I got a call from a client to attend the UNCF benefit."

"Oh, yeah, I heard the advertisement on V103 last week. How was it?"

"It was nice. As a matter of fact, I met one of the dancers in the show. Her name is Antoinette. And boy was she fine! Smooth brown skin, long pretty legs, and the most beautiful light brown eyes you ever want to see. And talk about talented! I've never seen a woman move with such style and grace."

"She sounds like a keeper."

"Yeah, that's what I thought, too, until she told me she already had a man."

"Since when did that stop you? Back in the day, you

would mack a woman down on her wedding night. Don't tell me you're starting to get a conscience."

"It's not always about sex," I said. "Men and women can be friends, too, you know."

"In other words, she didn't give you any play."

"No, she didn't." I laughed and gave him dap. "But she did promise to come to the club tonight."

"I can't wait to meet her. Any woman who can put Mr. Smooth in the 'friend zone' has got to be something special."

"She's something special all right," I said. "If she wasn't already taken I might consider putting a ring on her finger myself."

Simon almost choked on his iced tea. "Where in the hell did that come from?"

"Maybe my biological clock is ticking," I said with a serious look on my face. "Here I am thirty-seven years old with no daughters or sons to carry on my name. Hell, I haven't taken a woman home to meet my mom since high school."

"That's the first time since I've known you that you've mentioned marriage," Simon said, sounding surprised. "You sure you're not on drugs?"

"I'm just getting tired of the game. The money is great but dealing with these emotionally scarred women is wearing me out. Lately, I've been giving some serious thought to hanging it up."

"Why don't you come into business with me? I've already made plans to open another club in Marietta. You could be the manager."

"No offense, but there ain't no way in hell I'm working as a nightclub manager. I wouldn't give a damn if Donald Trump was the owner."

Simon's face turned as red as a black man's could. "Fuck you, Malcolm!" he said, raising his voice. "If you want to die of AIDS or end up shot in the head like your old man, be my guest."

I sat back in my seat to absorb what he had said. Simon knew how deeply I felt about what happened to my father. It was the first time in twelve years either of us had ever brought it up.

"Damn, Malcolm, I'm sorry," he said, looking sad. "You know I didn't mean that the way it came out. It's just that I love you like a brother and I don't want anything to happen to you."

"Simon, I realize that you're only trying to help, but this is something I've got to work out for myself."

"I understand, partner. Just remember I'm here for you if you need me," he said as we shook hands.

After a minute or so, the waitress returned with our orders. We bowed our heads in prayer to give thanks, then we dug in.

"So are we still on for tonight?" Simon asked reluctantly.

"Of course," I said while smearing sour cream on my baked potato. "I can't wait to see the new club!"

"Well, if it will make you feel any better, Cynthia won't be able to make it. She's in New Orleans for the weekend."

"That's the best news I've heard all day," I said, sounding cheerful. "Do me a favor and pass the salt."

Chapter 10

The Marriott Hotel in New Orleans was buzzing with activity. Hundreds of men and women gathered in the lobby waiting for the shuttle buses to take them over to the convention center where the seminars and book signings were being held. Cynthia and her girlfriend Debra were killing time at the bar sipping on Coronas.

"Girl, look at all these phony women," Debra said. "I haven't seen a woman yet who has her own eyes, hair, and breasts."

"We all can't be blessed with natural beauty," Cynthia said with conceit as she threw back her long brown hair.

"I guess not." Debra lifted her perfectly round 36DD breasts. "Who needs a Wonderbra?"

They gave each other a high five and toasted with their beers. "Here's to a week away from work, the traffic on Interstate 85, and our men," Debra said.

"I'll drink to that!"

"Excuse me, ladies and gentleman!" a short, chubby woman wearing a bright orange vest yelled. "The shuttle buses have been delayed. There seems to have been some sort of car accident on Canal Street and traffic is backed up for miles. So please be patient and we'll get you over to the convention center as soon as possible. Thank you."

"That's fine with me," Cynthia said. "It's too damned hot out there anyway."

"Hey, bartender, two more Coronas!" Debra yelled.

"I'll have a Long Island iced tea this time. All this beer does is make me wanna pee."

"Girl, it's only three in the afternoon!"

"And?"

Debra looked at Cynthia and smiled. "Hey, bartender, make that two Long Islands instead. I'm not gonna let my girl get shit-faced by herself."

After the bartender brought over their drinks, they continued to criticize and break down every woman who walked by, making fun of their outfits, body shapes, and what they called project-penitentiary hairstyles. But their signifying came to an abrupt end when a group of five men came strutting in from the parking area. They were all wearing sandals and shorts, which showed off their thick, hairy legs. The entire room suddenly got quiet as the men walked up to the front desk to check in.

"Now, see, that's the kind of shit that can get a woman in trouble," Debra said as she stared shamelessly.

"You need to get a grip. Remember you have a man at home."

"Cynthia, why are you fronting? You know damn well you want to break off some of that dark meat."

"That was the old Cynthia. I'm engaged now," she said, while admiring the three-carat diamond ring Simon had given her. "My *hoein'* days are over."

"Bitch, please," Debra said, laughing. "Just last month you were fuckin' that light-skinned brotha from accounting.

Now all of a sudden you've turn into Ms. Goody Two-shoes?"

"This time I'm going to be faithful to Simon," Cynthia said in a serious tone. "I want to settle down and raise a family. I'm not getting any younger, you know."

Debra got quiet realizing that Cynthia was serious. She reached over and held her hand. "I hope everything works out for you and Simon. He's a damn good man and he really loves you."

"I know," Cynthia said, sounding somber. "Sometimes I don't think I deserve him."

Just then, two of the five men who had attracted all the attention, walked up behind them. One of them was tall and muscular with a fraternity symbol branded on his right arm. His shirt was unbuttoned halfway, exposing his hairy chest. The other was five-ten with piercing brown eyes and short wavy hair. He wore a well-groomed beard that reminded Cynthia of Teddy Pendergrass.

"Excuse me, are these seats taken?" the one with the brown eyes asked Cynthia. His voice was deep.

"I don't think so," she replied.

The two men sat down and ordered orange juice and water. All eyes were on them as they drank and chatted with each other. Debra wanted to say something to the tall one but she was nervous. Cynthia decided to instigate just for fun.

"Excuse me, gentlemen, my name is Cynthia and this is my best friend, Debra."

"Pleased to meet you, ladies," the tall one said as he shook their hands. "I'm Randall."

"And my name is James," the other said. He shook their hands, too. "Are you ladies here for the Essence Festival?"

"Yes, we are," Cynthia said. "We come every year."

"This is our first time," James said. "But it won't be the last. I've never seen so many beautiful women in my entire life. Present company included."

"Why thank you." Cynthia blushed. "You gentlemen look quite handsome yourselves."

James smiled as he took a sip of his orange juice. His eyes never left Cynthia.

"So, are you ladies here with your husbands?" Randall asked.

"I'm not married!" Debra said promptly.

"That's a shame," he said as he walked over and sat on the stool next to her.

Debra turned around on her stool and talked with Randall in private.

"What about you, Cynthia?" James asked. "Where is your husband?" he asked, while looking down at her engagement ring.

"I'm not married. Not yet, anyway," she said, sounding dull.

"Congratulations!" he said. "When is the big day?"

"We haven't set an exact date."

"Well, I wish you all the best," he said, looking deep into her eyes. "Marriage can be a wonderful thing, with the right man."

"What about you, James, are you married?"

"Yes, I am."

That response made Cynthia's heart skip a beat. Although she was engaged, she was enjoying the idea of him being available.

"So, how long have you and your wife been together?"

"I'm not married to a woman, I'm married to the Lord." He reached inside his pocket and pulled out a business card.

"Reverend James Young, marriage and substance abuse counselor, Atlanta, Georgia," Cynthia read off the card. "That's where I live."

"I know," James said while stroking his beard. "I watch you on the five o'clock news every night. You're very talented."

"Thank you, Reverend."

"Do me a favor and call me James. 'Reverend' sounds so formal."

"Okay, James," she said, while handing him back his card.

"No, keep it," he said, closing her hands around it. "Give me a call if you ever need marital advice. The first appointment is on the house."

"I'm sure I won't be in need of any counseling, but thanks anyway." She tried to pass the card back again.

"Keep it just in case," he said. He stood up from his stool. "You never know when you might need someone to talk to."

He placed ten dollars on the bar to pay for his drink, then he shook her hand and walked away. Randall said good-bye to Debra and followed behind him.

"Girl, I've got his room number!" Debra said, sounding excited.

"He's sanctified," Cynthia said, while staring at James's card.

"So what! He has needs just like any other man."

"Well, I don't know about you but I don't do church men," Cynthia said as she took a long sip of her drink. "Besides, I'm happily engaged."

"I guess that's why you just slipped his card inside your purse. You ain't slick."

"I was saving it for a friend."

"Friend, my ass," Debra said. "Take my advice Cynthia, don't even think about getting married. Your hoein' days aren't over yet."

Chapter 11

It was half past eight in the evening when I awoke from my nap. I told Simon to wake me no later then seven-thirty but he must have forgotten. I slipped on my boxer shorts and went to see what he was up to. "Hey, Simon!" I yelled as I walked into the living room. But he didn't answer. I checked his bedroom then the basement, but he wasn't there either. When I went into the kitchen to get something to drink, I saw a letter taped to the refrigerator door. The paper was bright yellow and the writing was in bold black marker. I guess he wanted to make sure I saw it. After pouring myself a glass of cranberry juice, I peeled the note off the door and read it.

Malcolm,
I had to leave early to handle some business at the club. If you're hungry, there's leftover curry chicken and rice in the fridge. The bar is stocked with beer, wine, and Absolut. Try not to get too drunk before I see you.

By the way, I need you at the club before ten o'clock tonight. I want to show you around before the crowd gets too thick. If you need to reach me, my new office number is on the back of this letter along with the directions. See you there!

Your Homie,
Simon

"You old fox," I said with a wide grin. "I know you're up to something." I went to the bar and pulled out the bottle of Absolut and mixed it in with my cranberry juice. *"Ahhh,"* I sighed as I took a long sip. I walked over to the stereo system and sat down on the floor to look through Simon's old LP collection. He had some real classics like, "Love Rollercoaster" by the Ohio Players, and "Footsteps" by the Isley Brothers. Finally, I ran across the perfect song for the occasion, "Trouble Man" by Marvin Gaye.

I pushed the power button to the five-hundred-watt digital Sony receiver and turned the Yamaha speakers toward the bathroom. I carefully brushed the dust off the needle and laid the record down gently on the turntable. When the song began to play, I turned the knob on the volume until the walls vibrated. "The neighbors can go to hell," I said. "It's Saturday night!" When Marvin began singing, I picked up my hairbrush and pretended like it was a microphone.

I've come of heart, baby, but now I'm cool
I didn't make it surely, playin' by the rules
I've come of heart, baby, but now I'm fine
I'm checking trouble, sure movin' down the line

That was the only part of the song I knew by heart and I sang the shit out of it. While the rest of the album played, I took a shower then slipped into my Versace suit. I sprayed my neck and hands with cologne and snapped my Movado watch onto my wrist. By nine o'clock I was dressed to a tee.

On my way out, I stopped in front of the mirror in the hallway to check myself one last time. *I'm a trouble man, baby, don't get in my way,* I sang as I admired myself in the hallway mirror. Then I strutted out the door, ready to raise hell.

• • •

It was just after nine-thirty when I arrived at the club. A dark blue van with V103 colorfully painted on the sides was parked out front. Two men were passing out T-shirts and

CDs, mostly to women wearing short, tight skirts. The entrance to the club was covered by a gold awning with Club Obsession emblazoned in bold black letters.

"Good evening, sir," the valet said while cordially opening my door.

"How much do I owe you?"

"It's on the house, Mr. Tremell."

"How do you know who I am?"

"Mr. Harris said you would be driving a Black Lincoln Town Car. He's expecting you," he said with a noticeable grin.

"Thank you," I told him. I slipped him a five-dollar tip for being so professional.

I walked through the double glass doors that led into a lavish foyer. Two burly security guards directed me over to a small booth where the receptionist was collecting money.

"Excuse me, I'm looking for Mr. Harris."

"He's busy right now," she said politely.

"I think he'll take time out to see me."

"Oh, really," she said with an attitude. "And who might you be."

"My name is Malcolm Tremell."

"I'm sorry, Mr. Tremell, I didn't know it was you," she said excitedly. "Mr. Harris is waiting for you upstairs in the Jazz Room."

"Where is that exactly?"

"Just go inside and you'll see the stairs to your right. The Jazz Room is on the second floor."

When I walked inside the club, I was impressed by how classy the place was laid out. The room was filled with round tables covered with white cloths. The bar was a perfect circle with a brass footrest and high-back leather stools. And on the back wall across from the deejay's booth was a built-in aquarium. It was twenty feet long and had an assortment of tropical fish swimming about.

As I made my way up the winding staircase, I noticed a

dim light coming from the Jazz Room. When I got to the door, it suddenly went out. I put my ear to the door but there was no sound. "Simon, you in there?" I yelled. I pushed the door open slowly and entered the dark room. Suddenly the lights flashed on and the room erupted with cheers. "Surprise!" people yelled. There must have been at least two hundred people clapping and screaming.

Simon was standing on the stage with a microphone leading the crowd in song. *Happy birthday to you. Happy birthday to you. Happy birthday, dear Malcolm. Happy birthday to you.*

I've never been so embarrassed in my entire life. And to make matters worse, Toni was in the corner singing right along. We made eye contact briefly before Simon called for me to join him onstage.

"Malcolm, over the years, we've gone through many wars together. Sometimes we agreed to disagree, other times we fought like hell. But in the end, we always remained friends," he said with his hand on my shoulder. "As a token of my friendship, I want to present you with a special gift."

Simon signaled one of his employees to draw the long velvet stage curtain. As it slowly drew back, I felt like a contestant on the *Price Is Right*. I couldn't believe my eyes when I saw what was behind it: a shiny black Steinway piano.

"Is this what I think it is?" I asked nervously.

"I don't know what you're talking about," Simon said, trying not to grin.

When I saw the intials M.T. engraved on the face I knew it was the same piano my father had given me on my eighteenth birthday. My jaw damn near hit the floor.

"I thought it was destroyed in the fire," I said as I gently ran my finger across the keys.

"It was burned pretty bad, but I had it restored."

"I don't know what to say."

"Don't say anything, just play something smooth."

"What do you want to hear?" I asked, still trying to get a grip.

"It's your night, partner, you decide."

The house band joined me onstage and took their places next to their instruments. I used to play with them back at Simon's old club, The Oasis, before it burned down. There were four members, Big Johnny on the upright bass, Jimmy on guitar, Ricky on saxophone, and the vocalist Francine. But we called her Billie because she sang like Billie Holiday. We exchanged emotional hugs, then prepared to turn the joint out.

While the band warmed up, the crowd took their seats and began ordering drinks. Simon escorted Toni to the front table where he had a bottle of champagne chilling in a bucket of ice. The strapless white cocktail dress she wore draped perfectly over her shapely frame. Her hair was pulled back in a tight bun, which showed off her long neck and soft shoulders. As I looked into her brown eyes, she seemed even more beautiful then she did the night before.

When we were ready to play, Simon signaled for the engineer to dim the floor lights. The audience suddenly faded behind the bright glare of the stage lamps. "I want to dedicate this piece to the man who changed my life by introducing me to music," I said somberly. "This one is for you, Dad." The song I chose was "Summertime" by George Gershwin. I learned how to play it after I saw *Porgy and Bess*. It was my father's favorite.

As I pressed down on the familiar ivory keys, Billie stepped into the spotlight wearing a fitted red sequined dress and matching pumps. She gently stroked the microphone in a circular motion as if making love to it. The crowd applauded wildly as her soft, smooth voice filled the room. "Sing that song, baby!" one man yelled. It had been months since I performed in front of an audience and I was a little nervous. I took a deep breath to settle down. When it was time for my solo, I pretended like my father was in the audience. He always brought out the best in me.

The room was quiet except for the sound of my piano keys striking their chords. I closed my eyes and allowed the spirit to move me. I wanted to play it perfectly, just in case my father was listening. As my fingers glided across the keys I felt myself getting emotional. I tried to hold back my feelings but I couldn't. There was too much pain built up inside. I missed my best friend and my mentor. Even after twelve years, I hadn't forgiven my father for dying.

I poured my innermost feelings out in front of a room full of perfect strangers, not giving a damn if they appreciated it or not. I played that solo piece like never before. My eyes watered as I pressed down on the keys with the final note. The audience erupted with applause. "Encore! Encore!" Even the band members were clapping. I stood up and took a bow. "Thank you," I said, inconspicuously wiping my eyes. "Thank you very much."

I exited the stage and went over to the table where Simon and Toni were seated.

"That was incredible!" Toni said. She gave me a friendly hug. "I've never seen anyone play with such passion."

"I was just trying to impress you."

"Mission accomplished!" she said. "You were great!"

"All right, that's enough with the compliments. His head is big enough as it is," Simon said, while aiming his disposable camera. "Now put your arms around that fine woman and say 'cheese.' "

"Speaking of big heads, whose bright idea was it to invite Toni?" I asked.

"It was mine," Ariel said, coming out of nowhere. "I told her about the party when she called for directions."

"And who might you be?" I asked, trying to adjust my eyes from the flash.

"Allow me to make the formal introductions," Simon said, cutting in. "Malcolm Tremell, this is my new manager, Ariel Daniels."

"So, this is Ariel?" I said, while looking her up and down. "Simon didn't tell me you were so beautiful."

"And he didn't tell me you were so handsome and talented."

Ahem. Toni cleared her throat.

"I'm sorry, I hope I didn't step on any toes," Ariel apologized.

"No, it's not that," Toni said, while reaching for her purse. "I just wanted to say good-bye. I've got to be leaving."

"Could you excuse us for a moment?" I said to Simon and Ariel.

"No problem!" Simon said. "It was a pleasure meeting you, Toni. Hope to see you again."

"I'm sure you will." She smiled then gave him a hug. "Thanks for the hospitality."

Once we were alone, I sat down with her at the table and poured us both a glass of champagne. "The least you could do is join me for a birthday toast."

"Okay, just one drink, then I have to be going."

"What's the hurry?" I asked. "The night is still young."

"I would love to stay but I've got to get up first thing in the morning to take my fiancé to the airport."

"So, am I going to see you again? I still owe you that rose, you know?"

"Tell you what," she said, pulling out a business card and handing it to me. "If you take me out to brunch next week, we'll call it even. That is, if you're still in Atlanta."

"I'll be here all right," I said, as we clinked glasses and drank. "Here's to friendship."

After she finished her drink, I offered to walk her downstairs to her car, but she insisted that I stay and enjoy myself. I gave her an affectionate hug and handed her one of my business cards. "Call me anytime," I told her.

Once she was out of sight, Ariel came over to the table with another bottle of champagne.

"You mind if I join you?" she asked.

"Be my guest."

"I hope I didn't get you into trouble," she said.

"It's not that serious. Toni and I are just friends," I said, sounding discouraged. "As a matter of fact, she's engaged."

"Engaged?" she said, puzzled. "That's strange. She was the first one here for your party, and . . ." She stopped abruptly.

"And, what?"

"Look, Malcolm, I don't know you well enough to get into your business, so I think I'll just keep my big mouth shut."

"It's too late for that, you're already in up to your neck."

"Look, Malcolm, a woman who is in a strong relationship wouldn't be hanging out at the club at eleven o'clock at night with a man she just met the night before."

"How did you know that."

"We had plenty of time to talk before you arrived. Like I told you, she was the first one here."

"That doesn't mean anything. Maybe she was already in the area."

"Okay, then explain to me why she wasn't wearing a ring," she said with an attitude. "If I had an engagement ring I would be sporting that bad boy for the whole world to see."

"Maybe she just forgot to put it on."

"Yeah, right. Or maybe she took it off to change a flat tire. Give me a break! When a woman is excited about getting married, she represents!"

Ariel was right. Toni wasn't happy, and she damn sure wasn't in love. At least not in the way a woman should be before getting married. It was obvious that her old man wasn't on his J-O-B. Either that or Toni was using him for money. Women in the new millennium had become experts at using their bodies for profit. White-collar whores, I call them. But that didn't seem like Toni's style. And I was a pretty good judge of character. I figured her fiancé was just one of the millions of men who get comfortable in their relationship once they put a ring on a woman's finger. They stop taking them out to dinner, stop telling them how beautiful they are, and stop eating their pussies. Next thing you know, my phone is ringing off the hook.

Whatever the reason, I wasn't sympathetic. He had something I wanted and it was every man for himself. All I had to do was make myself available, be patient, and wait for him to slip up.

Chapter 12

D amn it's hot!" Ariel said as she stepped outside bare-
foot to get her Sunday morning paper. "No wonder
they call it Hotlanta." She rushed back into her living
room to finish watching one of her favorite programs,
Heart and Soul on BET. She belonged to a book club
and was looking for a new title to suggest for their meeting in August. Lately, they had begun reading books by
male authors like Eric Jerome Dickey, Omar Tyree, and
E. Lynn Harris. She almost choked on her food when the
host of the show mentioned a novel called *Men Cry in
the Dark*. "They should cry in the fuckin' light with all
the hell they put you through," she yelled at the television.

Just as the show was about to end, her phone rang.
She looked at the Caller ID to see who it was. "Oh, no,
I'm not in the mood today," she said as she picked up the
phone. "Hi, Mama, how you doing!"

"How did you know it was me?"

"It's called Caller ID, Mama. Get rid of that old rotary
phone and come out of the Stone Age."

"I just called to see how you were doing. I hope I wasn't interrupting anything."

"Anything like what?" Ariel asked. "It's eleven o'clock in the morning."

"I thought you might have company."

"Mama, please don't start preaching to me about finding a husband. I keep telling you, I'm not ready to share my space. And besides, these immature men can't handle a strong woman."

"That's exactly your problem, you need to stop being so damned strong!"

"What's that supposed to mean?"

"It means that your sisters have good jobs and college degrees. And they've each been married twice."

"Joyce and Sheila are just settling," Ariel said with an attitude. "I'm not going to spend the rest of my life with some overweight postal employee or an underpaid elementary school teacher. I need someone who complements me."

"Ariel, you know I love you with all my heart, and I'm proud of you for accomplishing so much on your own, but, baby, you ain't all that!"

"Excuse me?"

"You heard what I said. Stop holding yourself up as if you're better than everybody else," she told her. "You're from the streets like all these other uppity negroes. And I should know, I raised your nappy-headed behind."

"I don't think I'm better than other people. I just want someone who accepts me for who I am," Ariel said, getting upset. "Why should I have to act like an airhead just to make a man feel secure?"

"Sweetheart, I'm not asking you to play dumb, but you've got to learn how to relax and let the man lead. Or at least let him think he's leading," she said. "Men have to feel a sense of power. They have to feel needed."

Ariel got up from the sofa and walked over to the fireplace where her college degrees and certificates were on display. "Why do women always have to be the one in the relationship to submit, even when they have more education?" she asked emotionally. "It's just not fair, Mama!"

"Baby, listen to what I'm about to say, and don't ever forget it. When you find a God-fearing man who is worthy, you won't even see it as submission," she said in a motherly tone. "It will happen naturally."

"Thanks for the pep talk, Mama. I'm going to take your advice and stop being so picky," Ariel said as she wiped the tears from her eyes. "In fact, I might even go out on a date tonight."

"With whom?" her mother asked, sounding surprised.

"I joined the V103 hookup line last week. After sorting through fifteen crazy messages, I think there might be three good prospects."

"Good for you, sweetheart. Just promise me you'll go easy on them. None of that 'I am woman, hear me roar' business."

"I'll be the perfect lady, Mama. I'll keep my mouth shut like a good little girl and allow them to lead," Ariel said in a soft tone.

"And what happens if none of those three men work out?"

"Then I'm going to buy myself an economy pack of double A batteries and practice being submissive to my vibrator," she said, laughing.

• • •

It was 7:30 P.M. when Ariel arrived at Justin's restaurant in Buckhead. She left her car with the valet and went inside to look for Jeff, her blind date. When she talked to him on the phone, he described himself as six-three, two hundred thirty pounds, and muscular. Ariel liked her men big. She was also impressed by the fact that he owned a landscaping business. With all the single women buying homes in Atlanta, she figured he was making a killing.

When she didn't spot anyone who fit his description, she reserved a table with the host and went over to the bar to get a drink.

"What can I get you?" the bartender asked.

"Martell on the rocks, please."

"Coming right up."

While Ariel waited for her drink, the men at the bar began raping her with their eyes. Even the ones who had dates sitting right next to them were giving her flirtatious smiles. Like any other woman, Ariel loved attention, but her baby face and large breasts always seemed to attract knuckleheads, mostly men under thirty. It wasn't long before one of them made his move.

"Excuse me, is anyone sitting here?" a short man wearing a loud red jacket asked. He looked like a Puerto Rican, but he moved and talked like a brother.

"No, but I am waiting for someone," Ariel said.

"I'll be happy to leave when he arrives," he said politely as he sat down. "My name is Chris, what's yours?"

"I'm Ariel. Nice to meet you, Chris." She extended her hand.

Ariel was surprised by how comfortable she was with him. She preferred to be left alone, especially when she was waiting for a date. But Chris had one of those bubbly personalities that made her feel relaxed. It didn't hurt that he was cute and smelled good. Ariel loved men who wore nice cologne.

"So what brings you out on a Sunday night, Chris?"

"I just dropped my daughter off at her mother's house down the street and decided to stop in for a bite before heading home."

"How old is your daughter?"

"She's seven," he said, while reaching for his wallet. "This is a picture of her when she was six."

"Aw, look at her. She's a real cutie."

"Yeah, that's my little princess. I don't know what I would do without her."

"It's always nice to see men taking care of their kids."

"For me, it wasn't even an option," he said passionately. "When her mother and I divorced, I made a commitment to be there for her, no matter what."

"I'm sorry it didn't work out," Ariel said compassionately. "You think you'll ever get back together?"

"Excuse my French, but hell naw! That woman drove me crazy. Every time I turned around she was spending money, mine and hers," he said, laughing. "Worst of all, she couldn't cook worth shit! Her idea of cooking from scratch was Hamburger Helper, and she burned that half the time."

"I'm glad to see you have such a positive attitude. Most men would be carrying around a lot of emotional baggage."

"The way I look at it, she did me a favor. I have a renewed appreciation for being single," he told her. "Now, that's enough about me, what's your story."

"Well, I'm single, no kids, no debt, and I just received my master's degree in business."

"Don't tell me you're one of those strong, independent black women who doesn't need a man?"

"For your information, Mr. Know-It-All, I'm here on a date tonight," Ariel said with her face frowned up.

"So, where is he?"

"That's a good question."

Ariel checked her watch, it was 8:05. Jeff was supposed to meet her between seven-thirty and eight. She had given him her cell-phone number, just in case he was going to be late, but he hadn't called. With the exception of bad hygiene, promptness was her biggest pet peeve. After waiting another fifteen minutes, Ariel wrote him off. When her table reservation was called, she invited Chris to join her for dinner, her treat. Although she wasn't attracted to him in a sexual way, she enjoyed his conversation.

By 9:00 Ariel and Chris were carrying on like old friends. She was surprised by how much they had in common. They both graduated from Howard University.

And they both grew up in Cleveland. Chris had her cracking up when he talked about basement parties and blue-light posters back in the seventies. She almost peed on herself when he reminded her of the zodiac poster with the different sex position. "I almost killed myself trying to imitate that Scorpio position," he joked. They even ordered the same dish off the menu, catfish and grits.

The evening was going perfectly until Ariel noticed a man glancing around the room as if he were looking for someone. She had a strange feeling it was Jeff. He was six-three, two hundred thirty pounds, but she didn't see any muscles. His stomach was protruding out of his slacks and his hairline was receding.

"Oh, shit!" Ariel said, sounding distressed. "It's him!"

"Who is him?"

"My blind date."

"You mean the fat baldheaded guy in the tight suit?" Chris said, looking over his shoulder.

"Yeah, that's the one. Stop looking, maybe he won't notice me."

When the hostess pointed in her direction, she was sure it was Jeff. Luckily, she changed out of the white dress she told him she would be wearing. All he knew was that Ariel was five-nine with cinnamon-brown skin, and her hair was cut short.

"Oh, my God, here he comes," Ariel whispered, while shielding her face.

Jeff approached the table apprehensively. First he stood there like an idiot trying to figure out what to say. Chris and Ariel ignored him and went on with their conversation. Finally, he worked up the courage to speak.

"Ah, excuse me, is your name Ariel?"

"Naw, my name is Aquanita," Ariel said, sounding ghetto. "And this is my man, Rico."

Chris had to cover his mouth to keep from spitting his food out. Ariel reached over to pat him on the back.

"You all right, baby?"

"Yeah, Aquanita, I'm fine," Chris said as he wiped the tears from his eyes with his napkin.

"You're sure your name isn't Ariel," Jeff asked again. "You sound an awful lot like her."

"Look, I know what my name is!" Ariel said, getting loud. "Why don't you step off!"

"I'm sorry to have disturbed you," Jeff said, while backing away. "Have a nice evening."

Chris was still wiping his face when Jeff left the restaurant.

"Now that's what I call an Oscar-winning performance!" he said, still laughing. "Two thumbs up!"

"What can I say? I'm a woman of many talents."

"You don't seem to have any talent when it comes to dating. Where did you meet that loser?"

"I told you it was a blind date. How was I supposed to know he was lying about his looks? When we talked over the phone, he said he was a cross between Denzel Washington and Wesley Snipes."

"He looked more like Fat Albert, if you ask me," Chris said, laughing.

"Very funny, Richard Pryor. Now stop talking for a minute so I can give you something," Ariel leaned over and kissed him on the cheek.

"What was that for?"

"For rescuing me and for being so much fun to hang out with. I really enjoyed your company."

"Does that mean I'll be seeing you again?"

"Please don't take this the wrong way, Chris, but you're not exactly my type," Ariel said reluctantly. "But I would like to stay in touch."

"That's fine with me," he said as he pulled out his business card. "Give me a call when you get some free time. Maybe we can get together and rent a video. I'll even bring the popcorn."

"Don't be surprised if I take you up on that offer," Ariel said. "With all the bad luck I'm having with men, it's probably the best offer I'll get all year. No offense."

"None taken."

PART III

Womanology

Chapter 13

Monday afternoon Teddy arrived at the Foxy nightclub to pick up his paycheck. The club was considered the raunchiest in Atlanta, but it was among the most profitable, thanks to Teddy. His dance group, Hot Chocolate, performed there regularly to standing-room-only crowds. The only complaint he had was getting paid by check instead of cash. The owner was paranoid after being audited by the IRS and wasn't taking any chances.

When he walked inside the double-glass doors, the club manager, Claudia, was standing behind the bar doing inventory. Teddy kneeled down before she could see him and creeped up on her.

"Boo!" he shouted as he sprung up out of nowhere.

"Oh, my goodness," she said as she spun around grabbing her chest. "Boy, you scared the shit out of me! You should know better than to frighten a woman my age. I could've had a heart attack!"

Claudia reached over the bar and gave Teddy a friendly hug. She was a burly forty-five-year-old black woman, standing six feet. Her hair was dyed blond and she walked with a slight pimp. Any blind man could tell she was gay, and proud of it.

"Stop whining, you old lesbian, and give me my money," Teddy said, laughing.

"I may be a lesbian, but at least I'm a good one," she told him.

"Yeah, so I've heard. That's why I don't bring my women around here. You might turn them out."

"You know what they say, a hole will outlast a pole anytime."

"That depends on the pole," Teddy said. "I've been known to transform lesbians with one stroke."

"You're an arrogant little so-and-so, aren't you?" she said, while handing him his check. "If I didn't mix business with pleasure I would try you."

"You can't handle this sweet young meat." Teddy grabbed his crotch. "I'd have your old ass walking around like *Dawn of the Dead.*"

"That's exactly your problem, these naive little girls are giving you a big head. One day you're going to run into a mature woman and she's going to put a mojo on you."

"The woman that I'm shacking with is forty-five years old and a successful attorney, and I've got her so sprung that if I tell her the sky is green, she'll believe it," he boasted. "Just last week she confronted me about a pair of panties she found in her drawer. By the end of the night she was giving me a bath and a blow job. So, who's putting the mojo on whom?"

"That's why so many women are walking around so angry!" she said, getting upset. "All men do is use women up and throw them away like garbage."

"Don't get mad at me! She knew what she was getting into," he said adamantly. "What the hell did she expect from a thirty-year-old stripper? When we met, I didn't have an apartment or a car, and I was dating three other women. It's not my fault if she wants to play Mother Teresa and try to reform me."

"That doesn't mean you have to take advantage of her."

"Any woman who is stupid enough to give a perfect stranger credit cards and keys to her house deserves to be played," he said angrily. "I'm going to ride this horse until it goes lame or until a better one comes along."

"You mean a richer one, don't you?" Claudia asked.

"Whatever," he said smugly. "Now if you will excuse me, I'm going to use the little boys' room."

Suddenly there was a loud knock on the glass door. Claudia pulled back the curtains and noticed a sheriff's vehicle parked out front. "Come in, it's open!" she yelled.

"Good afternoon, ma'am. I'm looking for Mr. Theodore Simmons," he said. "Is he employed here?"

"Yes, he is, officer. Is he in some kind of trouble?" she asked, sounding concerned.

"That's for the judge to decide." He handed Claudia a clipboard with a pen and white envelope attached to it. "I need you to sign here."

"What's this?"

"It's a summons for him to appear in family court."

Claudia signed on the dotted line and handed him back his pen. "Is there anything you want me to tell him?" she asked.

"You can tell him that if he doesn't show up I'll be back with a warrant and handcuffs. Have a good day, ma'am." He tipped his cap and walked out.

Right after he drove off, Teddy came out of the bathroom and sat down at the bar. He buried his face in his hands for a moment then burst out laughing.

"What's so funny?" Claudia asked. "Didn't you hear what the officer said?"

"I heard him," he said calmly. "You mind if I make a phone call?"

"Be my guest?"

Teddy pulled a small black book out of his pants pocket and turned the tiny pages until he found the listing for Club Obsession. After dialing the number, he took a deep breath and cleared his throat.

"Hello, this is Teddy Simmons, may I please speak to Mr. Harris?"

While he waited to be connected, he whistled like he didn't have a care in the world. Claudia watched him, totally perplexed by his attitude.

"Hello, Mr. Harris. How are you?" I just called to let you know I'm interested in that gig on Thursday nights," he said cheerfully. "I just have one condition, I need to be paid in cash. Is that a problem?"

He paused for a second while Simon answered. "You've got yourself a deal! Me and the fellahs will see you Thursday. Nice doing business with you." Then he hung up.

"I can't believe you're so calm and cool considering what just happened."

"I knew it was coming," he said casually. "The baby's mother called me a few months ago and told me she had my baby."

"Why didn't you get a blood test to see if the baby was yours?"

"I already did. It's a boy."

"So why are you being served with papers?"

"Because I told that bitch she wasn't getting a single, solitary dime of my money, that's why!"

"That's not right, Teddy," she said. "No matter what you think or feel about the woman, your child shouldn't have to suffer."

"Look, I never asked for this baby," he said, agitated. "Hell, I hardly even know that heifer. I met her last year after I stripped at her bachelorette party."

"You mean she's married!"

"No, she *was* married. That love affair was over nine months after the honeymoon. I wish I could have seen the look on her husband's face when his son came out brown, not white," he said, laughing.

"Get the hell out of here, you no-good bastard!" Claudia yelled. "I don't want your kind around here. I don't give a damn how much money you bring in!"

"I was tired of this rundown dump anyway," he said arrogantly as he walked backward toward the door. "Besides, I got a better offer."

"You need to grow up and stop running away from responsibility."

"Fuck you, Claudia, you pussy-eating dyke."

"I may be a dyke, but at least I'm not a deadbeat parent." She tossed the summons in his face. "One day all the pain you cause is going to come back on you. I just hope I'm around when it happens."

Chapter 14

Iwas so pissed, I nearly wore a hole in the carpet with all my pacing. Like a fool, I let Simon talk me into returning my rental car on Sunday. My flight to Los Angeles was scheduled to depart at 7:40 P.M. and it was already 6:30. "Where is that knucklehead?" I said, while staring out the living room window. "I'm going to kill him if I miss this flight."

By 6:45 I was out of patience. I grabbed the yellow pages out of the closet and checked the listing under taxi service. Just as I was about to dial a number, Simon pulled into the driveway. "Let's go!" he yelled as he blew the horn. I threw my bags over my shoulder and rushed out the door.

He had the top down on the Dodge Viper, and "Pull Up to the Bumper" by Grace Jones was blasting over the speakers. I didn't know whether to hug him or smack him upside his big head. "Where have you been?" I asked, tossing my bags into the trunk.

"I had a few things to straighten out at the club," he said, trying to talk over the music. "But don't worry, I'll get you there in plenty of time."

"You'd better!" I said. "If I miss that flight I'm going to keep your ass up all night complaining."

"In that case, buckle your seat belt. I know a shortcut."

Simon slid on his shades and pulled out of the driveway like a madman. We sped down the street with the music blaring. The bass was so high on the stereo that the entire car was vibrating. Once we reached I-85, Simon swerved in and out of the HOV lane trying to make up time. People were blowing their horns and cursing us out. "Watch where you're going, you dumb son of a bitch!" an old woman yelled as she gave us the finger. I was laughing so hard tears were running down my face. Once we reached the I-20 merge, traffic began to lighten up.

"Now, that's what I call driving," I said, wiping my eyes with my shirt sleeve.

"That was a piece of cake compared to rush hour on the Dan Ryan in Chicago."

"A piece of cake? You damn near got us killed," I said, laughing. "What's gotten into you anyway?"

"I'm having one of those exceptional days where everything is going right," Simon said with a wide grin. "The revenue from the club is up, Ariel is working out perfectly as manager, and I just booked this stripper named Teddy Bear for Ladies' Night. Too bad you can't stick around to see him perform."

"Why would I want to watch some guy swinging his dick in front of a room full of sexually deprived women?"

"He put on one hell of a show last week. I've never seen professional women act so uncivilized."

"Well, you can tell Teddy Bear, Yogi Bear, or whatever his name is, that I said good luck," I said, laughing. "I've got my own hustle to deal with."

"Speaking of your hustle, does Toni know what you do for a living?"

"No, she doesn't. And she never will, not if I can help it."

"That's like trying to keep it a secret that the pope is Catholic," Simon said, laughing.

"What's your point?"

"My point is, there must be at least two hundred women in Atlanta that you've escorted professionally or fucked casually. It's only a matter of time before your name comes up."

"Toni is new to Atlanta. And I doubt that she's the type to gossip."

"Yeah, right! I haven't met a female yet that didn't listen to a rumor or two," Simon said wisely. "They can't help it. They're nosy by nature."

"I probably won't have to worry about her finding out anyway," I said, sounding discouraged. "I left her a message yesterday and today and she never returned my calls."

"Maybe she had an emergency. You never know. Why don't you give her another call, just in case." He tried to hand me his cell phone.

"Are you crazy?" I yelled. "Didn't you hear me say I already left two messages."

"And?"

"Rule number one in the *Player's Handbook,* never, ever call a woman more than twice," I said to him. "If she doesn't return your call after two messages, she's not interested."

"Fine, have it your way," he said, while slamming the phone into the holder. "I just hope your stubbornness doesn't backfire on you."

By the time we arrived at the airport, it was seven-fifteen. The traffic was much lighter than I expected for Monday. Simon pulled up to the American Airlines curbside check-in and popped the trunk.

"Thanks for making the trip to see me, partner," Simon said as he walked over and gave me a brotherly hug.

"I'm the one who should be thanking you for such a great birthday gift. You know how much I cherish that piano," I told him. "Just make sure it doesn't get burned up before I can have it shipped to L.A."

"Don't worry, I'll keep a fire extinguisher right next to it," Simon said as he got back inside the car. "And by the way, I'll be sure to tell my fiancée that you said hello."

"Oh, I almost forgot about the love of your life," I said, trying to play dumb. "Isn't she supposed to be back from New Orleans today?"

"She called me this afternoon and said she was staying another night. I told her I didn't have a problem with that."

"Do you honestly think she would have come home even if you did have a problem with it?"

"Of course," Simon said with confidence. "Cynthia would never do anything to disrespect me."

"That's rule number two in the *Player's Handbook*," I said as I picked up my bags and headed toward the door.

"What's that?" he yelled.

"Never say never!"

Chapter 15

It was half past midnight. The dimly lit tavern on Bourbon Street was still overflowing with intoxicated tourists. Cynthia and Debra blended in perfectly as they sipped on Coronas and turned over shots of tequila. "Happy Fourth of July!" they yelled. Technically it was July third, but that was close enough.

"Girl, I'm drunk as hell," Debra said, while checking herself in the dingy mirror behind the bar. "I hope we don't get pulled over for WWI."

"What the hell is WWI?"

"Walking while intoxicated," Debra joked.

They burst out laughing and tried to give high fives, missing each other's hands twice before finally connecting. The white patrons sitting next to them moved down a stool. Cynthia and Debra thought it was funny. They laughed in their faces and kept on clowning.

"It must be my perfume," Cynthia said, laughing.

"Excuse me, ladies," the bartender said, "could you please keep it down?"

"I didn't come all the way to New Orleans to keep it down," Debra said, getting upset. "And besides, I don't see you asking those rowdy white boys at the end of the bar to keep it down and they're twice as loud as us!"

"Look, miss, I don't want any trouble." He tried to sound more cordial. "I'm just trying to do my job."

"Well, do your job and get the hell out of my face before I have a Rodney King flashback!"

"Calm down, Deb, it's not worth it," Cynthia said.

"Fuck that!" Debra said, getting loud. "I paid my money just like everybody else."

The bouncer, who was six-five and as wide as a refrigerator, came over and stood behind Debra, trying to be intimidating. He had a baby face and wore an old Texas Rangers baseball cap and a dingy white T-shirt that read COWBOYS DO IT BEST.

"Is there a problem?" he asked. He had an annoying southern drawl.

"You're damn right, there's a problem," Debra said, stretching her neck to look him in the eye. "You're in my space."

"I'm going to have to ask you ladies to pay for your drinks and leave."

"On what grounds?" Cynthia asked.

"I don't have to give you black bitches any explanation. Now get out, before I throw you out!"

"No you didn't call me a bitch, you redneck motherfucker." Debra swung her glass of beer with all her might, barely missing his face.

The customers sitting at the bar quickly ran for cover as beer went flying everywhere. The bouncer grabbed her by the arm and picked her up like a rag doll. He put her in a bear hug and began carrying her toward the door.

"Let her go!" Cynthia yelled as she pounded on his back with her tiny fists.

"You want some, too?" he asked as he turned toward her with his fist balled.

"I wouldn't do that if I were you," a deep voice said out of nowhere.

It was Reverends James and Randall. The two men they met at the Marriott.

"Mind your own business, nigger," the bouncer said.

"If I weren't a man of God, I would make you sorry for using that word. But since I am, I'm going to ask you politely to put that woman down," James said with conviction. "And I'm only going to ask you once."

"And if I don't, then what?"

"Let's just say, I'll be praying for forgiveness tomorrow," he said.

Although the tavern was more than ninety percent white, the other patrons wanted no part of this standoff. Some were afraid but most felt the bouncer was out of line. It didn't take him long to realize that if he took it any further, he was on his own.

"You're lucky I'm in a good mood tonight," the bouncer said as he let go of Debra.

Debra straightened her clothes and gave him the finger.

"You're not so cocky now, are you, Baby Huey," she said as she picked up her purse off the floor.

"Just get the hell out before I call the police."

Cynthia walked over to the bar and sipped down the last of her beer. Then she slammed down a twenty-dollar bill. "Thanks for the warm southern hospitality," she said. "Keep the change."

They strutted out of the tavern with their heads held high, feeling like queens who had been rescued by their black kings. The moment they made it outside they laughed and slapped five.

"Girl, that was some shit right out of a *Shaft* movie," Debra said, laughing.

"Did you see the look on that white boy's face when he saw all those brothas," Cynthia added. "I bet he's never been in the same room with that many black folks in his entire life."

James and Randall didn't find it amusing. Neither did the other ministers who walked away shortly after the altercation.

"Now, what was that all about?" James asked, sounding upset.

"We were just having a little fun, that's all," Cynthia said.

"I think that's enough fun for one night," Randall said. "Let's go."

"Where are we going?" Debra asked.

"Back to the hotel, that's where. You two are in no condition to be walking around these streets."

"Okay, I'll go peacefully, reverend," Debra said as she pressed her large breasts against him. "But first I need to stop at the store for some aspirin."

"Good, now let's go," James said, leading the way.

"Hold up," Debra said, pulling James in the opposite direction. "It doesn't take four people to buy a bottle of Tylenol. Randall will take care of me. We'll meet you back at the hotel."

"I don't know, Debra," Cynthia said nervously. "Are you sure?"

"Yes, I'm sure!" Debra winked at Cynthia and led Randall away by the hand. "Don't wait up!"

Cynthia was as nervous as a teenager on her first date as she stood alone with James. She tried not to make eye contact with him knowing her eyes would reveal how much she was attracted to him. She tried looking down at his feet but that didn't help. James had on a pair of shorts that showed off his hairy, muscular legs. Cynthia couldn't help getting moist.

"So what do we do now?" she asked timidly.

"We're going home!" James said.

Although Cynthia wasn't expecting anything but an escort to her room, she loved the way home sounded.

• • •

Early the next morning, Cynthia awoke to the voice of a radio personality on Q93 FM. He was on the phone with a female caller who admitted to having an affair.

"So why did you cheat on your husband?" he asked.

"He wasn't giving me any attention," she said. "When we first met, he would take me everywhere, to the movies, to dinner, and out dancing. I love to dance. But now he's so preoccupied with running his business that we hardly ever see each other."

"Why not get a divorce instead of cheating?"

"Because I love my husband. And he's a good man. But a sistah has needs!" she emphasized. "Every now and then you need a little maintenance."

"I heard that!" Cynthia agreed.

She was tempted to call the radio station to tell her story. She had experienced the same problem with Simon over the years. Although he tried to include her in functions at the club, she felt left out. It was only a matter of time before another man . . .

Ahem. James cleared his throat. He was sitting on the foot of the bed putting on his socks.

"Oh, you scared me to death."

"Sorry. I was just listening to the program. Kind of ironic, isn't it?"

"Yes, it is," she said. "You think God is trying to tell us something?"

"Could be. The Good Book says He works in mysterious ways."

Suddenly the phone rang. James grabbed the rest of his clothes and went into the bathroom to give Cynthia some privacy. She turned down the radio and picked up the receiver.

"Hello?"

"Good morning, sweetheart."

"Oh, good morning, Simon. Where are you?" she asked nervously.

"I'm downstairs in the lobby."

"Oh, shit!" She covered the phone with her hand. "I mean, oh really."

"I'm only kidding," he said, laughing. "I'm at the club. I had to come in and take care of some paperwork. How's everything in New Orleans?"

"It's going great." Cynthia put her hand over her chest, trying to calm herself.

"So what time are you flying in today?"

"Debra booked us on the eleven o'clock. If you consider the change in the time zone, we should be there no later than one-thirty."

"Where is old loud mouth Debra, anyway? I'm surprised she's not yapping in the background."

"She's in the bathroom."

At that moment, James decided to take a piss. The sound of him hitting the water echoed through the room.

"What's that noise I hear?" Simon asked.

"What noise?" Cynthia said as she rushed over to close the bathroom door.

"That splashing sound I hear in the background."

"Oh, that's just Debra running some bathwater."

Simon paused as if he was trying to decide whether or not to accept that explanation.

"Well, be sure to tell her I said hello," he said, laughing. "I'll see you in Atlanta at the gate. Have a safe flight, sweetheart. Love you."

"Love you, too. Bye."

Cynthia covered her face with a pillow and screamed. "That was too close." James came out of the bathroom fully clothed with his Bible in hand.

"Was that your fiancé?"

"Yes, it was."

"Sorry about that. I guess I wasn't thinking."

"I don't think either one of us was thinking last night," she said with her hand on her forehead. "That was a big mistake."

"I agree."

"If you thought it was such a big mistake, why did you go through with it in the first place? You're supposed to be able to resist temptation. At least I have the excuse of being drunk."

"First of all, I'm imperfect just like any other man. Being involved in the church doesn't magically remove lust from your heart," he said seriously. "And as far as your excuse goes, alcohol only makes you do what you don't have the courage to do when you're sober. So don't try to lay all the responsibility on me."

"You're right. We both should have known better," she said, while putting on her robe. "The best thing to do is put this behind us and go on with our lives."

"That's a good idea. And I'll be sure to pray for both of us." He kissed her gently on the forehead and walked toward the door. "By the way, you're still my favorite news reporter." Then he left.

No sooner did the door close behind him than Debra burst into the room with a big smile on her face and singing, *I shot the sheriff!*

Cynthia was staring out the window shaking her head.

"What's wrong with you?" she asked, putting her arms around Cynthia. "I know you got some last night. I can smell sex in the air." Then she sniffed comically.

"I got some all right, and I'm already starting to feel guilty."

"Girl, you need to stop tripping. Men do this kind of shit all the time and they get married with a clear conscious. Just consider it as your last fling, your bachelorette party," Debra said.

"Maybe you're right."

"I know I'm right. Now get dressed so we can get something to eat before we fly out. All those orgasms last night made me hungry."

"I guess I could use a bagel and a glass of orange juice myself," Cynthia said with a sly grin. "But you know we're going straight to hell for what we did last night."

"Yeah, I know, but at least we'll go on a full stomach."

Chapter 16

Ariel was feeling like a million bucks as she drove down Lenox Road listening to "Joy and Pain" by Frankie Beverly and Maze. "Sing that song, Frankie!" she shouted as she snapped her fingers to the music. It was the Fourth of July and the weather was gorgeous. Her hair was freshly cut and she was enjoying her first full day after resigning from Coca-Cola. She was living her dream working as manager of Club Obsession. This was as far from corporate America as she had been and she was determined never to go back. As she looked over at the passenger seat, her old office ID was sticking out of her purse. She quickly let down the window and threw it out, "Free at last, free at last. Thank God almighty, I'm free at last!" she screamed.

To celebrate, she had gone on a shopping spree. The backseat of her Mercedes was packed with all kinds of goodies from Lenox Mall: a Coach bag, a Versace dress, and four boxes of Donna Karan shoes. She even bought two sets of white lace bras and panties from Victoria's Secret and she already had a drawerful.

She was still singing and bouncing in her seat as she approached the stoplight at Buford Highway. Suddenly, a white Lexus pulled up beside her. Two men waved their hands frantically, signaling her to let down her window. They appeared to be young. About twenty-five, she estimated. She turned down her music and cracked the window to hear what they were trying to say.

"Excuse me, baby. Can I talk to you for a minute?" the driver screamed.

"Come on, sistah, don't be like that. I just want to get those seven digits," the passenger hollered.

Ariel couldn't believe they had the audacity to even speak to her. They looked like two escapees from a bad rap video. The man driving had bumps on his face and was cross-eyed. And the scrub on the passenger's side had a row of gold teeth and the wildest hair she had ever seen. He could put Busta Rhymes to shame, she was thinking.

Ariel rolled up her window, put on her Gucci sunglasses, and turned up the volume on her music. It was just another harsh example of the lack of quality men in Atlanta. Since she moved from DC four years ago, she had been trying to find all the wonderful men her cousin bragged about. The same cousin who became so frustrated with men that she turned to women.

Ariel wasn't about to start bumping nipples. Having a man wasn't that serious, not as long as she had a vibrator and a strong middle finger. And when that didn't work she positioned herself underneath the spout in the bathtub and let the water do the job. She called it The Waterfall Technique.

While she waited impatiently for the light to change, her cell phone rang. She checked the Caller ID to make sure it wasn't Jeff, aka Fat Albert. He had been calling five times a day ever since their encounter at Justin's.

"Ms. Ariel Daniels," she answered, sounding proper.

"Good afternoon, Ms. Daniels, this is Simon Harris,"

he said with perfect diction to make fun of her. "Are you having a bad day or are you always this stuffy?"

"Sorry, boss. I guess I'm used to answering the phone at my office. It's going to take me a while to adjust."

"While you're adjusting, I need a couple of favors."

"I've only been on the job four days and you're already asking me to work overtime?"

"Well, you know what they say, you have to work eighteen hours a day for yourself if you don't want to work eight hours a day for someone else," Simon said.

"All right, Les Brown, now that you've motivated me, what do you want?" she asked, laughing.

"I have to pick up Cynthia from the airport, so could you please stop by the club and sign for the shipment? The liquor truck is going to make a special delivery for me today. It should be there at one o'clock."

"No problem. I'm in Buckhead right now," she said. "What's the other favor."

"The stripper I told you about is going to stop by to drop off some costumes and props. Just show him where the storage area is."

"You mean Theodore?"

"Yeah, that's him. But he prefers to be called Teddy, or Teddy Bear."

"I don't care what he prefers to be called," she said with an attitude. "His mama named him Theodore and that's what I'm going to call him."

"I wish I could be there to see you two go at it," Simon said, laughing. "This should be better than Ali and Frazier."

"It'll be more like Ali and Sammy Davis, Jr.," Ariel said, laughing. "These strippers may have great bodies but most of them are mental midgets."

"Try not to break him down too badly, okay? Remember, he works for us now."

"Don't worry, I'll leave him enough self-esteem to

shake his ass on Thursday," Ariel said. "But if he steps out of line, I'm gonna put him in check."

• • •

The vendors were waiting outside the club when Ariel arrived at 12:45. She turned off the building alarm and let them in the back door to unload the cases of liquor. "Put the Heineken over there," she directed. "And you, stack those cases of Courvoisier over here!" The vendors knew the routine but Ariel got a kick out of bossing the burly men around.

Within twenty minutes everything was unloaded and signed for. Ariel locked the back door and put the paperwork in Simon's office. "Now where is Mr. Theodore?" she wondered aloud while looking down at her watch. "I've got to get ready for my date." The club was stuffy, so she waited outside in her car to take advantage of the beautiful weather. She turned on her Frankie Beverly and Maze CD and started singing like she was in concert. *Joy and pain, like sunshine and rain.* She was seriously getting her groove on, snapping her fingers and clapping.

Suddenly a black Lincoln Navigator pulled up beside her with the music blaring. Her smooth Frankie Beverly was drowned out by Master P. She knew it could only be one person, Theodore.

"Wuz up?" he yelled, while rocking back and forth to the beat.

"Wuz up, nothing. Turn that damn music down," she yelled back.

"What?" He pretended like he didn't hear her.

"I said turn that music down before you wake the dead."

He gave her a conniving smile as he turned off the ignition.

"I'm looking for Mr. Harris. Is he in?" he asked.

"He couldn't make it," Ariel said as she got out of her car.

"He asked me to meet you. My name is Ariel Daniels. I'm the new manager."

"Well, hello, Ariel. It's nice to meet you," he said with enthusiasm as he got out of the truck.

He was wearing a pair of long white shorts and a tight body shirt that showed off his muscles. Ariel couldn't believe how incredible his physique was. His bald head was clean shaven and shiny. Ariel was impressed but she wasn't about to let him know it.

"You can call me Ms. Daniels, Theodore."

"Oh, so it's like that, huh?" he said, while looking her up and down.

"It's exactly like that, Theodore." She emphasized his name to annoy him. "Now get your things out of the car and I'll show you where the storage closet is."

Teddy's ego was bruised. When he flexed his biceps, even the strongest of women would bow down. Ariel's attitude was intriguing and challenging. He was determined to break her down.

"You mind if I ask you a personal question, Ms. Daniels?" He followed closely behind her carrying two large boxes.

"What is it, Theodore?"

"Are you married?"

"No?"

"Have any kids?"

"No."

"Do you have a man?"

"None of your business."

"Ah-hah!" he said, sounding excited. "So that's why you're so tense. You haven't had your annual tune-up, have you?"

"Are you always this obnoxious?"

"Look, I'm just trying to get to know you," he said with a flirtatious smile. "I'm single, you're single, what's the problem?"

Ariel didn't say a word, she just pointed him in the direction of the storage closet. Teddy set the boxes down and closed the door. By the time he turned around, Ariel was already walking toward the front.

"Look, I promise I'll never bug you again if you'll give me one good reason why we can't hook up," he said.

"Okay, I'll give you two reasons," she told him. "One, I don't sleep with the help. And two, you're not my type."

"Why, because I don't wear a suit and tie to work?"

"No, because you're arrogant and self-centered. But the biggest reason is you're a player."

"Who me?" he asked, playing dumb. "I'm the most monogamous man in America."

"Look, brotha, I grew up with three uncles who were the biggest whores in DC. So I know a player when I see one," she said seriously. "Now some women may see you as a challenge, believing they can change you. But one look at you and any sane woman could see that you're a bona fide player for life."

Teddy burst out laughing and gave her a high five. "Well, you can't blame a guy for trying."

"I ain't mad at you. It's not your fault these women are stupid."

She gave Teddy a friendly handshake and escorted him outside to his car.

"See you Thursday, Ariel—I mean, Ms. Daniels," he said as he stepped inside his truck. "I might lap dance for you."

"Bye, Theodore," she said as she waved. "Try to go easy on these country girls. I know you're breaking their hearts."

"Their hearts and their wallets!" he said, laughing.

Ariel watched as Teddy drove off in his Navigator with his music blasting away. Once he was out of sight, she shook her head, still trying to get over how incredible his body was.

"What a waste of good meat," she said, while locking the doors to the club. "Why can't I find a man with a body like that and a brain to match?"

Chapter 17

Later on that afternoon, Ariel was getting dressed to meet Lawrence at his home for a barbecue. He was the second blind date from the radio station hookup line. The next batter up. It had only been two days since her disastrous encounter with Jeff, but Ariel was eager to get it over with. "What the hell!" she said, while putting on her makeup. "No guts, no glory."

This time she took precautions. She insisted on seeing a photo, a recent one. Lawrence scanned a picture he had taken in Cancun and e-mailed it to her. He was wearing a pair of skimpy swim trunks and sandals. Ariel was pleased with what she saw: no love handles, no flabby ass, and most important, no beer belly. He was the perfect height, too, six-one. Although looks weren't number one on her list of priorities, Ariel wanted a man she was sexually and financially attracted to.

By five-thirty she was dressed and ready to go. She checked herself one last time in the full-length mirror then grabbed her purse off the kitchen counter. Just as she was reaching for the doorknob, the phone rang. Something told her not to answer it, but she did anyway.

"Hello?"

"Hi, sweetheart, hope I'm not interrupting anything."

"Mama, how do you always manage to call me at the most inopportune time?"

"I guess I'm psychic."

"If you're psychic, then you should know that I'm late for a date."

"That's great, honey!" she said excitedly. "Is it the same guy you went out with on Sunday?"

"No, Mama, it's someone else."

"Glad to see you're getting out more often. Before you know it, I'll have another son-in-law and some grand-babies."

"I wish you would stop putting so much pressure on me to get knocked up." Ariel was getting frustrated. "It's hard enough to find a man to date, let alone have kids with."

"It's not so hard to find a good man if you know where to look. There are plenty of nice men out here ready to settle down."

"They're nice all right—nice and boring. I need a man who is romantic but knows how to handle himself on the streets. You, know, a combination of Brian McKnight and Tupac."

"Brian who? And what the hell is a Twopuck?"

"A combination of Nat King Cole and Johnny Taylor, Mama."

"Aw, I understand, a pretty boy and a roughneck."

"Something like that," Ariel said, laughing. "Look, I've got to get going. I'll call you later in the week, okay?"

"Okay, baby, have a good time. And don't forget what I told you."

"Yeah, yeah, I remember. Don't be so strong!" she said. "Bye, Mama."

• • •

The drive out to Lawrence's home took a little more than thirty-five minutes. He lived in Alpharetta, an affluent suburb just north of downtown Atlanta. Ariel was impressed as she drove through the well-manicured gated community. Many of the homes were still under construction and had For Sale signs on the lawns that read NEW HOMES STARTING AT $350,000.

The last two numbers of his street address were hard to read on the scratch piece of paper she had. But finding his house was easy. There were several cars parked in the driveway and on the street. And the unmistakable beat of Parliament Funkadelics confirmed where the only black man on the block resided.

After she finally managed to find a parking space nearly a block away, she grabbed her bag out of the car and walked toward the lavish two-story home. As she got closer, she could see a group of women standing in the driveway. They were drinking beer and talking way too loud. Ariel wanted to walk by them without saying a word, but she knew that was asking for trouble. So she took a deep breath and walked into the lionesses' den.

"Excuse me, I'm looking for Lawrence," Ariel said cordially.

They turned in her direction but didn't say a single word. It was checkout time. Most of the women were average-looking, at best, and their bodies were out of shape. Three of them wore long weaves, and had the nerve to wear thongs that revealed stretch marks on their stomachs and behinds.

Ariel could feel the tension in the air. Without even knowing her name, they had already judged her. It wasn't her fault that she was looking cute in her bright yellow shorts and matching halter top. Her waistline was a firm twenty-four inches, which made her firm breasts stand out even more. *Bitch,* she could practically hear them thinking.

"Lawrence went to the liquor store to pick up some more beer, sweetheart," one of the women with the stretch marks said with a nasty attitude.

"He'll be back in a little while," another woman said, seeming more polite. "You can wait around back by the pool. That's where everybody is hanging out."

"Thank you very much," Ariel said.

"You're welcome."

The minute Ariel turned the corner, she could hear the ugly comments and snickering.

"Who does that hoe think she is?" one woman said.

"She needs to go take off that loud-ass yellow outfit," another remarked.

Ariel just kept stepping. She understood how some women could be. They felt threatened when another woman came on the scene who was more attractive. That was one of the main reasons why she was having a hard time dating in Atlanta. Women were constantly competing with one another.

She received a better reception in the backyard. Men were giving her compliments left and right. Several men came over to introduce themselves during the first ten minutes she was there. One guy even brought her a plate of food and a glass of Kool-Aid. Of course, all that attention only made the women even more jealous.

Ariel was so turned off by the hostile atmosphere that she decided to leave. Just as she was gathering her things and was about to stand up, a strong hand pressed down on her shoulder from behind.

"And where do you think you're going?" a deep, sexy voice asked.

Ariel looked up and saw a tall and tanned god towering over her. It was Lawrence. He was even more attractive than his picture. And his thighs seemed more muscular. *Um, um, good,* she was thinking.

"I guess I'm not going anywhere." Ariel was blushing.

"Good, now let me go put this beer in the fridge and I'll be right back," he said as he walked toward the back door.

"I'll be waiting," Ariel said flirtatiously as she sat back down.

Before he made it to the door, he turned around and came back. "By the way, did anybody give you a hard time?" he asked.

"No, everybody has been very nice," Ariel said.

"Well, you be sure to let me know, because I'll kick their asses," he said seriously. "I'm not going to have anybody bothering my baby." Then he kissed her on the cheek and went inside.

Ariel was somewhat disturbed by what he said. She didn't know him that well and he was already staking a claim. But she brushed it off figuring he was just kidding. Besides, she was flattered that he was being so protective. After dealing with so many wimps, she needed a man who would take charge.

"Theodore was right, I need a tune-up," she said, while reclining in the lawn chair. "If Lawrence plays his cards right, I might get my tires rotated and my oil changed, too."

Chapter 18

It was 10:00 Tuesday night and I was sitting at home bored to death. I could see the fireworks over the marina and it made me homesick. I wished I had gone home for the Taste of Chicago and the fireworks downtown on the lakefront. Anything would've been better than doing nothing. I thought about calling Toni again to leave another message but my pride wouldn't let me. It didn't help that I had her picture on my bedroom dresser, the one we took at my birthday party at Club Obsession. I looked at it every day to remind me of how lovely she was that night.

I decided to stop acting like a chump and go over to Melvin's Jazz Club to get into some mischief. Tuesday nights were popular with the Hollywood types—actors, musicians, producers, etc. It was the ideal crowd to attract another wealthy client. Since Helen fired me in Atlanta, I had to compensate for the two thousand dollars a month she was paying. There should be a law against cutting a man off that kind of money, I was thinking.

I opened the double doors to my walk-in closet to check my wardrobe. I needed an outfit that would reflect my mood. Something dark and sinful. I chose a pair of black Canali slacks and a black sheer top. I preferred a two-piece suit but it was too humid. The forecast was a sticky eighty-two degrees, and that was the low.

By 10:30 I was ready to hit the streets. I sprayed my neck with Dolce & Gabbana cologne and popped two multivitamins, just in case I got lucky. On the way out of the door, I looked over at Toni's picture on the dresser. "What are you looking at?" I said with contempt. "I can't sit around waiting on you. I've got bills to pay."

• • •

The drive from Marina del Rey to Melvin's Jazz Club took only fifteen minutes. As usual, there was a line of scantily dressed groupies that was nearly a block long. I cruised pass them in my black Porsche, slowing down just enough for them to get a good look.

"Who is that fine nigga?" a woman shouted.

"I don't know, but he's got a nice ride," another woman replied.

Los Angeles was the materialistic capital of America. If a man had a few dollars, drove an expensive car, and was halfway decent-looking, he could practically have any woman he wanted. Sometimes he didn't even need money, just the appearance of money. In L.A. it was all about knowing how to perpetrate.

When I rolled up to the front entrance, it was blocked off with orange cones and a sign in bold letters that read VALET PARKING FULL. Some of the jealous brothas waiting in line were laughing because they assumed I had to park two blocks down the street like everybody else.

I let them have their laugh for a minute then I blew the horn and flashed my headlights three times. The valet removed the bright orange cones and directed me to pull up to the curb. "Ain't that a bitch?" I heard one of them say.

"Good evening, Mr. Tremell," Rosco said as he opened my door. "I can see you drove the Batmobile tonight."

"It was time to take old Betsy out for a spin," I said, laughing. "How's it going this evening?"

"It's crazy as usual. I'll be glad when it's time to go home."

"Hang in there," I said, while slipping him a ten. "The night's still young."

My adrenaline was pumping the moment I walked through the door. The deejay was playing "Mr. Magic" by Grover Washington, Jr., and a few people were on the dance floor trying to step. I wanted to cut in and show them how we did it in Chi-town but I was too busy scoping out the ladies. Melvin's was packed with beautiful women of every nationality: black, white, Hispanic, and Asian. It was a man's paradise. Not surprisingly, most of the men were holding up the wall sipping on empty drinks, too chicken to strike up a conversation. "Look at these pussies," I said to myself. "No wonder so many women are paying for sex."

While I waited for the hostess to seat me, I made eye contact with an attractive woman seated in the VIP section. She had light brown skin, long black hair, and slanted green eyes. She was definitely mixed with something. I had seen her somewhere before, either on television or a magazine cover. We stared at each other without losing eye contact until the waiter came to serve her drink. Once he was gone, she looked around to make sure no one was watching. Then she took the cherry out of her drink and tied the stem in a knot with her tongue. My dick got as hard as a pack of Now and Laters. I had to put my hand in my pocket to hide my erection.

Just as I was about to make my move, I felt a heavy slap on the shoulder.

"What the—" I said as I turned around with my dukes up.

"Melvin wants to see you in his office," Scottie said. He was head of security and Melvin's personal assistant.

"You scared the shit out of me, Scottie," I said. "Next time how about a simple 'excuse me'?"

The woman in the VIP section was watching me and Scottie go at it, and she was cracking up. I gave her a wink and mouthed to her "I'll be right back." She read my lips and mouthed back "I'll be here."

While I followed Scottie back to Melvin's office, I had a strange feeling something was wrong. Melvin didn't usually work on Tuesday nights. When we arrived at the office, I knocked on the door.

"Who is it?" Melvin shouted in his deep, raspy voice.

"It's Malcolm."

"Come on in, Cool Breeze."

He pushed the release button for the door and I rushed in expecting the worse. Melvin was leaning out the window with his shirt unbuttoned trying to get some air.

"What's wrong, old man?" I said, sounding concerned. "And don't tell me it was something you ate."

"I'll be fine. I just need to catch my breath." He began to breathe easier.

"That's it! You're going to see a doctor!"

"Those doctors don't know squat," he said angrily. "According to them, I was supposed to be dead ten years ago."

"Well, if you don't stop smoking those cigars and working so hard, you won't last another ten months."

"I didn't ask you to come back here to give medical advice. I have something for you."

He pulled a box from under his desk and handed it to me. It was wrapped with a large bow on it.

"What's this?"

"It's your birthday present," he said. "I wanted to give it to you last week but you were in too big a hurry."

"What is it?"

"If I told you what it was, it wouldn't be a surprise, now would it?"

I was about to tear it open like a kid on Christmas, but he stopped me.

"Don't open it now!" he shouted. "Wait until you get home."

"Why? Is it going to explode?" I asked, laughing.

"I just prefer that you wait. Is that too much to ask?"

"Okay, you old grouch, I'll wait."

I walked over and embraced him. He held me tighter than ever before, and he wouldn't let go. When he finally stepped back, I saw tears in his eyes. That was the first time I had ever seen him cry.

"What's wrong, Melvin," I asked, sounding concerned.

"I'm fine, Cool Breeze. Really I am."

I knew he was lying. But Melvin was from the old school and believed in keeping his emotions pinned up. Until he was ready to talk, there was no point in pressing the issue.

"Is there anything I can do for you?"

"How about playing something for me," he said, wiping the tears from his eyes with a Kleenex. "Something upbeat and happy."

"Anything for you, old man."

I escorted Melvin from his office and sat him directly in front of the stage. Since there was no band performing that night I hopped onstage and started warming up on the piano. I didn't even bother making an announcement. "Testing, one, two," I said into the mike. The deejay finally caught on and turned off the music.

"Excuse me, ladies and gentleman. Can I please have your attention?"

The crowd suddenly got quiet, and all eyes were on me.

"Tonight I want to take time out to recognize a man who has supported me when I was down, who taught me about music, and most important, a man who took me into his home and treated me like a son. This one's for you, Melvin. I love you, old man."

The song I chose was the classic "My Favorite Things" by Oscar Hammerstein II. It was an upbeat song. And it was old school, like Melvin. When I began to play, you could feel the positive vibes blanket the room. It was like family. Some of the old timers began singing along. And those who didn't know all the lyrics, faked it. Before long the whole room was serenading Melvin. It was an emotional experience.

During the song, I gazed deep into Melvin's weary old eyes and expressed my love as much as I possibly could through those piano keys. His face lit up as I improvised on the notes and made the song my own, just like he had taught me.

When the song ended, the crowd gave him a standing ovation. Melvin's face was completely red and covered with tears. He didn't bother trying to hold them back. I took my bow and rushed over and embraced him. This time it was me who didn't want to let go. "Thank you, Cool Breeze," he said, crying. "That was the best gift you could've ever given me."

Melvin and I said our good-byes and Scottie escorted him outside to his car and drove him home. I was so emotionally spent that I was ready to leave, too. I said my good-byes to the staff and deejay and headed for the door. Before I reached the exit, the woman who was staring at me from the VIP section came up behind me and grabbed my arm.

"Hey, I hope you're not leaving without me," she said.

"That depends," I said.

"On what?"

"On how much money you have to spend."

I was tired and in no mood for games. I came at her very aggressively, hoping to scare her away. But to my surprise she didn't scare easily.

"Is this enough?" She pulled two crisp thousand-dollar bills from her purse.

"That will get you more than a church hug," I said, laughing. "Where do you want to go?"

"I own a beach house in Malibu, about thirty minutes down Pacific Coast Highway," she said. "You can follow me."

"Lead the way."

While we waited outside for the valet to bring our cars, it finally dawned on me where I recognized her from. She was an actress on one of the daytime soap operas.

She never did tell me her name, and I never told her mine. Maybe that's the way we both wanted it.

Chapter 19

It was six-thirty the next morning when I made it home from Malibu. I put my gift from Melvin in the closet, then I peeled off my clothes, making a trail of socks and drawers that led straight to the shower. After washing away the scent of perfume and sex, I closed my thick black curtains to block out the sunlight. Just as I was about to pass out on my king-size bed, I noticed the message light on my answering machine was blinking. The digital counter read 3. As I pushed the play button, I took a deep breath hoping one of them was from Toni.

"Wuz up, partner. It's Simon. I haven't heard from you since Monday. Give me a call to let me know you're still alive. Peace." *Beep.*

"Malcolm, this is your mother. I just wanted to let you know I received your check. Thanks for the extra money, sweetheart. Hope everything is going okay with the real-estate business. Talk to you later in the week. Love you." *Beep.*

"Malcolm, this is Ms. Ruby. I wanted to remind you that tomorrow is my cleaning day. Could you please remember to remove your funky gym shoes from the living room? I'd like to vacuum the floor without using a gas mask. Thank you." *Beep.*

"I'll be damned," I said to myself. "I can't believe she still hasn't called!" My feelings were hurt and my masculine ego was bruised. I went to my office and searched through my organizer for her phone number. When I found it, I tore it into tiny pieces and threw them in the garbage.

"That's rule number three in the *Player's Handbook*," I said to myself as I stormed back to my bedroom. "Never be more interested in a woman then she is in you."

Then I slammed the door shut and went to bed.

• • •

It seemed like I only had my eyes closed for a split second when I was awakened by the loud humming of the vacuum cleaner. I glanced over at my clock. It read 7:00 A.M. "Lord, please let me get some sleep," I said to myself. I put on my robe and charged out of my bedroom ready to strangle Ms. Ruby.

"Why are you torturing me?" I shouted.

Ms. Ruby was startled. She released the handle to the vacuum cleaner and placed her hand over her chest. "Malcolm, you almost gave me a heart attack."

"Now we're even!" I said angrily. "Why are you vacuuming at seven o'clock in the morning?"

"I didn't know you were here," she explained. "I wanted to get my work done early so I could watch the soaps."

"Look, I understand you have a job to do, but could you please take care of the housework that doesn't require making a lot of noise?"

"No problem, sir. Sorry I woke you."

Ms. Ruby put away the vacuum cleaner and began collecting the trash to dump in the incinerator. As I turned to go back to my bedroom, I noticed a FedEx envelope on the kitchen counter. Ms. Ruby must have picked it up from the security desk on her way up. I hadn't checked my mail in two days. When I looked at the name on the airbill, I was surprised to see Antoinette Grayson at the top. I sat down at the dining room table and opened it.

Dear Malcolm,

I know I'm the last person on earth you wanted to hear from, but please allow me to explain before you tear up this letter. Ever since I met you at the Fox Theatre, I haven't been able to stop thinking about you. I haven't been able to choreograph a single dance step in two days. Even my fiancé, Eric, has noticed a change in how I respond to him. No, I'm not trying to tell you that I'm in love with you, but you've definitely had an impact on me. I was moved by your confidence and your passion. Not many men have the ability to inspire me.

I guess what I'm trying to say is, I'm afraid. Afraid because I don't understand what I'm feeling. At first I thought it was infatuation, but since I'm a little too old for that, I'm sure it's something more. If you're interested in talking about it, call me before Friday. I'll be leaving for Chicago to do a show at the DuSable Museum on Saturday afternoon. If I don't hear from you, I'll understand.

Yours truly,
Antoinette Grayson

P.S. I realize a phone call would've been simpler, but I'm much better at communicating on paper.

My head blew up like a helium balloon. "Who's the man?" I shouted. It took four days for her to finally bow down, but it was well worth the wait. I decided to leave a message on her voice mail while I was still gloating. I went into my office and pulled out my organizer to find her phone number. But when I opened it, I realized that I had torn the number up and thrown it away.

I looked beneath the desk for the garbage. But Ms. Ruby had already collected the garbage and was on her way down the hall to the incinerator. I charged out of my apartment like a madman, determined to catch up with her in time.

"Ms. Ruby, wait!" I yelled.

By the time I caught up with her, she was emptying the garbage into the chute.

"Damn!" I said, gasping for air.

"What's wrong?" Ms. Ruby asked, looking bewildered. "Was there something valuable in there?"

"More valuable then you'll ever know."

I walked back to the apartment feeling like a jerk. There was no way for me to contact Toni to let her know I was coming to Chicago next week. All because I was too damned impatient. Like my mama always said, "There's a lesson in every situation." My lesson was to stop being so egotistical and appreciate that Toni was back in my life.

I picked up the letter off the table and read it again, just to make sure I wasn't dreaming. Ms. Ruby walked in and quietly shut the door. Then she eased up behind me and began reading the letter over my shoulder.

"Do you mind?" I asked.

"That must be one hell of a letter to have you running down the hallway with your Johnson swinging all over the place."

"For your information, it's from a very special lady."

"Excuse me, but did I hear you call her *special*?"

"Yeah, and?"

"That's the first time in six years you've ever expressed any interest in a woman. And it's definitely the first time you've ever called a woman special," she said adamantly. "To be honest with you, Malcolm, I was beginning to think you were gay."

"I'm about as gay as Hugh Heffner," I said, laughing as I walked toward my bedroom. "Now I'm going back to bed."

Just before I closed my door, I paused. "And by the way, I'm sorry for raising my voice at you. It won't happen again," I said emotionally. "You know I couldn't manage without you."

"It's okay, Malcolm. I know you work very hard and need your rest," she said. "But I'm not going to be around forever. Hopefully that special lady will be here to take care of you when I'm gone."

"Strange that you would say that, Ms. Ruby, because that's exactly what I was hoping."

PART IV

Every Man for Himself

Chapter 20

Simon woke up just after 10:00 A.M. horny as hell. Two weeks had passed since he last had sex and he was ready to explode. Cynthia was lying next to him completely naked, except for a pair of thong panties. He brushed up against her to give her the hint that he wanted some. When that didn't work, he kissed her on the back of the neck and fondled her breasts.

"Come on, baby," he whispered in her ear. "I need some lovin'."

"Not now, baby, I'm tired." Cynthia said as she rolled over onto her stomach.

After a few more attempts Simon became frustrated. He jumped on top of Cynthia's back and tried to pry her legs open.

"What are you doing, Simon!" Cynthia yelled.

"I'm skydiving. What the hell does it look like I'm doing?"

"Get off me!" she screamed. "I can't have sex right now."

"Why not?"

"Because it's close to my period and I've got bad cramps."

Simon rolled off her and sat on the edge of the bed. He covered his face with his hands trying to calm himself.

"Since you got back from New Orleans yesterday, we haven't even kissed. When you got off the plane, you said you were tired. Last night you said you had a headache. Now you're telling me it's cramps. I know damn well your period isn't for another two weeks!" he said furiously. "Now do you want to keep playing games or do you want to tell me what the hell is going on?"

Cynthia was speechless. Simon had never spoken to her so forcefully. She had to come up with an answer, and fast.

"I'm sorry, sweetheart. Don't get upset," she said, while leaning over and stroking the back of his head. "Nothing is going on. I'm just getting a little nervous over this whole idea of being married. You know how emotional women can get."

Simon was a sucker for an apology. He was in love with Cynthia. Any decent explanation was good enough for him.

"I wish you would talk to me instead of leaving me in the dark. I was beginning to think there was someone else."

"You know I would never do anything to disrespect you," she said convincingly. "You're the only man I ever want inside of me."

Cynthia led him back into the bed and laid him down on his back. Then she stripped off her thong panties and jumped on top. She really didn't want to have sex with him, but she knew Simon would forgive her for anything after she gave him a little pussy.

"Is it good?" he asked.

"Yes, it's good, baby," she moaned unenthusiastically.

"Is it mine?"

"Sure, it is."

Simon moaned and squirmed for a few minutes, then he climaxed. Cynthia looked over at the clock and shook her head. It lasted ten minutes flat. Right on schedule, she was thinking. Cynthia immediately got up and went to the bathroom to wash off the sex smell.

"Where're you going, baby?" Simon asked. "I want to cuddle."

"I'll be right back," she told him. "I have to pee."

Simon lay back against the pillow with his arms behind his head feeling like Don Juan. Meanwhile, Cynthia was looking at herself in the bathroom mirror trying to decide if she was making the right decision marrying a man who couldn't satisfy her sexually. Simon had his moments when the sex was great, but those moments had become few and far between.

When Cynthia came out of the bathroom, she planned to tell Simon a lie about needing to go home to do extra work. But before she could tell him, the phone rang.

"Hello?"

"Mr. Harris, this is Ariel. I know it's early to be calling you at home, but I need to call in that favor."

"What is it, Ariel?"

"I scheduled a private party at the club this evening but something has come up. Can you handle it for me?"

"Hold on, Ariel. I've got to consult the boss." Simon put his hand over the phone.

"Cynthia, do you mind if I run over to the club for a few hours?" he asked.

"No problem, sweetheart," she said, while rushing to get dressed. "Take care of your business."

He took his hand away from the phone. "I've got you covered, Ariel. Enjoy your evening."

"Thanks, boss."

After he hung up with Ariel, Simon walked Cynthia to her car. She gave him a peck on the cheek and quickly jumped in her Range Rover.

"You sure you don't want to come hang out with me at the club?"

"No, I would only be in the way," she said as she turned the ignition. "Besides, I have a ton of work to do."

"How about dinner tomorrow night?"

"I would love to, honey, but I promised Debra I would go to church with her."

"Since when did you turn religious?" he asked, looking surprised.

"Since today," she told him. "When I woke up this morning, I finally realized the importance of a strong spiritual foundation."

"Well, make sure you say a prayer for me."

"Oh, don't worry, sweetheart, I will."

Chapter 21

At 8:00 A.M. Teddy gathered his most recent pay stubs and his tax returns and rushed out the door. The hearing for his child-support case was at nine o'clock at the Dekalb County Superior Courthouse. The drive was only twenty minutes from his girlfriend's house but he didn't want to take a chance on being late.

As he drove down I-20, the traffic was heavy and moving slowly. He tuned in to 103.3 on the radio and tried to relax. Ironically, the topic of the day was "Deadbeat Dads." "This is definitely a bad omen," he said to himself.

He turned up the volume and listened as a man and woman argued over the issue of child support.

"Whether a man pays child support or not, he should have access to his kids," the man said. "Why should money be a factor?"

"Because kids cost money, that's why!" the woman angrily replied. "Men don't realize how expensive it is to raise children. I pay five hundred a month just for child care."

They bickered back and forth for a few minutes, then the radio personality jumped in.

"Both of you have valid points. But I have another question," he said. "Should a man have to pay child support even if he tells the woman up front that he doesn't want kids?" he asked. "Call in and tell us what you think." He gave the number to the studio line and then went to a commercial break.

Teddy couldn't resist. He picked up his cell phone and dialed the radio station as fast as he could. The first few times the line was busy but eventually he got through. He reached into the glove compartment for a napkin and placed it over the receiver to help disguise his voice.

"V103, what's your issue?" the producer asked.

"Yeah, uh, I want to respond to the question about men paying child support to women who trapped them."

"Are you being sued for child support?"

"Hell, yeah," he said. "As a matter of fact, I'm on my way to court, right now!"

"Perfect!" she said excitedly. "I'm going to put you on hold and we'll come right to you after the commercial break. Give me your name."

"My name is, uh, Tyrone."

"Okay, Tyrone, hold on."

When the commercials ended, the radio personality repeated the question to get the listeners stirred up. Teddy cleared his throat and put the napkin to the phone and waited anxiously to be connected.

"On the phone, we have a man who claims he was trapped. And he's on his way to court for child support as we speak. Are you there, Tyrone?"

"Yeah, I'm here."

"So, what's your story?"

"Well, I was hired to strip at this bachelorette party and I met this very attractive woman. We talked, had a few drinks, and one thing led to another," he said. "Now she expects me to pay child support."

"Let me get this right," the female jock joined in. "You met a perfect stranger at a party and you had sex with her that same night? And without a condom? Haven't you heard of AIDS?"

"For your information, I had on a condom, but it broke. That happens sometimes when you're well endowed," he said arrogantly.

"But the question is, did you tell her up front that you didn't want kids?"

"That should've been understood."

"And why is that?"

"Because she was the bachelorette who was getting married."

"Now that's a trifling wench," the female personality said. "Let's go to the phones and see what the listeners have to say. V103, what's your question or comment."

"I'm so upset with Tyrone I don't even know where to begin," a woman said.

"Just take a deep breath and say what's on your mind."

"First of all, you're right about the woman, she played herself by having sex with a complete stranger on the night before her wedding. Second, it doesn't matter what the circumstances were, it's all about the welfare of the child. After all, that baby didn't choose to be born," she went on. "And last, I'm fed up with these tired negroes running away from their responsibilities. If you don't want kids, practice celibacy or get a vasectomy."

"I heard that, sistah!" the female jock said.

"Let's not turn this into a *Waiting to Exhale* show," the male jock said, laughing. "Let's take another caller. What's your question or comment?"

"I agree with Tyrone!" a male caller said. "The problem with the child-support system is that it rewards women for having babies out of wedlock. All these lazy tramps have to do is get pregnant by a man with money and they can lay on their asses and collect a paycheck for eighteen years."

"So, what's your solution?" the jock asked.

"They should pass a law stating that if a man doesn't sign an agreement to have children then he's not liable for child support. I guarantee you the birth rate would drop by ninety percent overnight," he said assertively. "And if I were you, Tyrone, I wouldn't pay that heifer one red cent. Maybe next time she'll think twice before she tries to trap another brotha."

"Whew!" It's getting hot up in *cheer*," the jock said.

"Thank God, neither one of you fools is my daddy," the female jock said, laughing. "I'd be on *Oprah* trying to get therapy."

"Well, Tyrone, thanks for your call. And good luck in court today."

"Good luck my ass," the female jock added. "I hope they take the shirt off your back, you old deadbeat."

"Go to hell, you playa hater!" Teddy screamed.

Then he hung up the phone and turned off the radio.

• • •

Teddy exited I-20 on Candler Road and made a left until he found McDonough Street where the courthouse was located. He parked his Navigator in the back of the lot and took off his diamond earring and Rolex watch. His lawyer advised him not to come into court looking too prosperous.

When he walked into the building, there were three deputies standing by the entrance directing people through a metal detector.

"What's up with the tight security," he asked one of the officers. "I thought this was a courthouse, not a prison."

"It's just a precaution," the officer said. "You'd be surprised how violent people can get in family court."

"No, I wouldn't," Teddy said as he emptied his pockets and walked through.

After he collected his belongings, Teddy walked toward the elevators where his lawyer, Steve Grundy, was waiting.

He was a short, thin white man with a long scar on the left side of his face. Rumor was he got it from a famous ballplayer after winning the wife a large alimony settlement.

Steve had on his trademark drab gray suit and scuffed-up shoes. His hair was unkempt and his shirt had a ring around the collar. Although he wasn't much to look at, Steve had a reputation for winning big cases. Teddy was hoping he could work his magic for him.

"Wuz up, counselor?" Teddy said as he shook his hand.

"Good morning, Mr. Simmons. Do you have a copy of your pay stubs and tax returns?"

"You get right down to business, don't you?" Teddy said as he handed over a large brown envelope.

"That's what I get paid for," he said.

They stepped into the elevator and rode it to the eighth floor. When the doors opened, Teddy followed Steve down a crowded hallway filled with people arguing and screaming at one another. It was a real war zone

"I want you to wait here," Steve said. "I have to go inside the courtroom and let them know you're here. We should be out of here in no time."

"That sounds good to me."

Shortly after Steve left, the elevator doors opened and a white woman with long blond hair stepped out. It was Donna, the mother of his child. She looked him dead in the eye and didn't say a word.

Moments later, Steve came out of the courtroom and signaled for Teddy to come inside. It was nine o'clock, the moment of truth. Teddy sat in the back of the courtroom to avoid attention. Donna walked in behind him and took a seat in the front row, directly across from the bench. Once the court was brought to order, Steve finally worked up the courage to give Teddy the bad news.

"We may have a slight problem," Steve whispered.

"What do you mean by *slight*?"

"Well, the judge who was supposed to hear our case had a family emergency."

"And?"

"And he was replaced by Judge Harris."

"So what's the problem?"

"Judge Harris is the toughest judge in the state on deadbeat parents. I mean really tough!"

"Can't we get a postponement?" Teddy asked nervously.

"That's what I've been trying to do for the last thirty minutes," Steve told him. "We're going to have to see this one through."

"Something told me this wasn't going to be my day."

As the door to the judge's chamber opened, the bailiff turned toward the gallery. "All rise, the Honorable Judge Ann Harris presiding," he announced. The second Teddy laid eyes on her he knew he was in trouble. Judge Harris was an attractive forty-something black woman. He knew his charm and good looks weren't going to do him any good. He leaned back against the hard wooden bench and prayed for a miracle. But like everything else that day, his situation was going from bad to worse. His case was the first one called.

Teddy looked awkward as he made his way toward the front of the courtroom. At six-five he stood out like a sore thumb. Everyone was staring and making comments, especially the women. "Isn't that the guy who strips at the Foxy?" one of them whispered. That made him even more uncomfortable.

All the attention didn't go unnoticed by the judge who quickly used it to give him a hard time.

"Good morning, Mr. Simmons," she said. "I can see you're quite the celebrity."

"Not me, Your Honor. I'm just trying to get by like everybody else."

"Is that right?" she said, while looking at him over the top of her glasses.

Teddy was sworn in then he stated his name for the record.

"So what's the situation here?" the judge asked Steve.

"Your Honor, my client has cooperated by taking a paternity test, which proved he was the father of the child," Steve said. "However, the five hundred dollars a month that the state is asking for is unreasonable. As you can see by his tax returns, Mr. Simmons only earned twelve thousand dollars last year. Even at the highest rate of twenty-three percent of his gross income that would only be equivalent to two hundred and thirty-nine dollars a month."

"I know how to do math, Mr. Grundy," she said curtly. "However, the court has an affidavit by your client's previous employer stating that his income from tips is much greater then he reported. And from what I understand these tips constitute the majority of his income as a stripper."

"I prefer to be called an exotic dancer," Teddy said sarcastically.

"Whatever!" the judge snapped back.

"Before you make a ruling, we would like to bring it to the court's attention that Mr. Simmons also has two other children that he provides for," Steve added. "A five-year-old daughter in Texas and a two-year-old son in Oklahoma."

"Just because his name is on the birth certificates doesn't mean he's providing support," she told him. "Do you have any proof?"

Teddy was speechless. He didn't have any proof because he wasn't providing support. Steve advised him not to include that information but Teddy insisted, hoping the judge would be sympathetic.

"Unless you have any additional information, I'm going to make a ruling for the five hundred per month."

"But, Your Honor, I don't even know this woman," Teddy said, getting loud. "Why should I have to give her five hundred dollars of my hard-earned money?"

"Because it's the law, Mr. Simmons. And furthermore, you'd better watch your tone in my courtroom. Do you understand?"

Teddy just gave her an angry stare.

"Now, according to the record, your son is six months old," she went on. "Have you been providing support during that time?"

"Yes, I have."

"You're a damned lie!" Donna shouted from the gallery.

She easily stood out in the mostly black gallery with her long blond hair and blue eyes.

"And who might you be, ms.?" the judge asked.

"My name is Donna Riley. I'm the child's mother."

The room was abuzz with chatter. The black women in the back stood up to get a better look at Donna.

"I can't wait to get home and call my girlfriend," one woman said.

"Sellout!" another yelled.

The judge slammed her gavel down on the bench to get order.

"Mr. Simmons, you'd better have proof that you are providing support," she said angrily, "Or I'll make you wish you never stepped foot in my courtroom!"

"I do have proof. I just don't have it with me."

"Your Honor, he hasn't given me a single penny. Not even when I asked him for ten dollars for a bag of Pampers," Donna said. "I know I should have taken him to court sooner, but he threatened to kill me."

The room erupted with chatter again. The expressions on the women's faces in the courtroom were fierce. Although Donna was white, they could relate to her predicament.

"I've heard enough!" the judge shouted. "My judgment is for seven hundred dollars a month, retroactive from the date of the paternity test. You will provide proof of health insurance for this child within thirty days. And if you don't begin payments immediately, Mr. Simmons, you will be held in contempt and sent to jail."

"I'm not a brain surgeon for Christ's sake," Teddy said, looking distressed. "How am I supposed to pay that kind of money?"

"Get a real job!" she said as she slammed her gavel down. "Next case!"

Teddy was furious. He stormed out of the courtroom with Steve trailing closely behind. On his way out, he saw Claudia sitting next to Donna holding her hand. "You lesbian bitch!" he said to her. Once they were out in the hallway, Steve assured him that he would win on appeal. A few minutes later, Donna and Claudia came out of the courtroom.

"Teddy, I don't want your money," she said sincerely. "I just want you to take care of your son and try to be a father to him."

"Look, you poor white trash, I can hardly remember your name. What makes you think I want to play daddy to your mutt-ass child? Now leave me alone and go back to your lily-white world," he said viciously. "And by the way, I ain't paying you a dime. I don't give a damn what that tight-ass judge says."

Teddy looked her up and down with disgust, then walked toward the elevators.

"I hope you burn in hell, you cold-blooded bastard," Donna screamed with tears rolling down her face. "I wouldn't want my child anywhere near you anyway!"

"Lower your voice, Donna. Court is still in session," Claudia said, trying to calm her down.

"I don't care," she screamed. "And I may be poor white trash, but at least I'm not running away from my responsibilities as a parent, like you are. You fuckin' coward!"

Teddy boarded the elevator with his lawyer then pressed the button for the lobby. Right before the doors closed, he dangled the keys to his Navigator and smiled like he didn't have a care in the world.

Chapter 22

Ariel arrived at Sylvia's Restaurant just before 7:00 P.M. She was wearing three-inch pumps and a black halter dress that showed off her shapely figure. When she walked through the door, all eyes were on her.

"How many?" the hostess asked.

"Table for two, something near the front."

The hostess grabbed two menus and escorted her to the corner table next to the window. Ariel wanted to get a good look at Lawrence's tight buns when he showed up. It had been a long time since she had a man to lust over and she wanted to make the most of it.

When the waitress came over to take her order, Ariel asked for a glass of white zinfandel. She wasn't thirsty, but it was a helpful prop to ignore all the rude looks from the men surrounding her. Some were totally disrespectful. They continued to stare even though their dates were sitting right next to them.

The man at the table across from her was more discreet. He waited until his date went to the rest room, then he sent the waitress over with a complimentary drink and his phone number. Ariel sent it back without even looking in his direction.

While she waited impatiently for Lawrence to come to her rescue, she pulled out her compact to check her makeup. When she looked into the mirror, a man's face appeared out of nowhere over her shoulder. It was Chris. She hadn't seen him since they had met at Justin's but she recognized him right away.

"Hello, stranger," he said.

"Chris, you scared the dickens out of me."

"Sorry about that. I saw you sitting over here and I wanted to say hello."

"How did you know it was me with my back to the door?"

"Not too many women can wear a short haircut and look as fine as you."

"Don't try to make up by complimenting me. I'm still shaking." Ariel sounded serious but she was blushing.

"Well, I didn't want to bother you," Chris said as he began to back away. "Enjoy your food."

"Oh, no you don't. Come back here and protect me from these vultures." Ariel waved for him to come back. "Unless of course, you're here with a date."

"No, I come here alone every Thursday after work to get my grub on."

"Well, pull up a chair and hang out with me for a minute," she said.

As soon as Chris sat down, the jealous stares began. Half the men in the room were checking him out as if he were sitting with their woman.

"Next time you might want to consider wearing a pair of coveralls," he said, laughing. "Those legs could get a brotha killed."

"I don't usually dress like a hoochie so early in the day, but I thought my friend would like it."

"Don't tell me you're here on another blind date?" he said. "I'm not going to play Rico the killer pimp again."

"No, I had enough of that drama," she said. "I've already met this one. And he seems pretty cool."

"I'm happy everything is working out for you," he said genuinely. "But I hope this doesn't mean we can't still be friends."

"Of course not," she said, reaching over and holding his hand.

At that moment Lawrence walked into the restaurant. He glanced around the room until he saw Ariel. He saw Chris, too. And he didn't appreciate his holding Ariel's hand. He rushed over to the table and lifted Chris up by his arm."

"Get your hands off my woman," he shouted.

"Hey, man, what's your fuckin' problem?" Chris yelled back.

He got in Lawrence's face and shoved him. Although he was only five-six and fifty pounds lighter, he didn't back down.

"Stop it, Lawrence!" Ariel said, stepping between them. "Chris is just a friend."

By now, everyone in the restaurant was watching the fight like they were ringside in Las Vegas. Even the waitresses stopped serving food to watch the show.

"Chris, I'm terribly sorry," Ariel apologized. "Please let me handle this. I'll talk to you later."

"You should do a better job of choosing who you go out with," he said, while fixing his clothes. "Your boyfriend isn't playing with a full deck."

He stared Lawrence down for a few seconds then he calmly walked away.

Ariel sat down at the table and tried to act normally. She took a sip of her wine and a deep breath. Lawrence was still standing as if he were waiting for an invitation to sit.

"Would you please sit down?" she asked. "I think you've already attracted enough attention for one day."

Lawrence picked the chair up from off the floor and sat down.

"Look, Ariel, I apologize for what happened with your little friend, but a man has got to protect what's his."

"I don't need protection when I'm in a crowded restaurant talking to a friend."

"I know, baby. And I'm sorry for overreacting," he said, looking pitiful. "It's just that men today don't have any respect for another man's woman. They will stare at your woman and even grab her ass if you don't put them in check."

Lawrence's behavior was out of line, but Ariel noticed that it was effective. The men who were gawking at her earlier were looking somewhere else. It must be a man thing, she was thinking.

"Every woman wants a hero, Lawrence," she told him, "but I'm a strong, independent woman who can take care of herself."

"I know you can, Ariel. But maybe it's time you let someone else be strong?" he said. He took her hand as if he were proposing. "I've got a great job, a big house, and enough money so that you don't have to work unless you want to."

"Lawrence, I'm flattered, I really am." Ariel was smiling from ear to ear. "But as romantic as that all sounds, you don't even know me. And I don't know you. Why don't we give it a few months and see what happens?"

"Maybe you're right, baby. It probably is a good idea to slow down and get to know each other better. After all, you're not going anywhere, right?" he said, looking her straight in the eyes.

"Right, baby," she said apprehensively.

"Good, now let's get out of here. I want to go to the mall before it closes and look at some rings." He stood up from the table.

"I thought we agreed to slow down."

"I was just kidding," he said, laughing. "But I would like to go to the mall. Maybe we can catch a movie."

"That sounds like fun, but don't you want to eat first?"

"No, I lost my appetite," he said.

Ariel put five dollars on the table for her drink and began walking toward the door.

"I got it, baby," he said, while pulling a wad of bills out of his pocket. "No woman of mine has to spend her own money."

Ariel didn't argue. She gladly picked up her hard-earned money and put it back inside her purse. There had been too many occasions when her dates stuck her with the bill. Any act of chivalry was greatly appreciated.

Before they left, Ariel noticed Chris was in the dining area in the back.

"Lawrence, why don't you wait for me outside. I want to go say good-bye to Chris," she said. "That's the least I can do after what happened."

"Go ahead. And tell the little fellah I said I was sorry for the misunderstanding," he said, laughing.

Ariel made her way through the thick crowd, trying to avoid brushing up against the horny men who were watching her every move. When she finally made it to the back dining area, she walked over to Chris's table and pulled up a chair.

"I can't tell you how embarrassed I am for what happened. I don't know what got into him," she said. "He's very protective of me."

Chris kept eating without even looking up at her.

"Anyway, we're getting ready to leave," she went on. "I'll give you a call later on this week to see how you're doing, okay?"

When he didn't respond, she stood up from the table and began to walk away.

"Wait a minute!" He stood up and slowly walked toward her. "Look, Ariel, I know you don't know me from Adam, but I do care about you. If you ever need someone to talk to, or just a shoulder to lean on, don't hesitate to call. Even if it's only for a Blockbuster video and popcorn," he said, laughing.

"Thanks for being so sweet, Chris." She gave him a kiss on the cheek then she backed away "I'll see you later."

"I hope so," he whispered to himself. "If that psycho doesn't kill you first."

Chapter 23

It was three o'clock Saturday afternoon. My flight arrived at Chicago O'Hare more than an hour late. I grabbed my garment bag from the overhead compartment and headed straight for the rental car shuttle bus. When the bus arrived, I sat in the back, pulled out my cell phone, and dialed the number to the Dusable Museum.

"DuSable Museum, how may I direct your call?" a cordial woman's voice said.

"I'm looking for information about a dance recital this afternoon. Can you tell me what time it starts?"

"I don't believe we have any recitals scheduled today, sir. But if you'll hold on for a moment, I'll double-check."

While I waited for her to return, I slapped myself on the forehead. I knew I should've called before coming all the way from Los Angeles, but I trusted Toni would be there. All I could do was hope that the receptionist was wrong.

"Hello, sir?" she said.

"Yes, I'm here."

"We don't have a dance recital today, but there is a youth group scheduled to use the auditorium for dance lessons between three and five this afternoon."

"That has to be it," I said to myself. "Thank you very much for your help."

After I hung up the phone, I began calculating how long it would take to get to the museum. It was already 3:20 P.M. and the Budget car lot was still five minutes away. I estimated a ten-minute wait in line when I got there. And the drive to Sixty-fifth Place was thirty minutes, under ideal conditions.

I tried to relax by looking out of the window at the CTA trains as they emerged from the tunnel underneath the airport. When I was a kid, I used to ride those same trains downtown to watch karate movies at McVickers Theater. I laughed out loud when I thought about how my friends and I used to kick and punch each other all the way to Ninety-fifth Street. "Those were the days," I thought.

But those childhood memories didn't last long. I was stressing over the idea of coming all the way from Los Angeles only to miss Toni by a few minutes. I looked down at my watch a hundred times as if I could make time stand still. Even the elderly bus driver seemed to be working against me. He was driving slowly and he stopped at the traffic light before it turned yellow.

"I'm going to kill this old bastard if he doesn't hurry up," I said to myself. "I could run backward and get there faster."

• • •

The traffic on the Dan Ryan Expressway was horrible. By the time I came off the ramp at Fifty-fifth Street, it was 4:59. I turned east and headed toward Cottage Grove Avenue, driving like a bat out of hell. I ran two red lights, three stop signs, and almost hit a little old lady crossing the street with her grocery cart.

When I finally made it to the museum, I jumped out of the car and rushed toward the entrance. Once inside, I approached the receptionist booth to get directions. An elderly black woman with long gray hair was sitting inside reading a magazine.

"Excuse me, could you tell me where the auditorium is?"

"It's around that corner and to your left," she said. "Are you the gentleman who called earlier?"

"Yes, ma'am."

"Well, you'd better hurry, there are only a few people still inside."

"Thanks again," I said as I hurried off.

The closer I got to the auditorium, the faster my heart pounded. I was excited at the thought of seeing Toni again but I dreaded the possibility of her not being there. As I got closer to the door, I could hear classical music playing softly in the background. I slowly pushed the door opened and peeked inside. And there was Toni, looking more beautiful than I had remembered. She was standing onstage giving dance lessons to a group of young girls.

I wanted to rush over and sweep her off her feet, but I didn't want to interrupt their lesson. So I crept upstairs to the balcony and watched from the back row. I admired the way Toni handled the energetic young girls. She was trying to teach them how to pirouette but they were getting discouraged. "You can do it," she told them. "Just pretend like you're a top and spin." The little girls turned as fast as they could, while balancing themselves on their toes. The parents, who were sitting near the stage, applauded as though their daughters had just won Olympic gold medals.

After about ten minutes, the lesson was over. The children collected their belongings and left with their parents. Toni turned off her portable CD player and began packing her large duffle bag. I was ready to rush downstairs to meet her at the door, but she suddenly stopped. She stood in the middle of the stage and looked around as if she were checking to see if anyone was still inside the auditorium. I slid down in my seat as low as possible to avoid being seen.

When she felt comfortable that she was alone, she put on her leggings and ballet slippers and began stretching. She did a series of splits then stood up and touched her head to her knees. I have never seen a woman so limber. After she had warmed up, she pulled another CD out of her bag and placed it inside the player. Then she rushed to center stage to get set.

I was expecting to hear something classical or possibly a modern dance song. But my guess wasn't close. The song was "Makeda" by Les Nubians. It was a popular cut about a year ago sung by two French sistahs. I couldn't understand the lyrics but the beat was hypnotic and smooth.

I sat up in my seat and watched Toni as she swayed to the rhythm of the music. Her motions were fluent and precise as if the dance were choreographed. And her facial expression was intense. It was obvious that the song had a special meaning. I couldn't help feeling like I was trespassing on a private moment. I wanted to look away, but I couldn't help myself. I was captivated by her passion and spirit.

As the song continued to play, Toni stopped ballet dancing and began bumping and grinding like she was at a nightclub. And she was doing it so nasty. "Um, um, um," I said to myself, while shaking my head. "God is good." I decided the time was right to make my move. I rushed down the balcony stairs and made my way backstage. Toni was so deep into the music that she didn't see me coming as I danced my way toward her from the shadows. But she must have sensed me coming because she suddenly turned in my direction. She was startled at first, but once she saw it was me, she kept dancing and waved for me to come closer.

"Aw, sookie, sookie, now!" I said as I moved toward her.

When I got right up on her, she put her arms around my neck, pressed up against me, and began to grind and sing in French.

La reine de Saba vit en moi
Makeda vit en moi.
Oh, oh, oh, oh.

I couldn't make out a damn thing she was singing but it didn't matter. I finally had her where I wanted her—in my arms. We hugged each other tightly as we danced around the stage like Ginger Rogers and Fred Astaire. When the song ended, we stood still in the center of the stage and looked into each other's eyes.

"I see you got my letter," she said.

"I got it, all right," I told her. "But you could've saved a few dollars by calling."

"I felt you were worth it."

"I hope I don't disappoint you."

"I hope you don't either," she said.

As we moved toward each other, we wet our lips at the same time. She smiled. I smiled. Then we kissed. It was the first time in twelve years that I was affectionate with a woman without getting paid for it. And it felt good.

After what seemed like forever, we finally came up for air.

"So now what?" Toni asked as she leaned into my chest.

"Well, we could run off and get married," I said jokingly. "Or we can get something to eat."

"As much as I would love to take you up on the marriage proposal, I'll have to take door number two."

"Oh, well, you can't blame a guy for trying. Let's get outta here."

"I've got a few people I have to see before I can leave," she said. "Why don't I give you a call on your cell phone and you can tell me where you want to meet?"

"Actually, I wanted to invite you over to my mom's

house for dinner," I said. "She makes the best peach cobbler in Chicago."

"Sounds like a plan!" she said, sounding delighted. "Will eight o'clock be too late?"

"I could wait on you forever, baby," I told her. "But for my mother's sake, eight o'clock will be fine."

I gave her a hug and a kiss on the forehead, then I began walking toward the exit. And as I walked out the door, I suddenly turned.

"By the way, did you come all the way to Chicago just to teach this class? Or was it an excuse to see me?"

"As much as I would love to stroke your gigantic male ego, I came as a favor to a friend. She had an important business trip and she didn't want to disappoint the girls."

"You're one hell of a friend."

"No, baby, I'm one hell of a woman."

"I heard that!" I said with a smile as I wrote down my mom's address. "See you at eight."

When I made it back to my car, I called my mom on my cell phone to tell her I was bringing company. The phone rang five times, which was unusual. When she finally picked up, I understood what was keeping her. She had "Love and Happiness" by Al Green blaring in the background.

"Love will make you do wrong," she sang loudly in my ear. "Hello!"

"Mama, it's me, Malcolm."

"Who?"

"It's Malcolm!" I yelled. "If you turn down that music maybe you could hear me."

"Hold on, baby."

She turned down the stereo and came back to the phone, still singing.

"Love will make you come home early, make you stay out all night long," she sang.

"I can see you're in a good mood today."

"Of course I am. The Lord blessed me with another day

and my favorite son is coming home to have dinner with me."

"I'm your only son, Mama," I reminded her. "Now, stop singing for a minute so I can ask a favor."

"The last time you asked me for a favor, I had to bail you and Simon out of jail," she said, laughing.

"I promise you, it's not that serious," I said. "I just want to know if it's okay to bring a lady friend over for dinner?"

I heard what sounded like a large skillet dropping in the background.

"Ouch!" Mama yelled.

"Are you all right?"

"I'm fine, son. I just need to make sure I heard you correctly. Did you say you were bringing a woman over for dinner?"

"Yes."

"Is this woman a friend, or a girlfriend?"

"I guess you could call her a girlfriend."

"Hallelujah!" she screamed.

"Why are you making such a big deal out of this?"

"I'm sorry I got carried away, sweetheart, but you haven't brought a girl home since high school. I was beginning to think you were gay."

"I'm not gay! I'm not gay!" I hollered.

"All right, son, I believe you," she said. "Now let me go so I can make something special for your guest. What time will you be over?"

"About eight."

"Okay, I'll see you then," she said, sounding excited. "This is a young lady I've got to meet." Then she abruptly hung up.

The phone was dead, but that didn't stop me from venting. I looked at my reflection in the rearview mirror and yelled, "I'm not gay, dammit!"

Chapter 24

I arrived at my mother's house in Hyde Park at 7:30 P.M. When I pulled into the driveway, I could hear "Let's Stay Together" by Al Green blaring from her living room window. "Mama is seriously getting her groove on," I said to myself. I rang the bell and pounded on the door for nearly five minutes before she finally heard me. "I'm coming!" she yelled. "Hold your horses!"

When she opened the door, I was overwhelmed by the aroma of freshly cooked collard greens and her famous peach cobbler.

"Is dinner ready yet?" I asked as I walked right past her.

"Boy, you better come back here and give your mama a hug."

"I was just kiddin', Mama. How's my favorite girl?" I said as I lifted her up by the waist and gave her a sloppy, wet kiss.

"Malcolm, you're so crazy. Put me down!"

My mother and I were very close, almost like brother and sister. We drank together, went out to clubs to dance, we even worked out at the gym together. At sixty-five, she was in excellent shape. If it wasn't for her distinctive gray hair, she could easily pass for a woman fifteen years younger.

"Where is your lady friend?" she asked after I gently let her down.

"Her name is Antoinette, and she should be here any minute."

"Oh, my goodness, I look a mess," she said, trying to fix her hair. "Watch the food while I go freshen up." Then she ran off to the bathroom.

"Mama, stop making such a big fuss. She's just a friend, not the President of the United States."

But there was no use arguing with her. Mama was very conscious of her appearance. If she took the garbage out to the corner she wanted to look her best. That attitude must have been hereditary because I was just as obsessive. I had worked out for an hour before my date with Toni. And I made sure to wear shorts and a tight Polo top to show off my chest and arms. I wanted Toni to get a good look at the merchandise.

While I was blowing into my hands to make sure my breath wasn't kickin', the doorbell rang. "I'll get it!" Mama yelled. I wanted to rush to the door myself, but I played it cool and sat down on the sofa. I picked up one of Mama's old *Ebony* magazines and acted like I was reading.

"Good evening, Mrs. Tremell," I heard Toni say.

"Malcolm, it's your friend Antoinette!" Mama yelled. "Come in, sweetheart."

I held my breath as I waited for Toni to turn the corner from the hallway. Although I had seen her three hours earlier, Toni had a presence about her that made every encounter feel like the first time. When she walked into the living room, I casually peeked from behind the magazine to check her out. As usual, she was looking fine. She had on a white tennis skirt and button-up collar blouse. Her hair was pulled back into a tight ponytail that came down just past her shoulder. I just shook my head wondering what the hell I ever did to deserve such a prize.

"Don't I get a hug or something?" Toni asked.

"Most definitely!"

I sprang up from the sofa and walked over and gave her a hug. At first I held her gently, trying to be respectful in front of Mama. But Toni was feeling so damned good that I tightened my grip until I could feel her heart beat. "Um," we sighed simultaneously.

"All right, you lovebirds, break it up," Mama said while taking Toni by the hand. "I think you better come with me, young lady."

"Where are you taking her?"

"Away from your hormones," she said as she led Toni toward the kitchen. "Can you cook, child?"

"Yes, ma'am," Toni said.

"Good, come on in here and give me a hand with these greens."

Toni and Mama stayed in the kitchen for nearly thirty minutes yapping it up like mother and daughter. Mama came out to grab the family album, then she retreated back inside the man-free zone. The next thing I heard was Mama bursting out in laughter. "Aw, look at him. He's so cute!" I heard Toni say.

I was praying Mama wasn't showing her my baby pictures, or those horrible photographs of my grammar school graduation. The thought of Toni seeing me wearing that big lopsided afro was driving me crazy. Just as I was about to barge in to see what was going on, they came out with plates and utensils to set the table.

"It's about time," I said. "I thought you forgot about me."

"How could I forget about you, Bam Bam!" Toni said, laughing.

"Mama, I can't believe you told her that nickname."

"Don't worry, baby, I won't tell anybody," Toni said. "I just wish I could've seen you banging away on that toy piano when you were a baby. I bet you were so cute."

"See what you started, Mama?" I asked. "I'll never live this down."

"It's okay, Bam Bam, your secret is safe with me," Toni said, laughing.

We all sat down to Mama's delicious dinner of red beans and rice, collard greens, neck bones, corn bread, and of course, her peach cobbler. We laughed and talked about my childhood and anything else my mother could think of to embarrass me.

"Malcolm was a real lady-killer," Mama said. "All the girls in the neighborhood had a crush on him."

"Tell me more, Mrs. Tremell," Toni said as she rested her arms on the table.

"When he graduated from high school, five different girls asked him to the prom."

"So how did he manage his little harem?"

"He charged them fifty dollars each and made them pay for his tuxedo and a limo."

"Did they pay?"

"Oh yeah! They were lined up. And if they didn't have the money, their parents were happy to foot the bill."

"Sounds like he had a nice little enterprise going on."

"I told him he should've gone into the escort business instead of real estate," Mama said. "He could've made a fortune."

When she made that comment, I nearly choked on my Kool-Aid.

"Are you all right, baby?" Toni asked, while patting me on the back.

I nodded yes, and went to the kitchen to get a paper towel to wipe my face. I made sure to leave the door cracked so I could hear the rest of the conversation.

"I thought Malcolm was a musician," Toni said. "I heard him play at Simon's club in Atlanta and he sounded great!"

"I've been trying to convince him to pursue his music full-time, but he won't listen to me," Mama said. "Maybe you can talk some sense into him."

"I'm surprised that someone with so much talent would have to be convinced. It seems like such a part of who he is."

"It is a part of him. A very important part," Mama said. "But when his father died, something inside of Malcolm died, too."

"I didn't know his father was dead," Toni said.

"Malcolm didn't tell you what happened?" Mama said, getting emotional.

"No ma'am. But we don't have to talk about it if it's going to upset you."

"It's okay, sweetheart. Maybe it's time I talk about it," she said. "I've been holding on to the pain for twelve years."

Mama reached for the family album and opened the page with her and my father's black-and-white wedding picture. It was taken back in 1961. Toni moved in closer and put her arms around Mama.

"He was such a handsome young man, wasn't he?" Mama said.

"Yes, ma'am," Toni said, while admiring the picture. "Did he die of natural causes?"

Mama chuckled as tears began to roll down her cheeks. "I guess you could call it natural. He was shot while screwing the next-door neighbor's wife."

"Oh, my God!" Toni sighed. "I'm sorry, Mrs. Tremell, I didn't know."

"The painful part is that I still blame myself for what happened. I knew what was going on and I didn't do anything to stop it."

"It's not your fault, Mrs. Tremell. You can't control a man's behavior."

"But I had a choice not to put up with it!" she said, getting upset with herself. "If I had taken a stand I believe my husband would be alive today. But like so many women raised back in those days, my mother taught me to hang in there no matter what. A man is going to be a man, she would preach."

"That's not right, Mrs. Tremell. And it's not right for you to torture yourself," Toni said. "I know there's someone else out there for you who can make you happy. You're so beautiful and full of energy."

"Thanks for being so sweet, Antoinette," Mama said, wiping her tears away with her hands. "But you don't understand how deeply I loved this man. He was truly my soul mate. I remember the first time I ever saw him. We were at a high school sock hop and he asked me to dance. All the other girls were so jealous," Mama said, smiling. "When I looked into his eyes, the same way you look into Malcolm's, I knew we would spend the rest of our lives together."

Mama gave Toni a hug and kiss on the forehead. "Sometimes true love only comes around once in a lifetime, sweetheart. When it comes around for you, don't ever let it go," she told her. Then she went upstairs to her bedroom.

I waited inside the kitchen for a couple of minutes trying to give Toni a chance to get herself together. She had been crying, too, and I didn't want to embarrass her. When I finally came out, I tried to act as if I hadn't hear a word of their conversation.

"So, where's Mama?"

"She went upstairs to lie down," Toni said, sounding depressed. "Maybe this would be a good time to say good night."

"Don't be ridiculous. It's not even ten o'clock yet. Besides, we haven't had a chance to talk."

"Well, can we at least go outside? I could use some fresh air."

"I've got a better idea. Why don't we walk over to the lakefront? I could use some fresh air myself."

• • •

Toni and I held hands as we crossed over the steel bridge on Lake Shore Drive. The gentle breeze coming off the lake and the full moon created the perfect romantic atmosphere. But Toni's mind was on the other side of town. She hadn't uttered a single word since we left the house. She just gazed off into the stars seemingly full of thought.

"Are you all right?" I asked her.

"To be honest with you, I'm pretty shaken up."

"Was it the conversation you had with Mama? I heard what she told you."

"Malcolm, why didn't you tell me what happened to your father?"

"What was I supposed to say: Hi, my name is Malcolm, and by the way, my father was shot in the head while fucking the next-door neighbor?" I said, getting loud.

"No, but you could've told me he was dead, especially if you were taking me to meet your mother. That's something that just might come up in casual conversation, don't you think?"

"You're right, Toni," I said. "I guess I'm out of dating practice. Believe it or not, I haven't brought a woman home to meet my mother since I was seventeen."

"Why has it been so long?"

"Because I haven't met anyone special enough, that's why. You don't just bring any old woman home to meet your mother."

"Amen to that."

By this time we had made it down to the beach. We took off our shoes and walked onto the cool sand. There were couples everywhere, holding hands and walking along the shoreline. Toni and I grasped hands tightly and walked toward the water.

"Malcolm, why haven't you asked me about my situation with Eric?"

"I didn't want to force the issue. I figured you would tell me when you were ready."

"Well, I think this would be a good time," she said.

We sat down on the sand near the water, folding our legs Indian-style.

"I've known Eric since college," she went on. "We dated for a while, but after we graduated we sort of grew apart. About a year ago we ran into each other at a fund-raiser and we started dating again. The night before I met you, he asked me to marry him. I didn't officially accept but I didn't turn him down either."

"Now I'm even more confused."

"What I'm trying to say is I love Eric, I really do. But not in the way a woman should love a man she's going to marry," she said passionately. "I struggled with my feelings all that night. Finally, I just put it in the Lord's hands and prayed. I asked God to give me a sign. Any sign that would tell me if I was making the right decision. The very next day is when I saw your handsome face sitting in the front row at the Fox Theatre. Through all the bright lights, loud music, and hundreds of people in the audience, something made me look your way. At first I dismissed it as simply a physical attraction. But when you showed up with those eleven roses after the show, I knew you were someone special."

"I don't know what to say."

"Don't say anything unless you feel the same way I do. I don't want to be in love by myself."

"I do feel the same way, baby. It's been a long time since I truly cared about someone. Maybe too long."

"Just promise me one thing, Malcolm," she said as she held my face gently in her hands.

"What's that?"

"That we'll always be honest with each other. That's very important to me. I don't ever want to experience the

pain your father put your mother through. I could never forgive you for that."

"I promise," I told her.

Then we kissed and held each other until the sun came
up. It was the first time in my life I felt that close to a
woman.

Chapter 25

Ariel woke up Sunday morning and immediately went into her ritual. She brewed a fresh pot of coffee, retrieved her Sunday morning paper, and curled up on the sofa to watch *Heart and Soul* on BET. The show focused on books about relationships and self-improvement. "What a coincidence," Ariel said as she ran to get a notepad and pen. "A sistah could use a little advice right about now." Just when they were about to interview Iyanla Vanzant, the phone rang. Ariel checked the Caller ID to see if it was her mother, but the number was blocked.

"Hello?" she said with an attitude.

"Hello, Ariel, this is Lawrence. I know it's a bit early to be calling, but I wanted to make sure you were okay. I was getting worried since I hadn't heard from you in a while."

"Lawrence, I need time-out from this relationship."

"Time-out for what?"

"Time to get my head together, that's what! Things are moving way too fast."

"Can't we sit down and talk about this like adults?" he asked.

"There's nothing to talk about," she told him.

"I hope you're not still upset with me about what happened with your little friend at Sylvia's."

"My little friend's name is Chris," she said defensively. "And it has nothing to do with him. I just need time to sort things out."

"Have it your way," he said. "But I'm not going to stop calling unless you accept these flowers as a token of our friendship."

"What flowers?"

"The ones I'm holding outside your door."

Ariel walked over to the window and pulled back the curtains. Lawrence's black Lexus was parked in her driveway. "I'll be damned," she said to herself. When she opened the door, Lawrence was holding a gift basket filled with whip cream, condoms, and other sexual paraphernalia.

"Surprise!"

"Surprise, my ass!" she said. "I don't appreciate your coming over here unannounced. And what the hell is that basket for?"

"I just wanted to show you how much I've missed you," he said, looking pitiful.

"Well, you've shown me, now good-bye!" she said, trying to slam the door in his face.

"Damn, baby, don't be so cold," he said, putting his foot in the doorway. "Can I at least set this basket down and get a glass of water?"

Ariel thought about it for a second, then she reluctantly let him. She made him stand in the hallway while she poured him a glass of water from the faucet. She wasn't about to treat him to her bottled spring water.

"Here!" she said, shoving it toward him. "And don't take all day sipping on it. I want to get back to my program."

Suddenly the phone rang. Ariel was hoping it was her

mother. She wanted to let someone know Lawrence was there, just in case he turned violent. She excused herself and rushed into the bedroom to answer it.

"Hello!"

"Good morning, Ms. Daniels. How's my favorite manager?"

"Simon, you won't believe who just showed up at my front door," she whispered.

"Who, Michael Jordan?"

"No, you smart aleck. It's Lawrence!"

"You mean the guy who went off on your friend at Sylvia's?"

"That's the one."

"I thought you dumped him."

"I've been trying to cut him loose since last week, but he's persistent."

"Well, if he starts choking the shit out of you, make sure you scratch him so the police can get a DNA sample," Simon said, laughing.

"That's not funny. I think this guy is really crazy."

"You want me to call the police?"

"No, I think I can handle it," she told him. "But if you don't hear back from me in ten minutes, dial 911."

"All right, Ariel, but be careful. I don't want to see you on *Unsolved Mysteries*."

When she went back into the living room, Lawrence was sitting on the sofa with his shoes off. His feet were propped up on her glass cocktail table.

"Lawrence, what the hell are you doing?"

"I was just watching BET," he said with a smile. "I love this program about black books."

"Well, the show is over." She turned off the television with the remote.

"Okay, okay," he said, slipping on his shoes. "I know when I'm not wanted. Just let me use your bathroom and I'm outta here."

Ariel didn't want to make matters worse, so she showed him to the bathroom. While he handled his business, she wiped off the table where he had smudged her glass with his sweaty feet. "You trifling bastard," she said to herself. Then she took his glass into the kitchen and washed it out in hot water.

While her back was turned toward the sink, Lawrence came out of the bathroom buck naked, wearing a bright green condom, and holding a can of whipped cream.

"Here's Johnny!" he said.

Ariel was so stunned the glass slipped out of her hand and shattered on the floor.

"What the hell do you think you're doing?" she asked.

"I thought you might want sausage for breakfast," he said, laughing.

"Lawrence, you've got about ten seconds to put on your clothes and get the fuck out of my house!"

"Come on, baby. Stop fighting it. You know you want some of this sweet meat." He walked toward her while stroking his penis.

Ariel pulled a butcher's knife out of the drawer and swung it at him.

"If you take another step, I'm going to cut that little crooked motherfucker off."

"All right, I'm leaving!" he yelled as he ran into the bathroom and grabbed his clothes. "Just stop making dick threats."

Ariel followed him to the door waving the knife like a samurai. She didn't even give him a chance to put on his clothes before she pushed him out. "And stay out, you fuckin' lunatic!" she yelled as she locked the door.

A few minutes later, Lawrence drove off. Ariel collapsed on the sofa and tried to calm herself down long enough to call Simon back.

"Simon, this is Ariel," she said nervously. "I just wanted to let you know that he's gone and I'm okay."

"Are you sure? You sound terrible."

"I always sound like this when a deranged man comes to my house first thing in the morning and pulls out his dick."

"I'm glad that's all he pulled out," Simon said.

"Don't worry, I've got protection and I know how to use it," she said, sounding cocky. "By the way, why were you calling me this morning?"

"With all the drama going on I almost forgot," Simon said, laughing. "I called to remind you about Ladies' Night on Thursday. I promised Teddy that you would personally take care of him."

"Thanks, boss. That's all I need in my life is another lunatic," she said.

Chapter 26

The line outside Club Obsession stretched two blocks down Peachtree Street. The crowd was so unruly the security guards had to set up barricades to keep the over-eager women from cutting the line. Thursday nights had become chaotic since Teddy and his dance group, Hot Chocolate, began performing. It was the third consecutive sellout week and the crowds were becoming unmanageable. Ariel and Simon watched from the second-floor window trying to decide what to do.

"You think we should cancel the show?" Ariel asked Simon.

"Are you crazy? That would cause a riot," he said. "But we've got to come up with something fast. We don't have enough seats for all those people."

Ariel looked around the club with her hand on her chin.

"I've got an idea," she said. "Why don't we open the balcony area and place chairs along the back wall? If we move those old boxes, we can accommodate another two hundred people."

"That could work, except for one problem," Simon said. "The view is obscured by partitions."

"Believe me, those horny women will look around a building to see a naked man," Ariel said, laughing.

"You're pretty sharp for a rookie," Simon said as he gave her a friendly peck on the cheek."

"What's that for?"

"For thinking fast on your feet," Simon said. "If we get through this night in one piece, I might even give you a raise."

While he hurried to get the chairs in place, Ariel went to the dressing room to check on Teddy. She knocked on the door twice but he didn't answer. "Theodore, you in there?" she yelled. When she put her ear to the door she heard a smacking sound. She knocked again, this time harder. When he didn't answer, she used her key to unlock the door.

"Theodore, I know you're in . . ."

She was too stunned to get out the rest of her sentence. Teddy had one of the waitresses bent over against the wall banging her doggie-style.

"Didn't your mama ever teach you to knock?" Teddy said with a sly grin.

"I'm sorry, Ms. Daniels," the waitress whined as she pulled down her skirt. "I came to give him a glass of water and well one thing led to another. It was an accident!"

"Yeah, right. I guess you accidentally slipped on a wet spot and fell on his dick," Ariel said sarcastically. "Go collect your belongings, you're fired!"

"But, Ms. Daniels, I need this job."

"You should've thought about that before you bent over against that wall and played yourself," she told her. "Now get to steppin'."

She stormed by Ariel and mumbled, "Stuck-up bitch."

"Excuse me?"

"I didn't say anything."

"I know you didn't," Ariel said, looking fierce. "If you open your filthy mouth again they'll be carrying your ass out of here!"

Teddy was getting a good laugh out of the situation. He had a wide grin on his face as he pulled up his pants.

"You shouldn't have fired that sweet young thang," Teddy said. "Good help is hard to find."

"I would fire your arrogant ass, too, if it weren't for all the money Simon invested in you."

"Well, since I still have a job, I'm sure you won't mind closing the door so I can get dressed. My public is waiting," he said smugly. "Of course, you're more than welcome to stick around and watch."

"That's quite all right. I've already seen your little show, and frankly, I'm not impressed." Then she slammed the door shut.

Ariel tried to compose herself as she walked out into the club. The doors had opened for business and hundreds of women were rushing in to get front-row seats. Ariel maneuvered her way over to the bar where Simon was standing. He had the cordless phone in his hand and was signaling that she had a phone call.

"Who is it?" she asked

Simon put his hand over the receiver.

"I think it's Lawrence," he whispered. "You want me to tell him you're not here?"

"No, I'll take it in the office," she told him. "I need to put this behind me once and for all."

Once Ariel was inside the office, she closed the door, and picked up. Simon kept the phone up to his ear to listen in.

"Hello?"

"Hello, Ariel. This is Lawrence."

"Didn't I tell you not to call me again?"

"I know, but I just wanted to talk."

"Talk about what?"

"About working things out."

"There's nothing to work out. So please stop stalking me, otherwise I'm going to call the police."

"I'm harmless, baby. But if you call the cops I might have to get ugly," he said, sounding crazy. "Now stop playing hard to get and tell me what time I should pick you up tomorrow. My mother is having us over for dinner at eight o'clock. I told her all about you."

"Lawrence, I don't want to meet your mother, your father, or your damned dog. I just want to be left alone!"

"I'm not going anywhere until I get some pussy," he said. "I invested time and money in you."

"Look, you sick bastard, you heard what the lady said, now leave her alone!" Simon said, cutting in.

"Is that you, Mr. Big-Shot Club Owner?"

"It's me," Simon said. "You got something to say, tough guy?"

"Yeah, mind your own damned business!"

"Ariel is my business! If you have anything else you have to say, you can say it to me!"

"Now I see what's going on," he said. "You and Ariel have been mixing business with pleasure. Well, I've got something for both of your asses!" Then he hung up.

Simon rushed to the office to see how Ariel was doing. When he opened the door, she had her head down on the desk.

"This is like a bad dream," she said. "Why can't I find a straight black man in Atlanta with a good job, who's not on Prozac?"

"He's just trying to scare you," Simon said. "Guys like that are all talk."

"I don't know, Simon. I've got a bad feeling about this," Ariel said. "And now that you're involved, you'd better watch your back, too."

"Don't worry about me, I'm from the Southside of Chicago."

"Being from the Southside of Chicago doesn't make you bulletproof," she told him.

• • •

By 10:00 P.M. the club was jam-packed. Hundreds of women waited impatiently for the show to begin. "We want Teddy! We want Teddy!" they yelled. Simon gave the signal for the deejay to start the music. The lights dimmed and clouds of artificial smoke rose from the stage. The crowd erupted in cheers. "Bring on the meat!" one woman hollered.

When the smoke cleared, a mock toolbox was sitting in the center of the stage. Suddenly, four muscular men burst out of the cardboard box dressed as a plumber, auto mechanic, painter, and electrician. Teddy came out last dressed as a construction worker. When they stripped off their costumes, hundreds of women rushed the stage to get a touch of their muscular physiques.

"How much for a tune-up, baby?" a woman yelled, while flashing a ten-dollar bill.

"I need my pipes unclogged," another screamed. "Can you help a sistah out?"

The security guards rushed onto the stage to keep the situation under control. One woman had hold of the penis of one of the strippers and wouldn't let go. Teddy was loving the attention. He licked out his tongue and massaged his penis working the crowd into a frenzy. Simon and Ariel stood on the upstairs balcony and watched in disbelief as professional women in business suits climbed over one another like teenagers to stuff the strippers' thongs with cash.

"I'm in the wrong line of work," Simon said. "I might have to put on a tight pair of drawers and get out there and shake it up myself."

"Don't even think about it," Ariel joked as she patted him on his slightly protruding stomach. "They don't make G-strings that hold nickels and dimes."

The evening was going better than Simon expected. The bartenders were selling drinks left and right and the customers were having a ball. Even the women sitting upstairs with the obstructed view were enjoying themselves.

"Looks like we're going to survive another wild-and-crazy night," Simon said to Ariel as he looked around the crowded room. "You might get that raise after all."

"Don't be so quick to count your chickens. The night's not over yet."

Suddenly, there was a loud crashing sound near the front entrance. The music abruptly stopped and the crowd began to panic. "Somebody is shooting!" a woman yelled. People scattered in all directions running for the emergency exits. Ariel and Simon ducked into the Jazz Room to keep from being run over.

"I hate when I'm right," Ariel said.

"Me, too. And by the way, you can forget about that raise."

Once the commotion settled down, they came out to check the damage. It wasn't as bad as they had thought. Most of the tables and chairs were knocked over, but the glass to the aquarium wasn't damaged. That was Simon's biggest concern. There were a few people lying on the floor hurt. Some of them bleeding. "Call 911," Simon told Ariel. "I'm going to go see what the hell happened."

When he made it to the club's entrance, he noticed the large picture window was completely shattered. Glass was everywhere. The police had a man outside in handcuffs lying facedown on the ground. He was wearing flannel pajamas and a pair of flip-flops.

"Is this the son of a bitch who did this?" Simon asked.

"Yes, sir," the officer said. "He threw a brick in the window and tried to make a run for it."

"Turn him over so I can see his punk ass."

"Wuz up, Mr. Big-Shot Club Owner?" the man said. "I hope I didn't ruin your little party."

"Lawrence?"

"In the flesh," he said. "Maybe that'll teach you not to fuck with another man's woman."

Ariel saw what was going on and came running over. When she saw Lawrence covered in his muddied pajamas and wearing flip-flops, she didn't know whether to laugh or cry.

"Don't just stand there, baby, come over here and give Big Daddy a kiss," Lawrence said with a smirk on his face.

"Lawrence, you need serious help," she said.

"All I need is you. And if I can't have you, nobody will."

"Get him outta here," Simon said to the officer.

"It ain't over!" Lawrence yelled, while being carried away. "I know where you live you two-timing bitch!"

Ariel broke down in tears and began to tremble. Simon walked over and held her in his arms. "It'll be all right," he said, stroking her shoulders. "I won't ever let him hurt you."

Just then, Teddy came out of the club with his bag slung over his shoulder.

"I heard about what happened," he said. "Are you all right, Ariel—I mean, Ms. Daniels?"

"I'll be fine, Theodore. Thanks for asking."

"So does this mean the show is canceled next Thursday?"

"It's hard to say right now," Simon said. "I'll get in touch with you after I evaluate the damage."

"Cool."

Teddy shook hands with Simon and began walking toward the parking lot. But he couldn't leave without making a wisecrack.

"You must have some good pussy to have a brotha trippin' like that," he said, laughing.

Ariel walked up to him and slapped the grin off his face.

"You'll never know, smart ass."

Chapter 27

The next morning Simon awoke just in time to watch Cynthia on the twelve o'clock news. She was interviewing a famous bodybuilder at a local health club. Simon couldn't help noticing how friendly they were. Too friendly for a television interview, he thought. The muscle-bound man inconspicuously stroked Cynthia's breast while showing her the proper way to bench press. It may have seemed innocent to most people but Simon knew he was getting his feel on. "Don't make me come down there and hit your big ass with a dumbbell!" he shouted at the television.

Just then, the phone rang. He glanced over at the Caller ID to make sure it wasn't a pesky telemarketer. When he saw the 310 area code, he knew who it was.

"Wuz up, fool?"

"It's all good!" Malcolm said. "How's everything in Hotlanta?"

"Not so good, partner. Last night Ariel's psychopathic boyfriend threw a brick through the front window of the club."

"What did he do that for?"

"He thought Ariel and I were fooling around."

"I wonder what gave him that idea?" Malcolm said sarcastically.

"Don't even go there," Simon said, laughing. "I'm a one-woman man, not a big-time player like you."

"Well, my playing days might be over. I just got back from my little rendezvous with Toni in Chicago."

"How did it go?"

"It was great! We had dinner at Mama's house, and chilled out on the lakefront."

"And?"

"And what?"

"Did you hit it?"

"No, I didn't hit it, you old freak," Malcolm said, laughing. "We just hung out for a few days and enjoyed each other's company. Having sex wasn't a priority."

"Now, that's a first," Simon joked. "I guess you're ready to settle down and get married."

"I don't know about getting married, but I'm definitely ready for a change! This gigolo game is getting played out," he told him. "As a matter of fact, Toni hooked me up with an agent friend of hers in New York. If I get a deal with a major record company, I'd seriously consider putting a ring on her finger."

"That's great news about the agent. I always told you, you could make a fortune in the music business!" Simon sounded excited. "But aren't you forgetting about Toni's fiancé? I do recall her mentioning that she was engaged."

"That's no big deal. Toni is giving him the boot as soon as she gets back to Atlanta."

"And I bet you don't feel an ounce of guilt, do you?"

"Hell, no! Why should I?" Malcolm said, sounding cocky. "He had his chance and he blew it. Or as my father used to say, if you snooze, you lose."

"That's cold-blooded," Simon said. "Whatever happened to brothers sticking together?"

"In the love game, it's every man for himself," Malcolm said. "I've got to look out for my own interests."

Simon was still watching Cynthia flirt with the bodybuilder. He wasn't the type to get intimidated by another man, but listening to Malcolm brag about stealing Toni had made him paranoid.

"You think Cynthia would dump me for another man?" Simon asked.

"I'm the wrong person to ask about Cynthia."

"Just answer yes or no," Simon said, sounding serious.

"Anything is possible," he told him. "I mean, you're not exactly the easiest man in the world to be in a relationship with."

"What's that supposed to mean?"

"You're a workaholic!" Malcolm said. "As much as I dislike Cynthia, I have to sympathize with her. You probably don't have sex unless it's on your itinerary."

"Unlike you, I have a business to run. I can't lay up in bed all day," he said, getting defensive. "Sometimes all I have time for is a quickie."

"Women need romance, not some guy slamming against her for five minutes like he just got out of prison," Malcolm said.

"All right, Mr. Ladies' Man, what do you suggest?"

"Try sending her flowers or surprising her with a hot bubble bath by candlelight. Women love that kind of shit," Malcolm told him. "But most important, you've got to lick that clit until her toes curl."

"You know I don't take nosedives," Simon said.

"When it comes to satisfying your woman, the word *don't* shouldn't exist in your vocabulary."

"Look, I don't eat pussy and nothing you say is going to change my mind."

"It's men like you that keep men like me in business. All

you care about is money, money, money! Meanwhile your woman is home alone with a vibrator and her old black book," he said. "It's only a matter of time before she steps out for some maintenance."

Simon was speechless. For the first time in his life he was faced with the truth about his obsession with money. His relationship with Cynthia was deteriorating because he hadn't made her a priority.

"You're right," Simon confessed. "And it might be too late to make things right."

"What do you mean?"

"I haven't talked to Cynthia in almost a week. Since her trip to New Orleans she doesn't return my calls. And when I do manage to reach her, she's on her way to church."

"Why don't you hire a private investigator? I have an associate in Atlanta who owns a detective agency. He's eccentric, but he's good."

"Maybe I'm just overreacting." Simon was trying to avoid dealing with the issue. "I mean, what could she possibly be getting into at church?"

"Don't be so naive. Church is a player's paradise," Malcolm said. "I know men who go to service every Sunday just to meet desperate and lonely women."

"Okay, you've made your point."

Simon rummaged through his briefcase for a pen and something to write on.

"Now, tell me where I can find this associate of yours."

• • •

Late that afternoon, Simon arrived at the detective agency on Stewart Avenue in his old Chevy. The office was located on the second floor of a dilapidated building that sat between a liquor store and a barbecue joint. Simon glanced down at his notepad hoping he'd written down another address. Unfortunately, it was a perfect match. He grabbed the large brown envelope off the passenger seat and made his way across the street.

The building was a haven for derelicts and drug addicts. The hallways reeked of urine. Simon covered his nose with the handkerchief from his suit pocket and rushed to the second floor, stepping over an intoxicated bum along the way. The investigator's office was the third door on the right, directly across from the janitor's closet. PRIVATE DICK DETECTIVE AGENCY was awkwardly painted on the door. Simon took a deep breath and knocked.

"Who is it?" a man with a deep voice yelled out.

"It's Simon Harris, Malcolm's friend."

The door made an annoying squeaking sound as it opened. And the slower Simon tried to open it, the louder it squeaked. The detective was trying to crack the door just enough to peek out. Once he was convinced the coast was clear, he directed Simon to come in. He was clutching a nine-millimeter pistol, which he quickly tucked into the back of his trousers.

"Sorry for the tight security, but I make a lot of enemies in my line of work."

"I can imagine."

The detective was a tall, thin black man. But his dark complexion couldn't disguise the jagged scar on the right side of his face. It was the type of scar made by a knife with a dull blade or broken glass. He must have really pissed someone off, Simon was thinking.

The inside of the drab office was filled with all kinds of seventies paraphernalia. It was like walking through a time warp. The walls were covered with blue-light posters and old album covers. The living room was a shrine to the so-called black exploitation movies. Huge theater posters from movies like *Claudine, Foxy Brown, Cleopatra Jones,* and *J.D.'s Revenge* were everywhere. Taped to the refrigerator door was a mint-condition Ohio Players album cover. The one with the woman pouring honey on her chest.

The detective was a throwback to the seventies himself. He wore a pair of tight polyester pants and was sporting a short, unkempt Afro. Simon damn near fell out when he saw the Afro pick with the retracting red-and-green handles sticking out of the back of his head. Simon would've paid anything for that antique.

"I guess we haven't been formally introduced. My name is Ricky," he said, while extending his hand, "but everybody calls me by my last name, Roundtree. You know, like Richard Roundtree in the movie *Shaft*."

"He's a bad mother . . ."

"Shut your mouth," Roundtree sang along.

It was impossible for black folks to say *Shaft* without throwing in the lyrics to the song. It was one of those black things. The humor was unexpected but it helped to relax the mood.

"So, Mr. Harris, what can I do for you?"

"As I told you briefly on the phone, I'm getting married and I want to find out if my fiancée is cheating."

"Sounds simple enough," Roundtree said, while popping open a can of Old English 800. "Did you bring the information I asked for?"

"I've got it right here."

Simon emptied the contents of the brown envelope onto the living room table. There were several pictures of him and Cynthia, Debra and Cynthia, and one of Cynthia's Range Rover.

"Can I offer you a brew?" Roundtree asked.

"No thanks. The last time I drank some Old E, I woke up in a vacant lot wearing nothing but my drawers."

"Suit yourself."

Roundtree sat down on the dingy black leather sofa and looked over the pictures carefully. He grunted a few times then took a long sip of his beer.

"Nice-looking lady you got there," he said casually.

"Thanks."

"Have you considered a prenuptial agreement?" he asked out of nowhere.

"What made you ask that?"

"Just curious."

"You sound as if you expect to find something negative."

"Let's just say, I'm intuitive about these things."

He looked at Simon and smiled uncomfortably. Then he stood up and began pacing.

"Okay, this is the deal," he said with his hand firmly pressed against his chin. "I'll follow her for the next thirty days to see what I can dig up. When I put together enough evidence, I'll give you a call."

"That sounds fair enough. So how much is this little investigation going to cost?"

Roundtree wrote down a figure on a piece of paper towel and handed it to Simon. The amount read $2,999.95.

"What's up with the ninety-five cents?"

"It's marketing," he explained. "I got the idea from watching those Tae-Bo infomercials. The workout video sells for nineteen ninety-five because it sounds cheaper than twenty."

He escorted Simon to the door. They shook hands and gave each other brotherly hugs. It was a man thing.

"I assume you want to be paid in cash?"

"If it's not a problem," Roundtree said. "I don't want Uncle Sam in my pocket, if you know what I mean."

"Any particular denominations?"

"How about two one-thousand-dollar bills, nine hundreds, one fifty, two twenties, nine singles, three quarters, two dimes, and five pennies."

"Tell you what," Simon said, pulling out a wad of money. "I'll pay you an even three thousand up front if you throw in that Afro pick with the red-and-green handles."

"You've got yourself a deal!"

PART V

Don't Hate the Player, Hate the Game

Chapter 28

It was a typical muggy summer night in August. I stepped out onto my twenty-fifth-story balcony and watched the sun set over the Pacific. The view was breathtaking. I wished that Toni could have been there to share that moment with me. It had been almost three weeks since she left for Europe with her dance company and I was really missing her. But I had to put all those romantic thoughts aside. I had an important appointment to keep, and I didn't want to be late. I took one last hit of my drink and slipped into my Armani suit jacket. It was 8:50 P.M. and my limo was supposed to meet me downstairs in the lobby at 9:00.

As I was going out the door, the phone rang. The double ring let me know it was my business line. I was hoping it wasn't one of my horny clients calling for a last-minute booty call.

"Tremell Agency," I answered.

"Aha!" Melvin yelled. "I called your business number to see if you quit the escort business like you said you would. I can see you're doing business as usual." He sounded disappointed.

"I am out of business after tonight," I said. "I couldn't turn down two thousand bucks just for escorting some rich broad to a dinner party for two hours. It's easy money."

"What do you need with two thousand dollars? I thought you told me you had a record deal in the works?"

"I told you I had an agent. Until I actually sign a contract, I still have a mortgage to pay on this expensive-ass condo. Not to mention my six-hundred-dollar-a-month car note. Besides, I'm doing it as a favor to Helen. We fell out on bad terms in Atlanta and I wanted to make it up to her."

"Stop making excuses, Cool Breeze. Why don't you just admit that you can't give up the life. You love playing mind games on these women too much. And you love the variety of sex, too," he said, laughing. "Face it, you're addicted to women!"

"The only thing I'm addicted to is money."

"Okay, then, I'll give you two thousand dollars to stay in tonight."

"Yeah, right."

"I'm dead serious," he said.

"So what's the catch?"

"There is no catch. I just wanna keep you from backsliding. One night can turn into two, then three, and so on. Next thing you know, you're caught up in the game again."

"Nice try with the morality speech, old man. But I'm still going through with this last engagement. It wouldn't be very professional to cancel on such short notice."

"Two thousand dollars is a lot of money to pass up just to stay at home, eat popcorn, and watch cable. You sure you don't want to think it over?"

"I'm sure," I told him. "But if you insist on spending

your hard-earned money, why don't you make a donation to a worthy charity, like Players Anonymous," I said, laughing.

Just then, my other line rang. I told Melvin to hold on while I answered it.

"Hello?"

"Mr. Tremell, your car is here," the doorman said.

"Thank you. I'll be right down."

When I clicked back over, Melvin was coughing uncontrollably.

"You all right?"

"I'm fine," he said still hacking. "I just need a drink of water."

"You don't sound fine to me. Have you been taking your medication?"

"I'm fine, I told you! I've been taking care of myself since before you were a twinkle in your daddy's eye. So stop trying to act like my mother!" he snapped.

"Stop trying to sound hard," I said, jokingly. "You don't scare me like you do those employees at the club. I know you're just a grumpy old teddy bear."

He was laughing so hard, he nearly choked himself to death. After a few more coughs, he managed to compose himself.

"You always did know what to say to make me smile, Cool Breeze," he said, as he cleared his throat. "Look, I know you have to get going. But the first chance you get, I want to meet this special lady of yours. Any woman who can make you retire from the gigolo game must be an angel."

"Well, when my angel comes back from touring in Europe, I'll ask her if she can fly in on her wings to meet you. But only if you promise to start taking better care of yourself," I scolded him. "I don't want to take any chances of losing you. You're the most important person in the world to me."

He paused.

"That's a promise, Cool Breeze," he said, getting

choked up. "Now, get your narrow behind outta there and go take care of business. And you'd better keep your dick in your pants tonight, you hear?"

"There you go again, old man, trying to play hard," I said, laughing.

• • •

As we approached the entrance to the Marriott near the airport, I checked myself in the mirror one last time. This was my retirement night from twelve years of the game and I wanted to look my best. As the stretch black limousine cruised slowly toward the front of the hotel, the valet rushed to open my door.

"Welcome to the Marriott," he said. "Do you need help with your luggage, sir?"

"No, thank you. I'm here to meet someone."

I tipped him ten bucks then walked inside to find my date. The lobby was buzzing with black folks dressed in formal attire talking among themselves about business. When I looked over at the red-and-white banner hanging on the wall, I understood why they were so stiff. It read WELCOME NATIONAL ASSOCIATION OF AFRICAN-AMERICAN FINANCIAL CONSULTANTS. "What a bunch of tight asses," I muttered to myself

"My sentiments exactly," a woman said from behind me. "Mr. Tremell, I presume?"

"You would presume correctly," I said as I turned to face her. "And you are?"

"Catherine Howard, your date for the evening." She extended her hand. "Nice to meet you."

"The pleasure is all mine."

Catherine was incredibly gorgeous. Or as my daddy used to say, she was so fine she made you wanna drink her bathwater. She bore a stark resemblance to a young Diahann Carroll. Her hair was in a French roll. And she wore a fitted royal blue dress, which accentuated her full figure and dark-chocolate complexion. I knew from reading the article about her software company in *Fortune* magazine that she was forty-five, but she could have easily passed for a woman in her early thirties.

"You look surprised," she said bluntly.

"You don't miss much do you?" I asked, laughing. "My facial expression must have given me away."

"Yes, it did," she said, smiling flirtatiously. "What were you expecting? A troll?"

"To be honest with you, I didn't know what to expect. Sometimes pictures can be deceiving. But I can tell you that the picture of you in the magazine didn't do you justice. You should have that photographer shot."

We continued to talk as we strolled hand in hand toward the restaurant. Along the way, Catherine attracted a great deal of attention. She was waving and shaking hands as if she were running for public office.

"Good evening, Ms. Howard," some said.

"I enjoyed your speech, Ms. Howard," others professed.

"Don't forget to e-mail me that report," a woman added.

Catherine just smiled and kept walking as if it were no big deal. Once we made it through the corporate gauntlet to the restaurant, the maître d' sat us at a reserved table in the back. It was obvious by the way Catherine carried herself that she was accustomed to this kind of preferential treatment.

"So do you come here often," I asked sarcastically.

"From time to time," she said, smiling. "What about you?"

"Touché!" I said, giving her credit for a good comeback line. "You don't pull any punches, do you?"

"No, I don't. That's why I'm the president of this male-dominated organization today. I go for what I want."

"Well, since we're being so direct, what does a beautiful and intelligent woman like yourself need with an escort service? It seems to me that you could have any man you wanted."

"Three simple reasons," she said, moving in close so no one could hear her. "One, I need a strong man who knows how to take charge. Although I'm surrounded by highly successful men who earn millions of dollars, behind closed doors most of them are wimps who allow you to treat them like dogs. I need a man who isn't afraid to tell me no sometimes. And one who will tell me to shut up. Even a woman of my caliber wants a man with a little street in him."

I damn near choked on the water I was drinking. "Could you please be a little more direct?" I said, trying to clear my throat.

"Don't act so surprised. If you read the article you should know I'm from the Garden Valley projects in Cleveland. And you know we keep it real on the east side."

We inconspicuously slapped five and then she went on.

"The second reason is most men are very insecure, especially black men. If they can't handle a sistah making fifty thousand, what makes you think they can handle a woman whose net worth is five million?"

She cleverly slid her hand underneath the table and began moving it slowly up my thigh.

"And what's number three?" I asked, trying to keep a straight face.

"I love attractive young men with big dicks," she said bluntly. "And yours came highly recommended."

My dick got as hard as a petrified jawbreaker. And it didn't help that Catherine had unzipped my pants and was massaging my balls. I tried to keep my composure as people began to stare. But Catherine didn't even flinch. She just kept stroking my Johnson and talking dirty.

"Why don't we stop wasting time and go upstairs to my suite. I have a bottle of Alizé chilling in a bucket of ice and a Bill Evans CD. I heard you love jazz."

"You sure did your homework."

"That's the first thing they teach you in Business 101: always have a plan."

"I'll tell you what, I'm going to the little boys' room to give you some time to cool down. And when I come back, we're going to have a nice dinner and good conversation. Then I'm outta here." I stood up from the table and put my hand in my pocket to conceal my erection.

"Can I order you anything to drink while you're gone? A screwdriver, perhaps?"

"Very cute," I said, smiling. "But I'll just have a shot of brandy. On second thought, make that a double."

On my way back to the rest room I saw a familiar face sitting inside the sports bar. I moved in closer to make sure my eyes weren't playing tricks on me. But when she turned to the side, I was sure it was psychotic Tina. "What the hell is she doing here," I said to myself. Last I heard, she had settled with her NBA husband for ten million cash and the house. I'm sure he would've paid twice that just to get rid of her crazy ass. She was having drinks with a gigolo named Dexter. He was an up-and-coming young player from the San Bernadino area. I quickly turned away and walked back toward the restaurant as fast as I could. I knew Tina would make a big scene if she saw me.

When I made it back to the table, Catherine was sipping on a margarita with that horny look in her eyes. I didn't want to lead her on by going upstairs to her room, but I couldn't take a chance of running into Tina.

"Boy, that was quick," she said.

"I think I'll take you up on that offer to go upstairs."

"What about dinner?"

"We can eat upstairs," I told her.

"I like the way that sounds," she said with a sly grin. "Just let me pay for these drinks and we can start with dessert."

While she charged the bill to her room, I was trying to devise a plan to separate myself from Catherine. In order to get to the elevators, we had to walk directly past the sports bar. I wasn't about to take that chance on Tina seeing Catherine and me together. I had to think of something fast.

"All right, let's go," she said.

"Aw, damn! I left my wallet in the limo," I said, patting my pockets. "Why don't you get a head start and I'll meet you upstairs?"

"I don't mind going with you. I wanted to get a breath of fresh air anyway."

"I'd rather do it myself," I told her. "Besides, that will give you time to slip into something more comfortable."

That idea must have appealed to her because she promptly wrote her room number down on a napkin and handed me an extra key.

"Now don't keep me waiting," she said seductively. "I've got a fire that needs to be put out."

"Don't worry, baby, I'll be right behind you with my hose."

She gave me a kiss on the cheek and rushed off to put on her little costume. Once she was out of sight I made my way toward the door feeling relieved. "That was too close for comfort," I said, sighing. Just then Tina and Dexter came strolling out of the bar headed straight for me. I stooped down and tried to mix in with the crowd, but at six-three I was hard to miss. Before I could make a getaway down the opposite side of the corridor, she spotted me. "Malcolm, is that you?" she hollered. I wanted to keep steppin' but I knew Tina could get ignorant and draw even more attention. So I played it off by waving and giving her a phony smile.

But Tina wasn't going for that. She grabbed Dexter by the hand and rushed over. There was no way she was going to let me get away without bragging about how much money she had gotten from her divorce. She also wanted to flaunt Dexter in my face. It was well known that we didn't get along.

"Well, well, well, if it isn't Malcolm the Lover," she said.

"Hello, Tina. Nice to see you."

"Don't give me that shit. You know I'm the last person on earth you want see."

"If you knew that why did you run your tired ass over here?"

"Watch your mouth when you're talking to a lady," Dexter said, trying to sound hard.

"Look, young buck, you need to stay out of grown folks' business," I said, getting in his face. "Now, I know you think you're hot shit down in San Bernadino but you're in L.A. with the big dogs now. So I suggest that you rest that chivalry role before I toss your young ass over that banister."

Dexter and I were about the same height but he was thin, at least fifteen pounds lighter than me. He saw the look in my eyes and quickly backed down. He knew I was one second away from dropping him. Men read one another's eyes that way. It's a street thing.

"Baby, could you excuse us for a second?" Tina said to Dexter. "I want to talk to Malcolm alone for a minute."

"Yeah, Dexter, why don't you go kick some rocks like a good little boy. I promise I won't keep her long," I said conceitedly.

Once Dexter was gone, Tina's whole attitude changed. Her tone was more polite and she began rubbing on my chest.

"Malcolm, why haven't you returned my calls? You know I need my monthly fix."

"I've been busy."

"For a whole month?"

"Look, Tina, You're not my wife. I don't owe you an explanation. Besides, I told you I can't deal with your dramatic mood swings."

"I'm much better now that my divorce is final. Didn't you hear about the settlement on ESPN?"

"Yes, I heard. Congratulations," I said sarcastically. "Now why don't you get a life and leave me alone?"

"Because I'm in love with you. And I just can't cut my feelings off like a faucet the way you do."

"Yeah, right. You're so in love with me that you've been laying up with a different gigolo every weekend. I heard it through the grapevine that you've been buying dick all over California." I looked her up and down like she was trash. "What's wrong? Your crazy ass can't get laid without paying for it?"

Smack. She slapped me right in the face. The entire room turned in our direction to see what was going on.

"Fuck you, Malcolm!" she shouted. "That rich bitch you came here to see is no better than me. How much did she pay for some dick tonight?"

"This conversation is over," I said as I began to walk away. "Have a good night."

"Don't you walk away from me, you arrogant bastard. I'm not through with you yet!"

People rushed out of the restaurant and the sports bar to watch the circus. Some of them even had the nerve to take pictures. I walked as fast as I could toward the elevator with Tina trailing me screaming obscenities. Luckily the elevator was waiting when I got there. I frantically pushed the button for the fifteenth floor trying to force the doors shut.

"It's not over between us!" she yelled. "I bought your ass before and I can buy you again. You ain't nothing but a piece of meat who sells to the highest bidder."

As the elevator doors closed, she took off her high-heeled shoe and flung it at me. It grazed me on the right side of the forehead drawing blood.

"Take that, you pretty motherfucker."

• • •

When I arrived at Catherine's suite, I went inside the bathroom to find a towel to put on my face. The bleeding wasn't bad, but it did require a bandage. After I patched myself up with the first-aid kit, I walked out into the candlelit room. "My Foolish Heart" by Bill Evans was playing softly in the background. Catherine was lying on the bed face up, wearing a see-through black negligee and sipping on a glass of Alizé. She looked me up and down like a piece of meat but she never acknowledged the bandage on my head.

"So, how do you like it?" Catherine stood up and modeled.

"That's very nice," I said, trying to be cool.

"Nice enough to eat?"

"Like I said, you get straight to the point."

I was about to go into a big discussion about our agreement not to have sex, but I thought, what the fuck, and began taking off my clothes. Catherine was looking good and I needed to let off a little steam. While I stripped out of my clothes, I tried to put Toni out of my mind. When that didn't work, I played head games with myself to justify what I was about to do. *She's probably screwing some guy in Europe right now,* I was thinking. *What she doesn't know won't hurt her* was another thought. And then there was the classic excuse, *It's not like we're married.* Those were just a few thoughts running through my mind while I ate Catherine out. After she climaxed, she lay me down on the bed and returned the favor.

For the next hour, we sucked, licked, and screwed like animals. It was some of the wildest sex I ever had, and some of the most obscene. Catherine insisted on having anal sex on the patio, right out in the open. I agreed because she offered to pay more money.

When it was all over, I put on my clothes, collected my twenty-five hundred dollars, and headed for the door. No thank-yous, and no good-byes, not even eye contact. Catherine just turned over, lit a cigarette, and ordered room service. She got what she wanted and she was through with me.

As I walked down the corridor toward the elevator, I rubbed the bandage on my head and tried to play it off like it was business as usual. But in the back of my mind I was replaying what Tina had said about me. And she was right, I was just a piece of meat who sold out to the highest bidder. But this time I sold more than my body. I sold my integrity.

Chapter 29

Teddy was naked except for his underwear and one sweat sock. "Come on, seven!" he yelled as he prepared to roll the dice. He and Cheryl were playing strip Monopoly and Teddy's dog game piece was sitting on Pennsylvania Avenue. He needed seven to pass Go and collect two hundred dollars. If he rolled a three or five, he would land on Park Place or Boardwalk, properties that belonged to Cheryl.

Teddy blew on the dice and rolled them gently onto the board. "Come on, lucky seven!" he hollered. The dice seemed to turn in slow motion and finally landed flush: the total was five.

"You landed on Boardwalk, now take off those drawers!" Cheryl screamed as she jumped up and down on the bed.

"Wait a minute, baby. Your braids got in my eyes," Teddy said, getting upset. "I get another turn!"

"I hate playing Monopoly with you, Teddy. You're such a sore loser."

"I'll show you who's a sore loser."

Teddy grabbed Cheryl by the hair and slammed her down onto the bed. He ripped off her panties and rammed his penis inside of her.

"Ouch, baby, not so rough," she screamed. "I'm still a little dry."

"Well you better start thinking wet because I'm not about to stop."

Just as Teddy was getting into a nice groove, he heard a car door shut in the driveway. He quickly hopped off Cheryl and peeped out the window.

"Guess who's coming to dinner?" Teddy said, jokingly.

It was Cheryl's husband, David. Cheryl slipped on a pair of shorts and a T-shirt and began straightening up the bed.

"Don't just stand there, Teddy, give me a hand."

"I don't do beds," he said arrogantly.

"Damn you, Teddy. I don't want to lose my family over this."

"You should have thought about that two years ago when you started fucking me in your husband's bed."

She didn't have time to argue. She fixed the bed herself and then sprayed the room with Lysol, all the while giving Teddy a dirty look. By the time she was finished, her husband had walked through the front door.

"Honey, I'm home!"

"I'll be right down, sweetheart!"

Teddy was still standing there in his drawers with one sock on, acting as if nothing was happening.

"Hurry up. Hide in the closet!"

"How do you expect me to get my big ass in that tiny space?"

"Teddy, please!" she begged.

"Who are you talking to, honey?" David asked.

"Nobody, sweetheart."

She could hear David coming up the stairs. She looked Teddy dead in the eyes and begged him again to hide. But he wouldn't budge.

"I'll never forgive you for this," she said as she rushed out into the hallway to intercept her husband. "Hey, baby, you're home early. What happened to your business trip?"

She greeted him halfway with hugs and kisses, hoping to turn him around but he was carrying a heavy suitcase and seemed determined to set it down in the bedroom.

"My meeting in Kansas City was canceled, so I decided to come home to my beautiful wife."

"Well, let me take your suitcase and you can recline in your chair in the living room while I make you something to eat."

"I'm not hungry," he said as he made it to the top of the stairs. "I just want to take off my clothes and get into bed."

Cheryl closed her eyes and put her hands over her ears as David walked into the bedroom. But nothing happened. When she nervously peeked into the room, Teddy was gone. The window was wide open, so she thought he had climbed out.

"What was all that screaming about?" David asked, while undressing.

"What screaming?"

"I heard you screaming when I pulled into the drive-way."

"Oh, I was just doing some crunches. You know I've been trying to stay in shape for you."

"And you look damn good, too, baby," David said reaching out his arms. "Now come here and give your old man a real hug."

While they were embracing, Cheryl saw a finger come out of the closet. It was Teddy and he was pointing toward the door. That was his signal telling her he wanted to get out.

"Honey, don't you want to take a shower before you go to bed?"

"I just had a shower before I got on the plane," he said, trying to unzip her shorts. "But what I think I could use is some good loving to knock me out."

That's not what Cheryl had in mind but she figured any distraction was better then none. So she began undressing herself and laid him down on the bed. Suddenly David sprang up out of the bed and headed toward the closet.

"Wait a minute, let me get my old High Karate cologne out of the closet. When we first met, that aroma used to drive you crazy."

"No!" she shouted as he went to open the door. "I mean, that was ten years ago, sweetheart. All I want to taste is you."

David took his hand off the knob and went back to bed. Right away Cheryl covered him with the blanket and jumped on top, blocking his view of the closet. Teddy came creeping out with his clothes balled up in his arms. But instead of rushing down the stairs, he stood in the doorway while he got dressed. Cheryl was irate at first but then she became turned on. It was the best sex she had with her husband in years.

When Teddy had seen enough, he blew Cheryl a kiss and nonchalantly walked down the stairs and out the door. As he walked across the street to his truck wearing a devilish smile, his pager went off. The number on the display read 2911. It was his girlfriend, Karen. As he headed home to deal with the latest crisis, he was his usual arrogant self. "Whatever the problem is, baby, I've got a perfectly good lie to explain it," he said, laughing.

• • •

Teddy was feeling cocky as he pulled into the circular driveway, until he saw the bright yellow Corvette parked behind Karen's Mercedes. It belonged to Karen's younger sister, Lisa. She was also a lawyer. He tried to straighten out his wrinkled clothes as best he could then he took a hard swallow and went inside.

He could hardly open the door with all the boxes piled up against it. On the side of each one was marked GARBAGE in bold black marker. Karen and Lisa were carrying the last box down when he walked into the living room.

"What's this supposed to be, spring cleaning?" he joked.

"I'm glad you think this is funny, you two-timing snake, because you'll be laughing on the streets tonight," Karen said as she set the box down.

"Okay, just calm down for a minute and tell me what's going on."

"Well, let me see." Karen began to count on her fingers. "First there were the phone numbers in your pocket, then there was the lipstick on your collar. Last month I found a pair of Victoria's Secret panties that mysteriously buried themselves in my drawer. And now I come home from a hard day's work and I hear a message on my machine from one of your tramps."

"What message?" Teddy asked, playing dumb.

"We don't even need to go there, Teddy. Just get your stuff and leave."

"So what is Lisa here for?"

"To make sure you don't try to talk me out of it. I usually don't make a fool of myself when people are around."

Lisa was standing off to the side quietly. It was obvious she didn't want to be there.

"How are you doing, Lisa," Teddy asked.

"I'm fine, Teddy," she said passively.

"How's business at the firm?"

"Business is fine, too."

"All right, that's enough of this family reunion. Get your boxes and get out!" Karen yelled.

"Can't we talk about it, baby? You know I love you."

"You don't love anybody but yourself, you bald-headed bastard. Now get out before I call the police and have you thrown out."

"So it's like that, huh? Okay, then, have it your way. I'm outta here."

Karen stood at the door like a drill sergeant until Teddy

loaded the last box into his truck. When he walked out of the door with the last one, she slammed the door shut behind him.

"And stay out!" she yelled.

"Don't you want your house keys back?"

"The locksmith is on his way over to change the locks. You can keep yours as souvenirs," she said to him from the window.

"You're really serious this time, aren't you?"

"Serious as a lawsuit. Speaking of which, I heard about all your kids. I hope they catch up with you one day and put you under the jail, you deadbeat!"

"I'd rather be a deadbeat than a lonely old woman with stretch marks and a worn-out pussy," he said, while opening the door to his truck. "And by the way, thanks for the Navigator, the credit cards, the Versace suits, and the Rolex. Thanks to you, I've finally saved enough money to get a place of my own."

Karen ran to the door, while trying to pull the ring he had given her off her finger.

"You go to hell, Theodore, and take this Cracker Jack ring with you!"

When she finally managed to get the ring off, she threw it at him. It ricocheted off the truck and fell onto the driveway.

"Hey, you need to be more careful. This truck cost a lot of money," he said, laughing. "But I guess I don't need to tell you that, now do I?"

As he was about to drive off, he looked over at Lisa as she walked across the lawn toward her car. She was wearing a yellow halter top and miniskirt to match her Vette. It was an outfit she wore for Teddy many times before while Karen was out of town. It was his favorite.

They made eye contact on the down low then he sped off. As he turned the corner, he laughed out loud knowing he had another place to go home to. That's probably what

Lisa wanted all along, he was thinking. Maybe that's why she'd buried her yellow Victoria's Secret panties in her sister's drawer.

Chapter 30

It was early Saturday afternoon. Ariel barely made it inside the door before she collapsed onto the living room floor. She had lifted weights at the gym for an hour, then she jogged five miles around Stone Mountain. It was the first time she had exercised all summer and it showed. She was so out of shape she had charley horses in both legs. After she caught her breath, she peeled out of her sweaty Howard University T-shirt and went upstairs to run a shower. While she was stripping off the rest of her clothes, she noticed the message light on her answering machine was blinking. Ariel was hoping it was her latest blind date, Raymond.

"Hey, baby, it's me," a man's smooth and masculine voice said. "Just wanted you to know that my plane landed safely. I've got to drop off some presents for my girls, then I'll be headed your way. I should be there by five o'clock. By the way, I brought you a souvenir from Mexico. I hope you like it. See you in a minute, baby. Bye."

Ariel smiled. It was the call that she had been waiting for all day. She rushed back into the bathroom and jumped into the shower. It was 3:30 P.M. and she wanted to have everything ready when Raymond got there.

• • •

By 4:45 P.M. Ariel had created a nice romantic atmosphere. The dining room table was set with long white candles and a bottle of white zinfandel chilling in a bucket of ice. She even broke out the good china to add a touch of class. But Ariel wanted Raymond to admire more than the place setting. After she checked on the shrimp casserole, she rushed upstairs to get changed. Instead of putting on the conservative sundress she had laid out, she put on a pair of black lace pants and a white cotton tube top to show off her pierced belly button. "Girl, you know you got it going on!" she said as she admired herself in the mirror.

While she waited impatiently for Raymond to arrive, she sipped on a glass of wine and masturbated. And the more she drank, the hornier she got. She was contemplating whether or not to break out her vibrator when the phone rang. "Please, God, don't let this be Raymond calling to cancel," she said to herself.

"Hello."

"Hey, sweetheart, just called to see how you were doing. Hope I wasn't interrupting anything."

"As a matter of fact you were!"

"Well, excuse me, Ms. Thang. I'll just let you go then." She sounded hurt. "Good-bye!"

"Wait a minute, Mama. I'm sorry for snapping at you," Ariel apologized. "I've got a quick minute to talk."

"I don't know what's going on with you, young lady, but I don't like it."

"I've been under a lot of pressure lately, you know with the situation with Lawrence and all."

"I thought you told me he stopped calling weeks ago."

"He did, but it's going to take me a while to adjust to going about my daily routine without having to look over my shoulder," she told her.

"You managed to adjust enough to go out with what's his name."

"His name is Raymond, Mama."

"Why haven't you brought him over to meet me?" she asked. "From what you told me about him, he sounds like a nice young man. Didn't you say he's a doctor?"

"Raymond is very busy, Mama. He spends a lot of spare time with his two daughters, and he runs his own practice," she told her. "And for your information, he's not just a regular doctor, he's a heart surgeon."

"Listen to you sounding all proud," Mama said, laughing. "I'd like to meet any man who can impress you."

"I'm impressed all right." Ariel was admiring the picture of Raymond hanging over her fireplace.

"It sounds to me like you finally met Mr. Right," Mama said. "I just find it hard to believe that a man with his credentials is still single."

Suddenly, the phone went silent. Ariel cleared her throat a few times then tried to change the subject.

"So have you talked to Joyce or Sheila lately? How are the kids doing?"

"Ariel Michelle Daniels!" Mama interrupted. "I know you're not messing around with no married man. I didn't raise you that way!"

"Calm, down, Mama. I'm not trying to take him away from his wife and kids. I just want to have a little fun, that's all."

"Lord, I know your father is rolling over in his grave," she said. "Why can't you find a nice single man to get involved with, like your friend Chris. What's wrong with him?"

"Chris is okay, but he's not my type. He's short, light skinned, and he's not aggressive enough for me," she explained. "Raymond is tall, dark, and handsome, and I admire what he's doing with his life. That's a combination hard to find in any man, married or single."

"But baby, what about having a family of your own. Don't you want to get married someday?"

"Mama, that whole fantasy of the all-American family with the four-bedroom house, the station wagon, and the two-point-five kids is the reason why I've been alone for all these years. Ever since I was a little girl, I've been sizing every man up as a potential husband. But what I should've been looking for was someone who makes me happy."

"And you think sleeping with a married man is going to make you happy?"

"Yes, it will, Mama. And it's damn sure better then being alone," Ariel said, getting emotional. "I'll be thirty years old next month and I'm going to spend my birthday with someone that I'm interested in, not some boring, watered-down substitute for a man."

"Don't you realize there are other people affected by your decision? He has a wife and two kids at home. Have you even stopped to think about them?"

"When I met Raymond through the dating service, he was up front about his marriage. But he said he was going through some problems. It's not my fault that his wife can't take care of her business."

"Don't be such a damn fool, Ariel. All married men lie about having problems. It's all a game."

"To be honest with you, Mama, I don't care if he's lying or not. All I know is he makes me laugh, we enjoy each other's company, and the sex is good," she said defiantly. "He may not be all mine, but half a man is better than no man."

Ariel heard Raymond's car pull into the driveway. She wiped the tears from her eyes and checked her makeup in the hallway mirror.

"I'm sorry, Mama, I've got to go now. Raymond is here."

"I'll let you go, Ariel, but you better take some time out to read your Bible. Galatians six, verse seven. A man reaps what he sows."

"Thanks for the sermon, Mama," she said, sounding smart. "Good-bye."

Chapter 31

Simon was in the kitchen cooking a pot of spaghetti when he realized Cynthia had been gone for more than twenty minutes. She told him she was feeling ill and needed to step outside for some fresh air. He looked for her on the patio but she was nowhere to be found. He figured she was lying down in bed again. For the past week she had complained about headaches and dizziness.

On his way to the bedroom, he noticed a light coming from the bathroom. He crept over to the door and put his ear next it. He could hear Cynthia talking on the phone, almost in a whisper. Then she began coughing violently and throwing up.

"You all right in there?" Simon pounded on the door.

"I'm fine," she said as she flushed the toilet.

A minute later she opened the door. Her skin was pale and her eyes were swollen and red.

"Cynthia, you look terrible." Simon tried to put his arm around her. "Are you sure you don't need to see a doctor?"

"I told you I was fine!" She backed away from him. "Stop babying me!"

"Who were you talking to on your cell phone?"

"What were you doing, eavesdropping?"

"You're damn right I was eavesdropping. This is my house!"

"For your information, I was talking to my doctor."

"Your doctor, huh? Why in the hell do you have to whisper to talk to your doctor?"

"Because I didn't want you to know I was sick, that's why!" she said angrily. "You always make such a big deal out of everything."

"Most women would love to have a man who cared enough about them to make a big deal over them."

"Well, I'm not most women!"

Cynthia stormed into the bedroom and began collecting her belongings. She packed her makeup bag, a toothbrush, and a set of silk pajamas that she always kept at Simon's house.

"I guess this means you're gone for good."

"I love you, Simon, but I need a break."

"If it's just a break, why are you taking your toothbrush and pajamas?"

Cynthia took a deep breath then unpacked her things. "Now, are you satisfied," she said as she picked up her bag.

She tried to hurry by him but he grabbed her car keys out of her hand.

"Give me back my keys, Simon."

"Not until you tell me what's going on."

"Nothing is going on. I'm sick, I told you, and want to go home and lie down."

"Why can't you lie down in my bed?"

"Because I want to be in my own bed, that's why. And besides, the smell of that spaghetti is making me throw up."

"If that's what's bothering you, just give me a minute and I'll get rid of it."

"Damn you, Simon! Stop trying to fix shit all the time!" she screamed. "Just give me my keys and let me go home!"

"Fine!" He tossed the keys at her.

Cynthia grabbed them out of the air with one hand and walked out the door. Simon tried to play hard letting her go without saying good-bye, but he was too caught up. He hurried out the door and caught up with her just as she was getting inside her car.

"Hold up, Cynthia," he said, holding on to the car door. "I'm sorry for trippin'. It's just that we haven't spent any time together lately and I miss you."

"I miss you, too, Simon, but sometimes people need space."

"Can we at least get together for lunch tomorrow and try to work things out?"

"I told you earlier this week that I was doing a live remote from my church tomorrow. After that, I have a meeting with my producers."

"At first I was the one who was busy all the time. Now that I've taken time out from the club to spend more time with you, you're the one who's too busy," he said, while looking deep into her eyes. "Funny how things can change, huh?"

"It'll all work out, Simon. Like I told you, I just need some space."

She gave him a dispassionate hug, got inside her Range Rover, and drove off.

Just as her taillights disappeared over the hill, Simon's pager went off. It was Roundtree, the private dick. He rushed back inside the house to return the call. His hands shook as he punched in the seven digits. He had a gut feeling that the verdict would not be in Cynthia's favor.

"Hello, Roundtree? It's me, Simon. What's the word?"

"Well, do you want the good news or the bad news?"

"Give me the bad news first."

"Your fiancée is definitely fucking around," he said bluntly. "And when I say fucking, I mean it literally."

"And what's the good news?"

"The good news is that it's not a white boy or another woman."

But that was no concession for Simon. The woman that he loved had allowed another man to defile her body. And she did it while sharing his bed and lying to his face. He felt like a fool. The phone went silent as the tears slowly trickled down his cheeks. First tears of pain, then of rage.

"Mr. Harris, are you still there?"

"Yeah, man, I'm here," he said, while trying to clear his throat.

"So what's your next move?" Roundtree asked him. "You want to get together tomorrow and look over the pictures, or what?"

"To hell with tomorrow! I want to see everything you got on that cheating bitch tonight! I'll be at your place in fifteen minutes."

• • •

Simon burned rubber as he came to an abrupt stop in front of Roundtree's rundown building. He jumped out of his old Chevy without bothering to lock it and hurried inside. He was so enraged that he didn't even notice the stench of urine and vomit in the hallway. When he arrived at the second floor, Roundtree was waiting with the door already open.

"Damn, that was fifteen minutes flat!" he said, while looking at his watch.

"Don't waste my time with the comedy, Chris Rock," he said irately as he walked past him into the office. "Let's get down to business."

Simon sat down on the black leather sofa while Roundtree went to get the pictures. He was expecting a few neatly packaged envelopes of black-and-white snapshots, like the private dicks in the movies. But Roundtree surprised him when he came back into the room carrying a small box.

"You wanna get down to business, huh?" He dumped the contents onto the raggedy cocktail table and shook the box until it spilled over onto the floor. "How's that?"

Simon was so overwhelmed he didn't know where to start. He had his choice of videotapes, photographs, and copies of hotel receipts. Everything was marked precisely with dates, times, locations, and even titles. Simon picked up the video-tape labeled 7/21, 11:30 P.M., LAKE LANIER, DEEP THROAT.

"Here, put this in the VCR."

"Why don't you start with the PG-13 tape and work your way up to the triple X?"

"Don't play games with me tonight. I'm not in the mood."

"Okay, it's your dime," he said as he put the tape into the VCR. "But remember, I tried to warn you."

The beginning of the tape was blurred. When it came into focus, Cynthia's Range Rover was parked out on the deck near the boats. The camera zoomed in on a man sitting in the passenger seat. It was too dark to see his face through the window but when they stepped out of the truck and into the moonlight his features were very distinguished. He stood about six feet tall and was of medium build. His hair was short and wavy, like he had a relaxer in it. And he wore a well-groomed beard.

Cynthia opened the hatch and pulled out a blanket and picnic basket. While she laid the basket on the deck, the man pulled out what looked like a bottle of wine and poured two glasses. They appeared to be very familiar with each other as they cuddled on the blanket and talked with their feet dangling over the deck. Cynthia occasionally laughed and gave him pecks on the cheek.

But the romantic scene soon turned erotic. Cynthia pulled up her short skirt and casually sat on his lap. From a distance it seemed innocent, but when the camera zoomed in, the expression on her face was a dead giveaway. She was frowning and biting down on her finger to keep from screaming. The man was slapping her on the ass forcefully and you could read his lips asking, "What's my name?"

But the most painful part was the passionate expression on Cynthia's face. She wasn't just screwing this man, she was making love. The camera equipment was state-of-the-art so Simon could see every detail, from the perspiration running down her back to the veins in her neck as she moaned in ecstasy.

"Okay, turn it off. I've seen enough."

"Hold up, here comes the part where he slaps her on the ass with his Bible," Roundtree joked.

"I said that's enough, goddammit!"

Roundtree pressed the stop button and stood by quietly. Simon put his hands over his face and leaned back against the sofa.

"Did you find out who he is?" Simon asked.

"I know everything there is to know," Roundtree boasted. "Where he works, where he lives, his Social Security number, his credit rating, and his shoe size."

"Why don't we just start with where he works."

Roundtree handed Simon a five-by-eight photo of the same man standing in a church pulpit.

"What is this?"

"That's a picture of our man at work. His name is Reverend James Young of the First United Baptist Church."

"He's a goddamned preacher?"

"A part-time preacher and full-time manipulator," Roundtree said. "He runs a bogus counseling service out of an office on Buford Highway. That's usually where he and your fiancée meet up for sex."

"I knew that heifer was lying when she told me she was going to Bible study."

"Oh, but there's more," Roundtree interrupted. "She's

not the only woman in the congregation that he's boning."

Roundtree pulled out another set of pictures. They were of the same man with different women. Some of the photos showed them kissing and hugging. And others were more explicit.

"This guy is a true player," Roundtree went on. "And he's very particular about the type of women he sleeps with. Most of them are married and have high-profile jobs such as politicians, lawyers, and TV personalities. In other words, he chooses women who have something to lose if they open their mouths."

"Well, you can call me a player hater because this son of a bitch is going down!" Simon said ruthlessly. He gathered the pictures and videotapes from off the cocktail table and angrily tossed them back into the cardboard box. He was so fired up, his hands were shaking.

"Whatever you plan to do, count me in," Roundtree said.

"Thanks for the offer, but I don't want to get you involved. What I'm about to do is pretty low-down."

"Low-down is my middle name!" Roundtree said enthusiastically. "Besides, there ain't nothing in the world I hate more than a hypocritical preacher."

Simon paused for a second to reconsider. There was no one else he trusted to go through with such a cruel deed, not even Malcolm.

"All right, you're in!" He gave Roundtree a high five. "Now go grab a couple of cans of Old E and I'll tell you the plan."

Chapter 32

It was 10:30 Sunday morning. The parking lot of the First United Baptist Church was filled with vans marked EYE-WITNESS NEWS. The church was holding a special service at 11:00 A.M. honoring a famous civil rights leader. Every television station in town was there for the big event, including Cynthia's station, WBBQ. Simon and Roundtree crept around the back disguised as technicians and blended in with the army of television people who were setting up for the live broadcast.

Once they were inside the building, Simon played look-out while Roundtree broke into the projection room. Most of the church members were so busy trying to get their faces on camera, they didn't pay them any attention. Their vanity played right into Simon's hands. Within fifteen minutes, the trap was set.

"Now what?" Roundtree asked.

"We go have a seat and wait for the fireworks to begin."

Services began promptly at 11:00 A.M. with the praise team firing up the congregation. The atmosphere was joyful and full of energy.

"Praise the Lord," some shouted.

"Thank you, Jesus!" others prayed.

As Simon watched the enthusiastic crowd, he wondered if he was doing the right thing, especially with so many children present. But his sympathetic feelings quickly faded once Reverend Young was introduced. He strutted onto the stage dressed in a bright red suit and matching red shoes. Simon wanted to choke the shit out of him as he charmed the mostly female audience with his self-righteous grin. "Smile while you can, you perpetrator," he said to himself. "Vengeance will be mine."

After the pastor lead the opening prayer, the choir rose to sing the musical selection "Someone's Knocking on My Door." They looked magnificent in their royal blue robes as they lined up perfectly on the steel tier. Once they were in place, the musical director give the signal and the serene church was transformed into a concert hall. From the back of the room, Simon could feel the power of their voices and the spirituality of the lyrics. By the second verse, he was singing along.

Even Roundtree was caught up in the moment. He was stomping his feet and shouting like he was at an old-fashioned revival. "Hallelujah!" he screamed. Simon gave him a puzzled stare then burst out laughing.

"I'm cool, I'm cool," Roundtree said, trying to play it off.

"Are you sure?" Simon asked. "For a minute there I thought you were going to start talking in tongues."

"For a minute there, I was," Roundtree said, laughing. "This music could have the biggest sinner rushing to the altar to get saved."

"We're both going to need saving after this," Simon told him as he checked his watch. "It's almost show time!"

When the song ended, Reverend Young swaggered up to the microphone in his flashy red suit to acknowledge the media and special guests. Meanwhile, the ushers hurried to set up the screen for the video presentation. The ceremony for the honoree was to begin with the showing of the civil rights documentary *Eyes on the Prize.* Simon's stomach was in knots as he watched and waited. He wondered if someone had discovered that the videotapes had been switched. If so, he had a plan B to mail the videotapes and pictures to the newspapers. But plan A would be so much sweeter.

Once the screen was set up, Reverend Young gave the signal for the ushers to dim the lights. As the room darkened, Simon caught a glimpse of Cynthia and her girlfriend Debra sitting up front in the VIP section. "I guess screwing the pastor has its privileges," Simon said to himself.

The opening of the tape was a series of quick snapshots of Reverend Young and the married women, kissing and having sex. Roundtree edited the tape perfectly so that each picture was distinct. There was no mistaking who was doing what. Almost immediately you could hear men screaming out from the darkness.

"Hey, that's my wife!" one man yelled.

"And that's mine!" another hollered.

But the show was only just beginning. The pictures were promptly followed by the videotape of Reverend Young and Cynthia having sex at Lake Lanier. You could hear the hands of parents slapping against their children's faces as they attempted to block their view.

"Turn that garbage off!" Reverend Young yelled out at the projectionist. But the tape continued to play. It was Reverend Young's bad luck that the projectionist was a horny seventeen-year-old boy who was learning more from watching three minutes of that tape than he had in four years of sex education. Someone else had to charge upstairs to the booth to turn off the tape. But by that time the tape had played up to the part where Reverend Young slapped Cynthia on the ass with the Bible and asked, "What's my name?" You could hear the entire congregation gasp.

When the lights came up, Reverend Young was standing at the pulpit sweating like a Klansman at a Black Panther rally. Cynthia was sweating, too, as the camera crews from every television station in Atlanta including her own, focused on her.

"Calm down, please. This whole thing is a big misunderstanding." Reverend Young pulled the handkerchief from his suit pocket and wiped his brow. "That tape was made many years ago when I was still living in sin."

"You must think I'm a damned fool," one man yelled out. "The truck in that video is a ninety-nine."

"And how do you explain those pictures with my wife, you crooked bastard," another man yelled.

The situation erupted into a free-for-all as several men charged the stage. Simon wanted a piece of him, too. He fought his way through the impassioned crowd until he reached the stage. But the burly security guards had created an impenetrable human wall around the pulpit to protect the pastor.

"Hey, preacher, over here!" Simon yelled until the pastor looked his way. The expression on his face left no doubt that he knew who Simon was.

"What the hell do you want?"

"I just wanted to quote a scripture to you. Exodus, chapter twenty, verse seventeen. 'Thou shalt not covet thy neighbor's wife.' "

"I've got a scripture to quote to you, too: Kiss my ass!"

"No thanks, I've seen your ashy black ass on video and it ain't nothing nice to look at," Simon told him.

The security guards quickly ushered the pastor out of the side doors away from the cameras. However, Cynthia wasn't so lucky. Reporters were swarming around her as though she were Monica Lewinsky. Simon could see the look of humiliation in her eyes, the same terrible humiliation he had felt. Debra was standing off to the side watching helplessly as her girlfriend was being ripped apart. Simon walked up from behind Debra and tapped her on the shoulder. She was stunned when she saw who it was.

"Simon wha—what are you doing here?" she stuttered.

"That's not important," he told her. "I just need you to give this to Cynthia." He handed her a plastic bag.

"What is this?"

"It's a going-away present," he said with a smirk. "She'll understand."

Simon walked toward the exit where Roundtree was waiting. Once they were out of sight, Debra ripped opened the sealed package. Inside was a pair of white silk pajamas, a toothbrush, and a blank white card. Being the nosy woman that she was, Debra couldn't resist opening it.

Inside the card was a caricature of a man kicking a woman out of a house, with her luggage flying. Printed underneath it in bold letters was *Enjoy your space. Yours truly, Simon.*

Chapter 33

It was 8:15 P.M. when I awoke from my nap. The six-hour flight from Los Angeles to New York had gone by very quickly. I had slept for nearly four of those hours to pass the time. It also helped keep my mind off the sexy flight attendant who was working first class. Ever since I boarded the plane she had raped me with her eyes. And when she set down my drink, she leaned over so I could see her breasts. That old devil was definitely at work. When she came by to pick up my glass, I stopped her to check on our arrival time.

"Excuse me, how long before we land?" I asked.

"We should be touching down at LaGuardia in about twenty minutes," she said, smiling flirtatiously. "Can I, ah, get you anything?"

She meant it just the way it sounded but I wasn't taking the bait.

"No, thank you," I told her politely.

"Let me know if you change your mind," she said, smiling.

Twenty minutes was plenty of time to get into trouble with such a lovely young woman. So I distracted myself by using the airphone to call Simon. It had been five days since he left me a message about the episode with the preacher, and I was beginning to worry. During our twenty years as best friends I don't recall ever having gone more then three days without talking to him. Something was up. As his phone rang, I was hoping not to get his answering machine again.

"Hello, this is Simon. Sorry I'm not available to take your call. Please leave a message at the tone and I'll return your call at my earliest convenience. Thank you." *Beep.*

The message sounded dry and cold. Not at all like Simon. I didn't bother to leave a message. I was sure he had received my previous ten.

I was desperate for answers, so I dialed the only other number where I knew he could be reached, Club Obsession. Normally, I respected his need for privacy, especially after such a traumatic experience. But I had a gut feeling that something was wrong. There was no telling what Simon was capable of when it came to Cynthia. His was the classic case of a man loving a woman more than he loved himself.

As the phone to the club rang, I took a deep breath and prepared myself for the worse.

"Hello, Club Obsession," a woman's voice answered.

"Is Mr. Harris in?"

"No, he isn't. Would you like to leave a message?"

"Yeah, tell him to call his buddy Malcolm, ASAP."

"Malcolm, thank goodness, it's you!" Her demeanor changed completely.

"Ariel, is that you?"

"Yes, and I can't tell you how hard I've been trying to reach you."

"Calm down and tell me what's wrong?"

"I haven't heard from Simon in three days," she said,

sounding stressed. "And the media has been camped outside the club looking for him. It looks like the O.J. Simpson trial out there."

"Did Simon say where he was going?"

"All he said was he needed to go home to get his head together. But when I drove by his house, his car was gone and all his lights were out."

I knew exactly where Simon was. He was in Chicago, back in the old neighborhood. That's where he always went to sort things out.

"Try not to worry, Ariel. I think I know where Simon is," I told her. "Just give him a few days and I'm sure he'll call to let you know he's okay."

"Malcolm, I wish you could be here for him. He really needs a friend right now."

"As soon as I meet with my agent in New York, I'll go track Simon down and have a long talk with him," I assured her.

"Simon told me about your record deal. Congratulations!"

"Well, it's not official yet. My agent had his final meeting with the record company today. Hopefully, we'll have something to celebrate when I meet up with him tonight."

"I know Toni is happy for you!" she said excitedly. "Is she in New York, too?"

"Unfortunately, she's on tour in Europe until next week," I said, sounding depressed. "I really wanted her to be here to celebrate with me. Without her, none of this would've been possible."

Just then, the flight attendant came over the intercom to announce our approach to LaGuardia. I pulled up my window shade to check out the awesome view of downtown Manhattan. The skyscrapers seemed more like mountains as they blocked out the setting sun. Even Chicago with the Sears Tower and John Hancock buildings paled in comparison to the immense New York skyline. It was truly Gotham City.

"Well, that's my cue," I said to Ariel. "Try not to worry about Simon. He's just working things out."

"Thanks for calling, Malcolm. You really put my mind at ease. And good luck with the record deal. I know it's going to happen for you."

"You sound more confident than me."

"I know a winner when I see one," she said bluntly. "Just don't forget where you came from when you make it to the big time. Some brothas develop a serious case of color blindness after that first million."

"You don't have to worry about me selling out. I prefer my coffee black, no sugar, no cream," I said, laughing.

• • •

When I walked out of the jetway, there was a short elderly black man holding up a sign with my name on it.

"I'm Malcolm Tremell," I told him.

"Hello, Mr. Tremell, I'm your driver, Otis. May I take your bag?"

"But I didn't order a limo."

"Your agent, Jerry Cross, thought it would be a nice surprise."

"In that case, here!" I handed him my heavy garment bag. "Lead on, Otis."

By the time we made it outside, it had begun to drizzle. Otis pulled out a tiny umbrella and handed it to me. I tried my best to cover the both of us from the rain but we were moving too fast. Once we were at the limousine he hurried to open my door.

"I'm sure you'll like the car, Mr. Tremell. Your agent ordered this one especially for you," he said, smiling.

"Especially for me, huh? I'm beginning to like this celebrity lifestyle already," I said as I stepped inside.

No sooner did the door shut than someone yelled out, "Surprise!" It was Toni. She was wearing a sexy short black dress and holding two glasses of champagne. I almost knocked them out of her hands as I leaned over to give her a hug.

"Surprise is right! When did you get back from Europe?"

"I flew in late last night. I wanted to call you but Jerry and I had this planned for weeks," she said as she kissed me. "I wanted to be here to celebrate with you just in case the deal went through. I hope you don't mind."

"There's no one else in the world I would rather share this moment with than you."

When we pulled apart from hugging, she noticed the gash on my forehead—the one from Tina's high-heeled shoe.

"Oh, Malcolm, what happened!"

"It's no big deal. A guy scratched me while I was playing ball."

"Are you sure you're okay, baby?" she asked in a motherly tone.

"I'm fine, Toni. So, where is Jerry now?" I was trying to change the subject.

"We're supposed to meet him at ten o'clock at a club in Manhattan called the Ritz. It's a popular hangout for black professionals. In the meantime, let's get our private celebration started."

She handed me a glass of champagne, dimmed the interior lights, and slid in a Lauryn Hill CD. As the song "Nothing Even Matters" played softly in the background, she lifted her glass to make a toast.

"Here's to you, Malcolm. May God bless you with all the success you deserve."

"No, here's to you," I rebutted. "Because there's no amount of success or money in the world that can replace the value you have in my life."

Her eyes became filled with tears as we clinked glasses and took a sip. But the taste of the champagne and the moment was bittersweet because I had told another lie. Deep in my heart I knew all my lies would come back to haunt me. Lies always do.

Chapter 34

It was raining heavily by the time we arrived at the Ritz nightclub in Manhattan. Otis pulled up as close as he could to the club and escorted us to the door with the small umbrella.

"I'll be parked across the street," he said. "Just step outside when you're ready to go."

"You can take a long nap, Otis," Toni said. "I'm in a party mood tonight!"

The moment we walked inside the club I could feel the walls vibrating. The song "Just Be Good to Me" by the SOS Band was playing and the dance floor was crowded with well-dressed black folks getting their groove on.

"This place is off the hook!" I shouted over the music.

"Yeah, I know. This used to be my regular hangout," she said. "Eric and I used to come here once a month for Old School Friday."

"You and Eric, huh?"

"I'm sorry, sweetheart, I didn't mean to bruise your ego," she said playfully. "I know how territorial men can be."

"I'm not one of those insecure men who gets jealous over ex-boyfriends," I said, getting defensive. "I wouldn't mind running into him tonight to say hello."

"Oh, no. I made sure he was out of town before I made reservations. I didn't want to take any chances on you two bumping heads tonight. Once that testosterone kicks in, it's all over."

"What does your former fiancé do for a living, anyway?"

"He tells rich people how to invest their money. As a matter of fact, he's at a convention in Los Angeles this week," she told me. "I'm surprised you two haven't crossed paths as often as he's in L.A. I think you would have a lot to talk about considering you have so much in common."

"Like what?"

"Both of you are very intelligent, attractive, and arrogant."

"Who me? Arrogant?"

"Malcolm, you love attention. I saw you flirting with your eyes the minute we walked in the door," she said, laughing.

I was getting ready to say something to defend myself but she cut me off.

"But it's okay, honey. You don't have to explain. I know it's a horrible disease and you can't help yourself," she said, laughing. "As long as you look and don't touch, I won't have to show the ghetto side of me."

She gave me a peck on the cheek and grabbed me by the hand.

"Now let's go find our table so I can set my purse down," she continued. "I'm going to wear your butt out on the dance floor tonight."

I was speechless. She read me like a book from cover to

cover. It was the first time I saw that homegirl side of her and I liked it. I liked it a lot.

The hostess escorted us over to our table, which overlooked the huge oval dance floor. Toni didn't waste any time taking off her shoes and dragging me out onto the floor. I guess she thought she was going to show me up, being a professional dancer and all. But what she didn't realize was that I was from the Southside of Chicago and I could party with the best of them. When the deejay mixed in the song "Shame" by Evelyn "Champagne" King, I took her to school.

"Come on, baby, show me what you got!" I said, while dancing circles around her.

"All right, Malcolm. Don't make me embarrass your old ass out here in front of all these people."

"I ain't scared of you, Ms. Ballerina. Come on with it."

Why did I go and say that? Toni broke out into a move right out of the movie *Flashdance*. She kicked her leg straight up over her head, did a pirouette, and came down into a split. I took a hard swallow and looked around to see if anybody saw her. They did!

"You go, girl!" the woman next to us shouted.

"Damn, did you see that?" the man on the other side yelled out.

The deejay must have known Toni personally because he got on the microphone and gave her a shout-out.

"Ms. Antoinette Grayson is in the house tonight, ladies and gentlemen. It's show time!"

The deejay mixed in "Bad Girls" by Donna Summer and the dance floor parted like the Red Sea. Before I knew it, I was standing alone in the middle of the floor with a professional dance machine. And she was making me look bad, too, spinning and sliding all over the place like she was on Broadway.

"Okay, sweetheart, you made your point," I whispered. "Can I please get the hell out of here now?"

"Not yet," she said, laughing. "One more song."

"You know you're wrong for this, don't you?"

"Yeah, I know. But you're secure enough to handle it," she said, laughing.

We danced for another song then we walked off the floor to a standing ovation. When we sat down at the table, I was drenched.

"Remind me to pay you for that lesson," I said, while wiping my face with a stack of napkins.

"You can write me a check after you see the private show I have planned for you at the hotel tonight."

The seductive look in her eyes gave me an immediate erection. If she had half as much energy in bed as she did on the dance floor, I was in for a long night.

"Look, I need to go to the bathroom to wash my arrogant face," I told her. "Do you want to go to the ladies' room while I watch the table?"

"I'm fine," she said, looking cool. "I haven't broken a sweat yet."

"Show off!" I said, walking toward the men's room.

When I arrived at the men's room, it was full of stuffy brothers smoking cigars. It was torturous listening to them bragging about their new cars and how much their homes cost. The most annoying of them all was a proper-talking jerk who was louder than everyone else. I wasn't halfway into the rest room and I could hear his big mouth.

"I wonder how the poor black folks are living," he said, laughing conceitedly.

"Yeah, those lazy niggas in the hood are probably drinking forty ounces right now," another man said.

"Well, let's make a toast to the brothas who couldn't be here," the loud one slurred.

I tried to ignore their snobbish comments while I took a pee, but it wasn't easy. The guy with the loud mouth wouldn't shut up for one minute. And the more he spoke the more familiar he began to sound. I knew I had heard his voice somewhere before, but I couldn't place him.

After I finished relieving myself, I maneuvered my way over to the sink to wash my hands. I damn near fell out when I saw who the loud mouth was. It was the same high-yellow negro from the Fox Theatre in Atlanta. When he saw my reflection, he recognized me right away. I intentionally stood right next to him while I squirted my hands with soap.

I could tell he and his drunk buddies had just arrived because they were wiping the rain from their jackets. I smiled back at him through the mirror, daring him to say something smart. He was one of those Uncle Tom negroes who needed a good ass whippin' and I was ready to oblige him, outnumbered or not. But surprisingly he didn't say a word. He just kept looking at me with that silly-ass expression on his face until I walked out. "Punk motherfucker," I said loud enough for him to hear.

When I made it back over to the table, Toni was signing autographs for her adoring fans. I just stood back and admired the way she handled the flirtatious men as they tried to mack her down for her number. She was so smooth and poised that they hardly realized they were being rejected. After a couple of minutes passed, I went to break up the party.

Ahem. I cleared my throat to announce my arrival.

"Hey, sweetheart." She sprang up from her seat to give me a kiss. That was her way of demonstrating that she belonged to me. Like I said, she was smooth. It wasn't long before the vultures began to scatter. Men can sense when another man's game is tight.

"So, are you having a good time tonight?" she asked, while sitting on my lap.

"As long as I'm with you, every night is a good time."

"Well, I promise you it's going to get even better. I have a big surprise for you when we get to the hotel."

"You're not a transsexual, are you?"

"No, silly. I was referring to your career."

"Speaking of my career, I'll be glad when Mr. Cross

gets here so I can find out what happened at the meeting. I'm getting impatient."

"Well, that's the surprise, Mr. Cross is . . ."

Suddenly a man walked up from behind us and stood still. Toni looked over my shoulder to see who it was. When she saw his face, she sprang up from my lap.

"Eric, what are you doing here?" she asked.

"You know I come here on Friday nights," he said. "The question is what are you doing here?"

"I'm here with Malcolm," she said proudly.

I played it cool and continued to face the dance floor. I recognized Eric's voice as the loud mouth from the bathroom and didn't have shit to say to him.

"So this is the man you left me for, huh?" Eric said. "He doesn't seem to be the sociable type."

"Hello, and good-bye," I said in a deep, angry voice.

"Aw, don't be like that, brother," he said with perfect diction. "I just want to meet the man who stole my woman."

"First of all, I'm not your brother. Second, I can't steal what you never possessed. Now for the last time, good-bye!"

"You can't talk to me like that." He grabbed me by the shoulder and spun me around. "I'll be damned, it's you!"

"You know each other?" Toni asked.

"Oh, I know him all right," Eric said. "I saw him in Atlanta at the Fox Theatre. And I saw him last week at the Marriott in Los Angeles. That's when I found out that he was a . . ."

I grabbed Eric's arm and twisted it behind his back before he could finish his sentence. "Thanks for giving me a reason to fuck you up!" I whispered in his ear. Then I smashed Eric's face into the table. The music suddenly stopped and all eyes were on us.

"Malcolm, stop!" Toni yelled.

"How does it feel, Mr. Big Shot? You got something to say to the poor black folks in the ghetto now?"

Eric's nose was broken and blood was dripping everywhere. His friends came to rescue him. When they tried to swing at me, I used Eric as a shield. Shortly after, the security guards rushed over to break us up.

"Malcolm, what's gotten into you?" Toni cried.

"I'll tell you what's gotten into him," Eric said. "He's a fucking prostitute!"

"You shut your damn mouth before I shut it for you!" I was trying to get my hands on Eric but the muscular security guards were holding me back.

"What are you saying, Eric?"

"I'm trying to tell you that your man is a professional gigolo. He was at the Marriott last Friday arguing with one of his tricks. I've got pictures of her throwing a shoe at him," he said while staring at me with a smirk on his face. "That's probably how he got that scar on his forehead."

Toni took one look into my eyes and knew Eric was telling the truth. She walked over to me and slapped me right in the face.

"How could you lie to me, Malcolm?" she said with tears in her eyes. "I believed in you." She picked up her purse off the floor and went over to help Eric.

"Toni, please wait! I can explain."

"There is no way to explain a lie between a man and the woman he's supposed to respect and cherish." She wiped her eyes with her hand. "I thought you were something special but you're nothing more than a high-priced hoe."

"Do you wanna press any charges?" the security guard asked Eric.

"No, he's already paid the ultimate price. Let him suffer."

The security guards waited until Eric and Toni were long gone, then they escorted me to the front door and tossed me onto the wet pavement. Otis must have seen what had happened because he sped over in the limo.

"Mr. Tremell, you all right?" he asked as he jumped out of the car.

I didn't bother to answer him. I just sat on the ground

in the pouring rain feeling numb. My expensive suit was getting soaked but I didn't give a damn.

"Mr. Tremell, please," Otis said, standing over me with the umbrella.

I didn't want to give that old man a heart attack, so I got up for his sake and stepped inside the car. Once Otis was inside, he let down the divider and handed me a white envelope.

"Ms. Grayson told me to give this to you."

In the upper left-hand corner it read Columbia Records. I began to open it then I suddenly stopped.

"Otis, where is Jerry Cross? And why did he rent this car and not show up tonight?"

"I wasn't supposed to tell you this, but Ms. Grayson rented the car."

Everything was beginning to make sense. I opened the envelope and found what I expected. It was a recording contract. I read the section under agent fees, but there was no name. That's when I realized that there was no such person as Jerry Cross. Toni had negotiated the deal herself. That was her surprise.

I put my head in my hands, disgusted with myself. Toni had made my lifelong dream come true and I rewarded her with a broken heart.

"Mr. Tremell, you okay?"

"No, I'm not okay, Otis. I'm pretty fucked up," I said, trying to regain my composure. "Let's get out of here."

"Where to?"

"Take me back to the airport."

"But there are no flights out to Los Angeles until six o'clock tomorrow morning."

"Good! That should give me plenty of time to figure out how I messed up the best thing that ever happened to me."

Ironically, the Lauryn Hill CD was still playing on the stereo. As we drove off into the dreary night, the lyrics to the song "Ex-Factor" were hitting home.

It could all be so simple, but you'd rather make it hard.
Loving you is like a battle, and we both end up with
scars.
Tell me who I have to be, to get some reciprocity. . . .

I knew reciprocity meant a mutual and honest exchange.
To give and get, to do for, and to feel. Something I was
unwilling or unable to do. And my selfishness had cost me
dearly. Maybe this whole thing was meant to happen, I was
thinking. Maybe it's God's way of telling me I didn't
deserve Toni after all.

PART VI

Submission

Chapter 35

It was just after two o'clock when Simon arrived at Club Obsession. Two weeks had passed since the incident at the church and he was ready to get back to work. When he drove around back to open the gates, three trucks were already backed against the dock making deliveries. He was wondering who was signing for the orders because he didn't recognize the Chrysler Sebring convertible parked in the manager's space.

"Take those crab legs to the kitchen!" he heard a woman shout. "And you, don't forget to replace those beer kegs in the upstairs bar."

It was Ariel. She was bossing the deliverymen around, as usual. Simon crept alongside the truck and picked up a large box of shrimp off the dock. He concealed his face with it and carried it inside. When he got close to Ariel, he deliberately stumbled and almost knocked her over.

"Hey, watch where you're going, you idiot!"

"Sorry, about that, boss. This is my first day on the job," he said, trying not to laugh.

"You refer to me as Ms. Daniel, not boss, understand?"

"Okay, boss."

"Oh, I see we've got a smart-ass," Ariel said. "Get back to work before I call your supervisor."

Simon moved the box from his face and burst out laughing.

"It's you!" she shouted as she dropped her clipboard. "I've been worried sick about you?" She threw her arms around his neck and kissed him on the lips.

Simon was stunned but he quickly recovered. He wrapped his arm around Ariel's small waist and pulled her closer to him. Both their eyes were closed tight and their hearts raced. It was more than a kiss between friends, it was passionate. Just as Simon began caressing Ariel's butt, she pushed away.

"I'm sorry," she said, trying to compose herself. "That was way out of line."

"You're right." Simon said, clearing his throat. "And I apologize for touching you on the . . . you know."

Ariel smiled nervously. She picked up the clipboard from the floor and began counting the cases on the dock like nothing had happened.

"So, where have you been?"

"I went home to Chicago. I needed time to meditate and think things over."

"Have you heard from Cynthia?"

"No, but her mother called and left a nasty message on my answering machine," Simon said, laughing. "I've never heard an old woman use so much profanity."

"I can't say that I blame her after what happened."

"Excuse me!"

"Never mind, Simon," she said, backing off. "This is none of my business."

"No, speak your mind. I wanna hear what you have to say."

"Simon, you embarrassed that woman on live TV. They replayed that video on *Nightline, Dateline NBC,* and *BET Tonight.* It created a nationwide controversy about infidelity in the black church. Now, don't get me wrong, it was about time somebody exposed these no-good preachers who use their positions to take advantage of women. But Cynthia was just your girlfriend, not your wife. Infidelity was no excuse for destroying her career. Because of what you did, she'll never work in television again. Never!"

"What the hell did you expect me to do, Ariel?" Simon said, getting upset. "I was hurt!"

"You should've simply let her go," she said calmly as she took him by the hand. "And counted your blessings that you found out before you married her."

Simon's first impulse was to lash out but Ariel had expressed herself so eloquently he had to submit. Not only had he ruined Cynthia's career but he jeopardized his own by abandoning his business for two weeks. If it weren't for Ariel holding things together, thousands of dollars would have been lost and his employees would have gone without paychecks.

"Sometimes it's hard for a man to admit when he's wrong," Simon said. "Thanks for telling me what I need to know instead of what I want to hear."

"No problem, boss. Now let me get back to work. It's Ladies' Night tonight and you know how crowded it gets when Teddy performs."

Ariel tried to walk away but Simon grabbed her by the arm.

"Oh no you don't! It was no coincidence that I came back today." He pulled a card out his suit pocket and handed it to her. "Happy birthday."

"You remembered," she screamed. "Thank you, thank you, thank you!"

"Now give me that clipboard and take your butt home. You've got the next two nights off."

"You mean it?"

"Yeah, I think I can run this place without you for a couple of nights."

"Thank you, Simon. You're the most decent man I know," she said as she kissed him softly on the cheek. "One day you'll find a woman who truly deserves you."

Ariel ran to her car screaming like a kid on the last day of school. Simon just shook his head as he watched her from the dock. She threw her purse into the car and rolled down the windows ready to get her groove on.

"Hey, birthday girl!" Simon yelled out. "What happened to the Benz?"

"It's in the shop. Some fool sliced my tires last week," she told him. "I just hope it wasn't that fool Lawrence trippin' again."

Chapter 36

Ariel was playing "Femininity" by Eric Benet while she got ready for her date with Raymond at the Shark Bar. She danced provocatively in the mirror as she combed her short Afro then slipped into her fitted white dress. "Just like wine, you keep getting better with time," she said with conceit. It was her thirtieth birthday, a landmark in a woman's life, and she wanted it to be memorable. On the way home, she stopped by Fredrick's of Hollywood to pick up a pair of handcuffs, massage gels, and a white teddy with garter straps for that whorish look. Raymond was staying overnight for the first time and she wanted to try something kinky.

By six-thirty she was dressed to kill. She sprayed her neck, wrists, and crotch with perfume and headed for the door. Before she could turn the knob, the phone rang. She was hoping it wasn't her mother calling to lecture her again about dating a married man. They hadn't spoken in weeks and Ariel wasn't in the mood to argue. "Please God, not on my birthday," she prayed.

"Hello?"

"Hello, stranger, this is Chris. I just called to wish you a happy birthday."

"That's very sweet of you, Chris. Thanks for remembering." She tried to sound cordial but she was looking down at her watch anxious to leave.

"Did you get the present I sent you?"

"Yes, I did. I meant to call you to say thanks but things have been hectic at the club lately. I'm sure you understand?"

"No, I don't," he said abruptly.

"Look, Chris, I don't have time to get into this right now. I'm late for a date. Can we talk about this later?"

He paused for a moment to collect himself. Then he stopped beating around the bush and said what he really wanted to say.

"Look, Ariel, there's no need for us to talk later. I spend two hours walking around the mall to buy you something special for your birthday and you didn't even have the common courtesy to call and say thank you," he said to her.

"Now, wait one damned minute!"

"No, you wait!" Chris said, cutting her off. "I may not have a master's degree or a fancy car but I do have a good heart. I know that doesn't mean very much in this materialistic-ass world but that's all I have to offer, that, and my friendship," he said, sounding dejected. "Now, I'm not going to take up any more of your valuable time, Ms. Daniels. Have a happy birthday. And I hope you find whatever it is that you're looking for." Then he hung up.

Ariel stood there with the dial tone ringing in her ear. It was bad enough that her mother was on her case. Now mild-mannered Chris was telling her off. But she knew she had it coming. She hadn't returned his calls in more than three weeks. Not even to say thank you for the gift.

The same gift that was still sitting on her dining room table unopened.

• • •

The Shark Bar was unusually crowded for a Thursday night. Ariel had to wait in line fifteen minutes just to get to the hostess. She was livid when she found out that Raymond had forgotten to call in their reservation. The wait for a table was almost forty-five minutes.

Ariel went over to the bar and ordered a Long Island iced tea to kill time until Raymond showed up. He was supposed to meet her at 7:00 P.M. But it was already 7:35 and he still hadn't shown up. "I did hundreds of sit-ups to fit into this tight-ass dress and he has the nerve not to show up on time to appreciate it," she said to herself. But her tight dress didn't go unnoticed by the men at the bar. They were gawking at her large breasts and round ass like she was a piece of meat.

It was the kind of attention Ariel didn't find flattering. She was careful not to dress too provocatively unless she was on a date with a secure man. Raymond had abandoned her in a den of wolves. And she knew it was only a matter of time before they drank up enough courage to come over to get their mack on. As usual, the young hip-hop types were the most aggressive.

"Excuse me, sweetheart. Can I buy you a drink?" a young man asked. He was wearing a bright orange jacket and had a gold tooth with the initial *M* engraved in it.

"No, thank you. I'm waiting on someone," she said politely.

"Well, if you change your mind, I'll be over there with my posse." He whipped out a business card and handed it to her. "My name is Marcus, but they call me Milk Dud."

"Okay, Mr. Dud," Ariel said, trying not to laugh. "Thanks for the offer."

Ariel put the card in her purse knowing it was going straight in the garbage. When she was younger, she would get into long discussions about why she couldn't accept a man's card. But as she matured, she realized the best thing to do was take the card and get rid of him. Besides, some men could become verbally abusive and violent toward women when they got dissed in front of their boys. She wasn't taking any chances on having any drama, especially not on her birthday.

By eight o'clock Ariel was furious. Raymond still hadn't arrived to rescue her from the knuckleheads who were circling her like vultures. One of her biggest pet peeves was promptness. As far as she was concerned, nothing short of death was excusable. When the hostess called out her reservation, she excused herself and went over to be seated. She was determined to enjoy her evening and have a nice dinner, even if it meant doing it alone.

Just as the hostess was leading her to her table, Raymond came rushing in. He waved his arms to get her attention. He was dressed very dapperly in a sharp dark blue suit and tie. Ariel made eye contact with him then turned her head and kept walking. She knew he would follow her over and she wanted to make his trip as uncomfortable as possible. Once they were alone at the table, Raymond gave her a kiss on the cheek and poured on the old charm.

"Baby, I can't tell you how sorry I am for being late. My wife was supposed to pick the girls up from dance class but she had to work overtime. I ran every red light on Peachtree Street trying to get here on time," he said, sounding sincere. "Please give me a chance to make it up to you."

Ariel couldn't help blushing whenever she looked into Raymond's light brown eyes. He was a pretty boy: six feet tall, light brown skin, wavy hair, athletic build, the whole nine, not usually her type. She preferred her men dark chocolate. But the dick was good and he had a deep, sexy voice. Not soft and squeaky like so many corporate black men she dated in Atlanta. Raymond could make her wet just by calling to say hello. But wet panties and all, she was still disappointed. It was the fifth time in the last month he was either late for a date or had to cancel.

"I'm getting sick and tired of you showing up late for our dates, Raymond" she said angrily. "If it's not the kids, it's one of your patients. It's always something!"

"Look, Ariel, I told you up front that my career and family came first," he said sternly. "I'm still a married man and a father and that means I have responsibilities. Now if you can't handle that, maybe we need to stop seeing each other."

Ariel wanted to tell him to go to hell. She wasn't accustomed to playing the role of the other woman. But she swallowed her pride because it was her birthday and she was horny as hell. Raymond hadn't given her any sex in almost two weeks and she needed some maintenance.

"Okay, I forgive you, this time," she said. "So are you still spending the night?"

"I can stay for a while, but I've got to get up early in the morning."

"For what?"

"I rushed out of the house and forgot to bring an extra set of clothes for work."

"I don't appreciate all these last-minute changes, Raymond. I may be your woman on the side but I have needs."

Raymond was facing the front of the restaurant. Ariel noticed he kept looking over her shoulder toward the door. She didn't pay it much attention until he did it a second and third time.

"Are you expecting somebody?"

"No, I thought I saw someone I knew," he said unconvincingly. Then he tried to change the subject. "Look, why don't we skip dinner and go to your place. That way we can spend more time together."

"But I'm starving! And I spent a lot of time getting myself together to come out tonight. Which reminds me, you haven't even complimented me on my dress."

"You look great, Ariel," he said, looking toward the door again. "When we get to your place, you can model it for me."

Suddenly there was a commotion outside. Ariel heard what sounded like a windshield being smashed in. Not long after, a woman came barging into the front door dragging two little girls along with her. Judging by the expression on Raymond's face, Ariel knew who it was.

"Just stay calm and let me handle this," Raymond said nervously.

The woman spotted Ariel and Raymond sitting at the corner table and stormed toward them, knocking over trays of food on her way. When she got up to the table, she walked right up to Raymond and smacked the shit out of him.

"How dare you!" she yelled.

"Calm down, sweetheart. I can explain."

"You can't explain a goddamn thing, you two-timing bastard. I know who this bitch is!"

Ariel held her tongue to avoid escalating the situation.

"I slave around that house all day raising your kids and washing your dirty-ass drawers. I'll be damned if you're going to disrespect me by bringing one of your hoes out in public."

"Who you calling a hoe, you fat heifer?"

Raymond's wife was a big woman and a strong one. She grabbed a bowl of peach cobbler à la mode off the table next to her and smashed it into Ariel's face. When Ariel tried to retaliate, she gave her a right cross and sent Ariel flying over the table.

"Take that, you slut!" she yelled. "Maybe next time you'll think twice before you fuck with a married man."

The women in the restaurant just stared—not even the female staff made an effort to help Ariel to her feet. It was as if they had vented their own frustrations for all the conniving other women in Atlanta. It was a town notorious for backstabbing women who celebrated the role of being mistresses. On that night Ariel was the scapegoat.

As Raymond's wife stormed out of the door with her girls in tow, there was muffled applause. No one called the police or even tried to stop her.

"I'm sorry about all this, Ariel," Raymond said as he picked her up.

"Just get away from me, Raymond. Go home to your wife."

With peach cobbler running down her face and onto her brand-new dress, Ariel calmly put two hundred dollars on the table for the damages and walked out. When she got out to her car, the windshield was smashed on the passenger's side and the antenna was broken. What was most embarrassing were the words *Home Wrecker* spray-painted on the hood and both doors. The bold red letters were accentuated against the white surface of the car.

Ariel didn't even react, not outwardly anyway. She got inside the car and drove off as most of the patrons in the Shark Bar looked on. She held up pretty well until she made it to North Druid Hill Road on 85. Then she broke down. When she looked at her face in the rearview mirror, she cried even harder. She had a deep cut below her left eye, and her top lip was busted. "That's what you get, stupid!" she said to herself.

After she wiped off her face, she pulled out her cell phone to call her best friend. She needed someone to talk to.

"Hello, Mama, it's me," Ariel said, crying.

"Baby, what's wrong?"

"Mama, I'm sorry. You were right. You were right about everything."

"We don't need to talk about that right now, sweetheart. Are you all right?"

"I'll be fine. Nothing that a dry cleaner and a bandage won't fix," she said, laughing.

"Why don't you come over and I'll pour us a glass of wine. We can stay up all night and talk like we used to. Remember?"

"Yeah, I remember, Mama," Ariel said with a smile on her face. "But there's something I have to do. Can I take a rain check for tomorrow night?"

"Sure you can, sweetheart," she said in that motherly tone. "But what are you about to do, if you don't mind me being nosy."

"I'm going to pick up a Blockbuster video and a bag of popcorn, and go visit Chris," she said. "I realized the hard way that what I'm missing in my life is not a husband, but a man who is truly a friend."

Chapter 37

It was 9:00 P.M. Ladies' Night at Club Obsession was going strong. Teddy and his dance group, Hot Chocolate, were putting on their best show ever. The room was wall to wall with enthusiastic women buying alcohol like it was going out of style. The restaurant was crowded, too. The kitchen sold out of buffalo wings and fried shrimp before the show began. It was the most successful night since the grand opening.

But Simon was in no mood to celebrate. He locked himself in his office with a bottle of cognac trying to think through his issues. Usually he would call Malcolm and talk about his problems. But since the incident in New York, they hadn't spoken much. Malcolm was still recovering from losing Toni. And although he tried to act as if it was no big deal, Simon knew he was devastated. Malcolm had not been so withdrawn since his father died.

The conversation with Ariel was also weighing on his mind. He never considered how his actions at the church would affect Cynthia's career. He only wanted revenge, not to destroy her livelihood. "What the hell have I done?" he asked himself as he stared at the large poster of Cynthia hanging on the wall behind his desk. The same poster he refused to take down and throw away. After all the trouble he went through to get even, he was still in love with her.

As he took another sip of cognac to quiet his conscience, there was a knock at the door.

"Who is it?" Simon yelled.

"Mr. Harris, come quick!" a waitress said frantically. "The police are arresting Teddy!"

Simon could hear the commotion as he made his way toward the front of the club. Women were booing and tossing paper plates at the two sheriff's deputies who were making the arrest. Simon hurried over to see what the deal was.

"Excuse me, officers, I'm the owner, Simon Harris. What seems to be the problem?"

"There's no problem," one of the deputies said. "Mr. Teddy Bear here is under arrest."

"This is bullshit, Mr. Harris. I'm innocent!" Teddy yelled. Besides the police handcuffs, all he had on was a leopard-print thong.

"Do you mind telling me what the charge is?"

"Contempt of court. He failed to appear in court after refusing to pay his child support."

A group of nosy women standing nearby overheard their conversation and quickly spread the word. It wasn't long before all the boos were focused on Teddy.

"Don't just stand there, Mr. Harris, say something," Teddy said as the policemen led him away.

"You're fired!" Simon yelled.

The police escorted Teddy out of the club as fast as they could for his own protection. Women were cursing him out and spitting in his face as he walked by.

"I hope they put your trifling butt under the jail, you deadbeat," a woman hollered.

Teddy was finished as a stripper in Atlanta. By Monday morning Simon knew Teddy's business would be all over the radio airwaves, Kiss 104, V103, and Hot 97.5.

Simon took advantage of the situation and closed the club. He refunded everyone's money and sent the employees home. It didn't matter to him that the club was a mess. He just wanted to be alone. Within thirty minutes, the club was deserted.

After he locked the doors, Simon put on his Heatwave CD and mixed himself a stiff Barcardi rum and Coke. While he listened to the smooth melody of "Star of a Story," he leaned back in a chair and propped his feet up onto the bar. "Ah, that's more like it," he said as he took a long sip.

Just as he was getting his relaxation on, there was a loud knock at the door. "Now what?" he said in disgust. As he went to answer the door, he was hoping it was Ariel. Although he wanted to be alone, he could finally finish giving her lessons on how to step, Chicago style. But when he peeked out the side window he didn't see Ariel's car. Instead there was a black Range Rover parked out front. It was Cynthia's.

He pulled the shades back on the doors and there she was, in a pair of dingy blue jeans, a T-shirt, and a Atlanta Falcons cap. She looked pitiful. Her eyes were red and puffy. He could tell that she'd been crying. She also seemed to have put on a little weight, especially in the face and arms. Simon thought about going to get his pistol just in case she turned fatal, but he decided not to. Cynthia was a no-good cheater but Simon doubted that she had turned murderous, too. As he unlocked the door to let her in, he could already feel the tension in the air.

"What do you want?" Simon asked before she could get into the door good.

"Don't worry, I'm not going to stay long. I just wanted

to tell you to your face how sorry I am for what happened."

"Apology accepted. Now, good-bye!" Simon said, sounding cold.

"How can you talk to me like that, Simon, after all we've been through?"

"It's easy, all I have to do is think about you screwing that phony preacher. By the way, where is your spiritual maintenance man?"

"For your information, I haven't seen him since that Sunday."

"Now why does that not surprise me?" Simon said sarcastically. "I thought you two would be in a big house in the suburbs with a white picket fence living happily ever after."

"Fuck you, Simon!"

"No, fuck you!" Simon yelled. "I trusted you and you went behind my back and lay down with another man. Not once, not twice, but several times. And you expect me to be sympathetic. Hell no!"

"What about you, Mr. Big-Shot Club Owner. When did you ever pay any attention to me?" she yelled back. "You've been cheating on me for three years with your damned business. Everything revolved around work. And when you finally came home, you were tired. I needed someone who was there for me, Simon. To hold me, tell me I was beautiful, and make passionate love to me," she said as tears rolled down her cheeks. "I'm not superwoman, goddammit. I need attention!"

Simon wanted to run over to her and hold her in his arms. He was in just as much pain as she was but his pride wouldn't allow him to show it.

"Is that all you have to say?" he asked callously. "I've got work to do."

"Fine, Simon. If that's the way you want it. Here, take it!"

She pulled the engagement ring off her finger and threw it at him. "But before I go, I want you to know that I never loved James. He was just a substitute for the man that I love."

Cynthia wiped the tears from her eyes with her hand then turned toward the door. But before she walked out, Simon yelled, "So, when is the baby due?"

Cynthia stopped dead in her tracks.

"How did you know?" she asked, while still facing the door.

"I have two sistahs who were teenaged mothers. And ten waitresses as employees. Didn't you think I would recognize when you had morning sickness?"

"The baby is due in April," she said, softly.

"Do you know whose it is?"

Cynthia took a deep breath as she turned to face him.

"To be honest with you, Simon, I don't know. But it doesn't matter. I'm putting it up for adoption after it's born. I'm not going to shame myself or my family any further by trying to raise a child without a father. Now if you're through breaking me down, I'm going to leave. Good-bye!" she said, crying.

"Wait, Cynthia!"

Before she could get inside her car, Simon chased her down and brought her back inside the club. Without saying a word, he cleared the chairs off the dance floor and turned up the volume on his Heatwave CD. He forwarded it to the song "Always and Forever" and led Cynthia out onto the floor.

"Simon, what are you doing?"

"What I should've done a long time ago," he whispered in her ear. "Giving you the love and attention that you need."

Chapter 38

It was just after 10:00 A.M. when Ms. Ruby rushed into my bedroom nearly hysterical.

"Malcolm, wake up!" she yelled as she shook me violently.

"What's wrong?"

"It's Melvin. He had a heart attack!"

I sprangout of my bed in one motion and began searching through my closet for something quick to slip into. I pulled out a wrinkled pair of blue jeans and a Malcolm X T-shirt.

"When did this happen?"

"About eight this morning. Scottie found him lying on the bathroom floor at his home. The ambulance had just arrived when he called."

"Why didn't you wake me sooner?" I asked, angrily.

"I turned off the ringer when I came in this morning," she said as tears began to pour down her brown cheeks. "I was only trying to make sure you weren't disturbed."

I felt like a heel for yelling at her. She was just as concerned as I was. She knew how much Melvin meant to me. I took a deep breath to calm myself down, then I walked over and put my arms around her.

"I'm sorry for snapping at you, Ms. Ruby," I told her. "Did Scottie mention which hospital they were taking him to?"

"King/Drew Medical Center in Compton."

"Was Melvin still breathing?"

"He didn't say."

"I want you to try to calm down," I said as I gave her a kiss on the forehead. "I'll call you from the hospital as soon as I know something."

I grabbed my car keys and cell phone off the kitchen counter and hurried out the door. My heart was racing one hundred miles an hour as I rode the elevator down to the lobby. The thought of losing what had become the most important man in my life again was unbearable. I frantically dialed Scottie's number trying to get through but there was no answer. "Pick up, goddammit!" I yelled. The people riding with me on the elevator were staring at me like I was going crazy. But I didn't give a damn. I needed to know if Melvin were still alive.

• • •

The emergency room at King Drew was a madhouse. Doctors and nurses scrambled to stabilize four gunshot victims, all young children no older then ten years old.

"Another drive by," I heard one nurse say. "And it's not even sundown yet. It's going to be a busy weekend."

"They don't call this place Killer King for nothing," another replied.

The sweltering Los Angeles heat had a way of increasing the body count in the black community. Although it was mid-September it was more than ninety degrees. After the commotion died down, I approached the nurse at the receptionist's desk. She was a crabby old white woman wearing wire-framed glasses.

"Excuse me, nurse. I'm looking for a patient who was brought in earlier this morning. His name is Melvin Butler."

She held up her index finger, indicating that she wanted me to wait until she had finished gossiping on the phone. I stood there for another minute or so trying to be courteous, but when she continued to ignore me, I snapped.

"Excuse me!" I said much louder. "Would you please get your ass off the phone and give me some assistance."

I must have scared her to death because she slammed the phone down and gave me her undivided attention.

"When was he admitted?" she asked, looking up at me timidly through her wire-framed glasses.

"This morning about nine o'clock."

"Here he is," she pointed out to me on the computer screen. "He's in intensive care."

"Which way is it?"

"Just go down that corridor and turn left."

Scottie was standing in the waiting room talking with the doctor. When I approached him, he turned and gave me a hug.

"How is he?" I asked the doctor.

"Not good. He had a hemorrhagic stroke, which means he has internal bleeding in the heart," he explained. "I'm sorry, there's nothing we can do."

"I need to see him," I said.

"No one is allowed to see him except his immediate family."

"I am the immediate family, goddammit! Now take me to him!"

Scottie waited in the hall while the doctor escorted me to Melvin's room. It was hard for me to see him lying there so helpless with all those tubes and electrodes attached to his body.

"Can you please give me a moment alone?"

"No problem, I'll be right outside," the doctor said.

I stood over the bed and held Melvin's clammy hands. His face was pale and his breathing was weak. I fought back the tears hoping he would open his wrinkled old eyes and tell me one of his dirty jokes. He had been the closest thing I had to a father in twelve years and I was losing him. I felt so helpless.

Suddenly his grip tightened around my hand. He cleared his throat and tried to speak.

"Did you open the present I gave you?" he whispered.

"Not yet, old man, but I will as soon as I get you back home." I was trying to be cheerful. "Did you get my message about my deal with Columbia Records."

"Yeah, I got it. Congratulations. I knew you would be a big star someday."

"Hey, slow down with all the hype. I haven't signed the contract yet."

"It's going to happen for you, Cool Breeze, because it's time. Just like it was time for you to meet that young lady," he said, sounding sure of himself. "I could tell by the way you talked about her that she was the one. You do love her, don't you?"

"Yes, I do," I told him. "She's everything I've ever wanted."

"I'm just glad I lived long enough to see you happy," he said as the tears welled up in his eyes. "Make sure you take good care of her. I don't want you to end up old and alone like me."

"You're not alone, I'm right here," I said as I watched him fade away. "Don't leave me, old man. I still need you!"

"Just remember, I'm proud of you, Malcolm. I've always loved you like my own son."

"And I've loved you as a father," I said, crying.

I held him in my arms as his eyes slowly shut. He took one last breath, then he was gone.

Chapter 39

The day of the funeral was dark and dreary, much like the day my father died. A light drizzle fell as the mile-long procession slowly made its way down Crenshaw Boulevard to the Inglewood Park Cemetery. The mayor himself would've been envious of the multitude of people who came out to pay their respects. Melvin was practically an institution in the black community and he was going to be dearly missed.

The reading of the eulogy took place underneath a small canvas tent. Only fifty or so people were able to stand out of the rain while the minister spoke words over Melvin's casket. I held hands with Scottie and the staff from the club, and we tried to comfort one another. Aside from a distant cousin, we were the only family Melvin had.

After the eulogy, we joined hands and sang "Amazing Grace." That was the toughest part of the service to get through. Everyone broke down crying, including the minister. But I held my tears for later, just like I did with my father. There were thoughts I wanted to share with Melvin that had to be shared alone.

As Melvin's casket was being lowered into the ground, we threw flowers on top of his ivory and gold-plated casket. It was our way of saying good-bye to a man who had been a father and a mentor to all of us. Once it was rested against the cold, dark ground, I threw in the first symbolic shovel of dirt. With every shovelful of dirt that fell, a part of my soul was being buried, too. "Rest in peace, old man," I said.

When the service was over, those who were outside the tent lined up to pay their last respects. There were at least two hundred people standing in the pouring rain waiting to lay down their floral wreaths and to bid Melvin a final good-bye. I had never seen such a show of devotion.

As the procession came to its end, I saw a familiar face. At first I thought my eyes were playing tricks on me. But after he laid down the bouquet of roses that were obscuring his face, I realized it was Simon. I had successfully held back my tears up until that point. But the moment we embraced, I let it all out.

"Déjà vu, huh, partner?" Simon said as we hugged.

"Yeah, déjà vu," I said. "How did you know I was here?"

"Ms. Ruby called me yesterday. I flew out of Atlanta this morning on the first available flight."

"I know I should've called you myself. But I didn't want to burden you. I know you have enough drama to deal with."

"If we weren't in a cemetery I would slap the hell out of you. I thought we were boys."

"You're right, Simon. I don't know why I'm trippin'," I told him. "My head hasn't been right for a while."

Simon waited outside while I received the last of the guests. Once they were all gone, I grabbed my umbrella and we took a short walk together. In a strange way it was the perfect reunion. Simon had been by my side to bury both my fathers. Having him there helped to alleviate some of the pain, just as it did twelve years before.

"So how are you holding up?" Simon asked.

"I'm hanging," I told him. "Although I've been through this before, it doesn't get any easier. Pain always feels brand-new, no matter how much experience you've had with it."

"Amen to that!" Simon said. "I've had all the pain I can handle for the next twenty years."

"Speaking of pain, you mind if I ask you a personal question?"

"Shoot!"

"Whatever happened to Cynthia?"

"I was hoping you wouldn't go there."

"Look, partner, we don't have to talk about it. I was just wondering how things worked out."

"I may as well tell you and get it over with. Cynthia's pregnant and we're getting married in Vegas next month," he said. "Now before you say anything . . ."

"Congratulations," I said, cutting him off.

"Excuse me?"

"I said congratulations. I wish you both all the best."

"I'm surprised you didn't try to talk me out of it, or ask whose baby it is."

"Who am I to criticize you or anybody else? My personal life is a disaster. I can't even go out on an appointment to get paid without my conscience kicking my ass," I said. "Would you believe I've been celibate for more than four weeks? That's the longest I've gone without sex since high school."

"Did Toni get that close to you?"

"Toni who? What are you talking about?"

"Don't try to run your game on me, Malcolm. I know you too well," he said. "And any blind man can see that you miss that woman. I'm sure Melvin saw it, too."

"Yeah, I miss her. But that page in my life has been turned."

"Listen to you trying to sound all hard. You ain't foolin'

nobody but yourself. Why don't you stop playing the role of big-time ladies' man and go after that woman. She loves you, you arrogant fool!"

I dropped the umbrella I was holding and grabbed Simon by the collar of his trench coat.

"Shut the fuck up! Shut up!" I yelled. "You have no idea what I'm feeling inside! There isn't an hour that goes by that I don't think about her. I can't even lie down with another woman without seeing her face. So don't you assume to know shit about me. I've got a heart, too, god-dammit!"

"Well, stop being so afraid and use it!" Simon said, pushing my hands away. "A good woman like Toni is not going to respond to your manipulating games. You have to be willing to be vulnerable and submit yourself to her the same way you want to be submitted to. Until you learn how to do that, you will always be alone. Alone or dead!"

Simon pulled a laminated piece of paper out of his coat pocket and handed to me. It was an article from the *Atlanta Journal Constitution.* The headline read LOCAL STRIPPER SHOT AND KILLED BY JEALOUS HUSBAND. I only had to read the first few lines to get the point. The man killed was Theodore Simmons. He was the stripper who worked at Club Obsession. He was shot in the head when a husband came home early and caught him in bed with his wife. Ironically, it was the same story of what happened to my father.

"There are no coincidences in life, Malcolm. Everything happens for a reason," Simon said. "You have to take advantage of all the hurt and pain in life and grow from it. I learned that lesson the hard way. And if your father or Melvin were alive they would tell you the exact same thing."

Simon had hit me over the head with a five-hundred-pound dose of reality. I walked down to the bench that was a few yards away and sat down. I didn't care that my umbrella had blown across the cemetery and I was getting soaked.

"I'll be damned!" I said, laughing nervously.

"What's so funny?" Simon asked as he came and sat down beside me.

"The student has finally become the teacher," I said. "I was trying to teach you the game and here I am breaking the cardinal rule in the *Player's Handbook.*"

"What's that?"

"Never fall in love."

We hugged in that brotherly way that men do to say they're sorry. I had learned more about myself that day than any other, and I had Simon to thank. Shortly after our talk, Simon left to catch his flight back to Atlanta. I stayed at the cemetery for another hour to say my good-byes to Melvin. I wanted to tell him that I was going to be okay. And that I would do everything in my power to get Toni back.

• • •

That night I took a long walk near the ocean to reflect on the meaning of life, the universe, and all that other philosophical shit you think about when you're trying to get your head together. I was in a creative mood, so I brought along a spiral notebook and my John Coltrane "Ballads" CD. I found a secluded spot away from the crowds and laid my blanket down along the shoreline. As I watched the full moon gleaming off the still ocean, I thought about the night Toni and I spent on the lakefront in Chicago. We stayed up all night holding each other and talking about our hopes and dreams.

That romantic evening seemed like such a distant memory. Since the incident in New York with Eric, I hadn't heard from her. When I tried calling to apologize, her home number had been changed. And so had the number to her pager. The thought crossed my mind to show up on her doorstep unannounced, but I quickly dismissed that idea. Not only was it inappropriate but it was the fastest way to get my feelings hurt.

My only chance at getting Toni back was to write her a letter from the heart. God had blessed me with the gift of writing music. All I had to do was transfer that same passion into words.

Dear Toni,

It's hard to know where to begin when you've lost a woman's trust. The words I'm sorry seem so inadequate, so empty. I would've preferred to express my love for you in song on the piano. But I doubt even a melody could express the degree of pain I feel for letting you down. Lately, I've been praying at night to rid myself of the guilt from that moment. You know how religious black folks can get when things get tough. I got on my knees and prayed for another chance to hold you again, and to show you that I am the man you need me to be: caring, affectionate, and most of all, honest. Toni, I am all those things, and much more. It just took someone like you to come along to bring out that part of me. That part that wants to love and be loved uncon-ditionally.

I know starting over would be hard. It always is when trust is involved. But I'm willing to do whatever it takes to rebuild that trust and make you happy. I miss holding you, and talking on the phone all night. And I miss watching you dance. I'll never forget the first time I saw you. You looked just like an angel. In a very short period of time, you have become a necessary part in my life, and without you nothing feels real.

Love always,
Malcolm

P.S. Whatever happens, please don't ever stop believing in me. That means more to me than anything else in the world, even more than your love.

When Players Pray

(2000)

It was a typical Thursday night. Melvin's Jazz Club was standing room only. Hundreds of people turned out for the special memorial party I was throwing for Melvin. My mother even flew in from Chicago, and she hated airplanes. Simon and Cynthia were there, too. They had just returned from Vegas and were sporting their diamond wedding bands. They never looked happier.

But behind all the champagne and celebration was a real concern that the club would be closing. Melvin didn't leave a will, which left his cousin as executor of his estate. He was a greedy old bastard who couldn't wait to sell the club to a condo developer. My lawyer had done everything in his power to block the judgment but we were running out of arguments.

I tried to put those thoughts aside as I relaxed in Melvin's office. It was a quarter to nine, fifteen minutes before show time. I wanted to stay focused on my music. To take my mind off the situation, I pulled out Melvin's old photo albums. As I turned the dingy pages, I was in awe of the artists who had performed at the club over the years. Ray Charles, Thelonious Monk, and Sarah Vaughn, just to name a few. Melvin was his usual flamboyant self, all decked out in his pinstriped suits with his hair slicked back. And of course, he was chewing on his trademark Cuban cigar. I smiled just thinking about how smooth he must have been back in the day. "Knock 'em dead in heaven, you old playa," I said.

The sudden roar of the crowd broke my concentration. The band had taken the stage to warm up. That was my cue. But I had promised myself the day before, and the day before that, to open the birthday present Melvin had given me. It was still wrapped tightly with the red bow on top, the same as it was back in June. I don't know why I waited so long to open it. Maybe I was afraid of the responsibility attached to whatever was inside.

As I tore away the colorful wrappings, my hands began to shake. It was as if I were opening some sacred artifact like Harrison Ford in *Raiders of the Lost Ark*. Once I got the paper off, I searched for something sharp to remove the thick tape. But before I could find a pair of scissors, someone pounded on the door. I knew it had to be Scottie.

"Malcolm, let's go! It's show time!"

"Give me a couple of minutes," I said, while trying to bite the tape off the box.

"You don't have a couple of minutes. Everybody is waiting."

"You're not getting away today," I said to the box. "I'll be back!"

As I made my way toward the stage, it finally hit me that it could be the last time I walked down these historic halls.

Forty years of blood, sweat, and tears, down the drain. All for the love of money. Just as I was being introduced, I bowed my head in silent prayer. If this was to be my last performance at Melvin's, I wanted it to be my best ever. "Don't forsake me, Lord," I prayed. "Not tonight!"

When I walked onto the stage, I was greeted with cheers and thunderous applause. My legal battle to keep the club open was well advertised in the local media. The *Los Angeles Times* dedicated an entire page to the story. "Thank you very much," I said as I took a bow.

When I sat down at the piano, I noticed something was different. The house piano had been switched. In its place was my Steinway, the one my father had given me on my eighteenth birthday. I ran my fingers across the engraved initials M.T. to make sure I wasn't dreaming. As I scanned the room through the bright stage lamps, I saw Simon sitting in the front row with a shit-eating grin on his face. I was so overwhelmed with gratitude that I walked over and gave him a hug.

The audience applauded us as we embraced, no doubt celebrating that two black men could openly show affection for each other. In a town like Los Angeles where brothers shoot one another over gym shoes, it was a welcome sight.

"I love you, man," I said to him.

"I love you, too, partner," he replied. "Now do me a favor and turn this place out."

"You got it!"

I walked back toward my piano, fired up and inspired. I had intended on playing a song by Cole Porter, or perhaps Thelonious Monk. But my spirit compelled me to play what was in my heart. As I pressed down on the keys, a hush came over the crowded smoke-filled room.

"This song is dedicated to the two men who taught me everything I know about music and life. My father, Joseph Tremell, and Melvin. And also, to the woman who without knowing it, taught me the meaning of love. The name of the song is 'When Players Pray.' "

It was the song I had written for my father before he had died twelve years ago. Ironically, I wrote the lyrics on the same night I wrote Toni the letter. I wasn't much of a singer, but I was going to give it my best shot. The melody of the song was similar to "Fortunate" by Maxwell.

I played the game for selfish reasons,
The love you gave so freely was for but one season.
My heart was so very cold and locked away,
Never to feel the warmth of a holy wedding day.

After that first verse, the audience was swaying back and forth to the rhythm and holding up their cigarette lighters. It was a very spiritual and emotional experience.

Never love more then she, that's the rule
A man who masters his sensitivities will seldom play the fool.
But the game is not eternal, there is always a spiritual price to pay,
Heavenly Father, is it too late to repent? Is it too late for a player to pray?

After that second verse, there wasn't a dry eye in the house. I continued to play, even though I was overwhelmed with grief. All the repressed feelings I had toward my father, Melvin, and Toni came pouring out onto the keys. It was my most intense performance ever. At the end of the song I was given a standing ovation. "Encore! Encore!" the crowd screamed. I inconspicuously wiped the tears from my eyes and stood up to take a bow. My mother, who was sitting at the table with Simon, was wiping the tears from her eyes, too. More than anyone else, she understood how significant that moment was for me.

As I exited the stage, one of the waitresses approached me, carrying a bouquet of red roses, eleven to be exact. Attached to the bouquet was a small card that read I STILL BELIEVE IN YOU!

"Where did you get these?" I asked, anxiously.

"The woman over there." She pointed in the direction of the bar, but no one was there. "At least that's where she was standing a minute ago," she said.

"What did she look like?"

"She was a very classy-looking lady about five-eight, medium-length hair, and brown skinned," she said.

I knew it had to be Toni. The card could have come from anyone, but the eleven roses were a dead giveaway. I gave her eleven roses when I met her for the first time at the Fox Theatre in Atlanta. I rushed through the thick crowd after her. The audience was still applauding as I made my way toward the front door. Judging by the sly expression on Simon's face as I passed by him, he knew what was going on. I suspected he was responsible for her being there.

Once I made it outside, I saw a woman in a long sheer black dress stepping inside a taxi. She was across the street, so it was hard to make her out. But just as her head disappeared inside, our eyes briefly met and I knew it was her. "Toni, wait!" I yelled. I ran across the busy intersection, almost getting myself run over. But I was able to catch her before her taxi drove off. Or maybe she was simply waiting. I didn't know for sure and I didn't care.

When I bent down to peek inside the taxi, she was staring at me with those beautiful brown eyes.

"Hello, stranger," she smiled nervously.

"Hello to you," I replied. "Leaving so soon?"

"I—I have another stop to make," she stuttered.

"I guess you were just in the neighborhood, huh?"

"Actually, I wanted to stop by and pay my respects to Melvin. I know how much he meant to you."

"How did you find out what happened?"

"I went by Club Obsession to say hello to Simon and he told me what happened."

"Look, I don't mean to break up this romantic reunion

but I've got a job to do," the taxi driver said. "Are you going or not, Ms.?"

"Yes," Toni said.

"No!" I quickly replied.

"Which one is it going to be?" the driver asked, sounding frustrated.

"Toni, don't go like this," I begged. "I know you didn't come all the way to Los Angeles just to give me flowers. Can I talk to you for just a minute, please!"

Toni sat there for a moment to contemplate. Then she gave the driver five dollars for his inconvenience and stepped out of the taxi.

"Malcolm, before you get started, I want you to know that I can't stay long. Eric is waiting for me at the hotel. We're engaged again."

"Eric?" I said in disgust.

That was the last name in the world I wanted to hear. Anybody but him, I was thinking. My heart all of a sudden became heavy.

"I guess there isn't much for me to say after all," I said. "I'll call you another taxi."

I escorted her back toward the club. I couldn't even look at her pretty face, knowing she was back with him. It was too painful an image. Just as we were about to cross the street, Toni grabbed me by the hand and pulled me back.

"Malcolm, why won't you look at me?"

"How could you go back to him?" I asked, trying my best to hide my pain.

"Because I can trust him, that's why!"

"Is that all you need to be happy?"

"No, but it's the most important thing in a relationship," she lashed out. "But I guess you wouldn't know anything about trust and honesty, now would you?"

"Why are you saying these things to me when you know how sorry I am. Didn't you get my letter?"

"They're just words!"

"Words are all I have since you won't let me close enough to look you in the eyes and tell you how I feel!" I said, as I grabbed her by the shoulders and looked her dead in the eyes.

"Well, here I am!"

Toni was trembling as she stared back into my eyes. Her strong and agile dancer's legs seemed limp as she tried to take a stance. I was tense, too. This was my final chance at redemption. I set aside my male insecurities and spoke from the heart.

"You are the most important person in my world. I didn't know how incomplete I was until you came along and filled that void. You taught me to believe in myself and to never give up on my dreams," I professed. "What I'm trying to say is, I love you, baby. And I need you in my life."

"I'm scared, Malcolm," she said, crying. "I don't want to end up hurt and alone."

"I'm scared, too. I've never been in love before. But I'm ready to take that chance in order to be happy. What about you?"

Tears rolled down her cheeks as she looked deep into my eyes. I held my breath and prayed she would give me another chance to be the man I knew I could be.

"I'm ready, baby," she said.

We embraced each other and kissed on the corner of that busy intersection. People were driving by blowing horns and whistling. But I didn't care. It had taken me thirty-seven years to find my soul mate. I wanted the whole world to know she was mine.

"Wait a minute," I said, after we came up for air. "What about Eric?"

"Eric who?" she said bluntly.

I didn't touch that. Hell, that was his issue, not mine. Toni and I ran across the street hand in hand back to the club.

"Wait right here," I told her. "I'll be right back."

"Where are you going?"

"I'm going to get something out of the office, then we're outta here!"

"Malcolm, this is an important night. You can't just leave."

"Watch me!"

I ran back inside the club to get my birthday present from Melvin's office. On the way out, I congratulated Simon and Cynthia on their marriage. It was the first time I ever kissed Cynthia. And it felt good to finally put my issues with her to rest. Then I gave my mother a kiss on the cheek and told her I loved her. She just looked at me and smiled. I had never seen her so happy. She knew Toni was good for me. Mothers always know what's good for their sons.

It felt strange walking out of those historic old doors knowing it was possibly for the last time. Melvin's Jazz Club had been my home for nine years. That was hard to handle. But I had to get on with my new life as a recording artist and as a man in a committed relationship. And I couldn't think of a better start than to drive down to the ocean and watch the sunrise, just like we did on our first date in Chicago.

It was another full moon that night and the breeze off the ocean was brisk, perfect for snuggling. With Toni by my side I finally worked up the courage to open my birthday present. The box contained a Bible and a white envelope. On the envelope were the words *To My Son* in cursive writing on the back. Inside was a copy of Melvin's Last Will and Testament. I couldn't make out the fine print but one thing was definitely clear, I was the beneficiary of Melvin's Jazz Club.

Maybe I should've been elated by my newfound wealth, but I wasn't. I celebrated within by holding Toni tight and giving thanks to God. I had been blessed so much that night and I wanted to remain humble.

Finally, I pulled out the old King James Bible. It was the same one Melvin's father had given him before he died.

There was a marker inside the Book of Proverbs with the inscription, 18:22. I turned to the chapter and read the verse out loud.

"Who so findeth a wife findeth a good thing, and obtaineth favor of the Lord."

"What a coincidence," Toni said.

But I knew better. Simon told me that there were no such things as coincidences. "Everything happens for a reason," he said. I had finally come to understand what that meant. In life, and especially in love, everything happens in God's time.